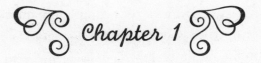

Chapter 1

It might be magic, it might be destiny. Or it might just prove that the universe is completely random. It doesn't matter. You're rich.

My mother kicked me out one minute after I won eight million pounds.

She didn't literally manhandle me over the threshold, she just stood there, arm pointing at the door, tears pouring down her face saying, 'Just. Get. Out. Now!' in a voice that sounded like she was taking huge gulps of vodka in between each word.

Actually, she was gargling red wine that evening. Burgundy, to match her lipstick and toenails.

It was totally random, this eviction. One of those fights that we'd been having a lot round about then. I thought they were all her fault. She seemed to think they were all mine. We'd been bickering all evening, and I was trying to stay cool and calm and totally reasonable. But the more I laid out my case for her to hand over twenty quid, the more quivery and emotional she became. It was completely unfair.

My little sister Natasha had struck gold when the evening was young and Mum was getting ready to go out to a party, humming Beyoncé, trying on earrings and admiring herself in her Karen Millen purple satin sheath dress. All Nat had to do was tell her how great she looked and Mum plunged into her diamanté clutch bag and handed over twenty pounds.

By the time I realised I was in desperate need of cash, having over-celebrated my birthday earlier in the month, Dad had announced that he had man flu. Their party outing was cancelled and Mum was back in her jeans, sulking in front of the telly.

'You're not actually doing anything, Lia,' she said, picking at her Weight Watcher's Shepherd's-Pie-free Pie. 'Why should I give you money? You've had your allowance for this month.'

I opened my mouth wide. 'But . . . you gave Nat twenty quid. That's so unfair. . . I want to go shopping tomorrow. I need twenty quid as well.'

I did need money. I always needed money. There was a fabulous 1960s leather jacket at my favourite stall in Camden – I'd dragged Mum there on my

Keren David

Lia's Guide to Winning the Lottery

F

FRANCES LINCOLN
CHILDREN'S BOOKS

birthday, begged her with tears in my eyes to buy it for me, but she'd said she wasn't paying eighty pounds for someone's tatty old leftovers. I couldn't believe it – that jacket was a *bargain*. She just couldn't bear letting me make my own decisions – she'd become downright mean and controlling over the last year or so. It was probably something to do with getting old – maybe she was bitter that she was getting all dried out and wrinkly while I looked reasonably OK in a good light and with the right jacket.

Anyway, that particular jacket was my latest ploy in the battle to get the attention of Raf, gorgeous, mysterious Raf, my latest crush. I had forty pounds all saved up. If I could get another twenty pounds . . . and then hit Dad for some more the next day. . .

'Natasha needed money to go out with her friends. It was an unexpected expense. And she doesn't get as much allowance as you do. Come off it, Lia.'

'You're only giving her money because you're desperate for her to *have* friends,' I said. I knew it was a little mean to point this out – it was really tough for Natters when she fell into the grip of bullies last year – but that still was no reason to award her totally unearned and unfair bonuses.

'*Don't* be so *vile*,' said Mum.

I took a big bite of spaghetti, slurping like a Dyson to pull in all the random threads.

'Must you?' she asked, with her bulimic face on.

'Well, it's true. You think Nat needs a load of extra financial help to bribe people into being friends with her. "Come on, everyone, popcorn's on me!" Actually, it'll just make her look desperate. No offence.'

I really didn't mean to be offensive. I could have given Natasha a lot of help with school politics if anyone had listened to me. Of course, no one ever did.

Anyway, I was older than Natasha by a full eighteen months and two days. Seniority should count for something. Anything she got, I should get more.

'It's not *fair*,' I said again, totally pointlessly, I knew. Whenever I pointed out basic, obvious, total inequalities, my parents just rolled their eyes and said, 'Life's not fair, Lia. Anyone ever told you that?' Possibly the most annoying phrase ever spoken.

Mum was getting a bit red in the face, and sloshing wine into her glass. I helpfully informed her that her mascara had run. She accused me of nicking her super-expensive waterproof wand. I blinked rapidly – to disguise the evidence – and launched into a full *Oh my God, how can you accuse me of stealing,*

OMG, your own daughter defence.

'And anyway,' I finished, 'if you just increased my incredibly tiny allowance then I'd be able to buy my own.'

'Oh, change the record, Lia,' she said. 'What's wrong with you earning some money? Dad's offered you a Saturday job.'

'Oh *please*,' I said, 'I've told you. I'm not interested.'

Just because Dad couldn't think of anything better to do with his life than take over the family bakery, didn't mean I had to devote every Saturday to pushing Danish pastries. I supposed I might decide to take over one day . . . one day far, far in the future. When I was about fifty and my life was over. But not every Saturday. That was bringing the inevitable far too near.

Mum rolled her eyes. 'You have the perfect Saturday job lined up for you, but you're too lazy to take advantage. Anyway, keep the volume down. Your dad's not very well.'

'Yeah, right,' I said. 'Poor old Dad.' We both knew he didn't really have flu. He was just permanently tired from getting up early every day – baker's hours, he called them – and allergic to most of her friends. Understandably.

'Not that you care about anyone except yourself,' she said, *whoosh!* out of *nowhere.*

I played an invisible violin. I could've been on *Britain's Got Talent.* The Amazing Lia! She mimes and winds up her mother at the same time.

Mum tutted. 'You really are horrible; I don't know what's happened to you.'

My mother's decided to hate me, that's what's happened to me, I thought, but I couldn't think of a way to say it that didn't make me sound pathetic. Instead I studied *Heat.* It's incredible how rubbish you can look and still achieve celebrity status.

'Anyway, Lia, it's cheeky of you to be asking for more cash because I think it was you who nicked that tenner from my purse on Thursday. I'm not made of money, you know.'

I yawned. What a fuss about nothing. How dare she accuse me of *theft* when I fully intended to pay back that trifling sum? I needed that money. I'd run out of lip balm. It was practically a medical emergency.

There didn't seem to be any hope of extracting any cash from her padlocked purse, so I went on the counter-attack just for the hell of it.

'You're the selfish one. What's so special about this party, eh, Paula? Crushing on a random pensioner?'

I'd been experimentally calling my parents Paula and Graham recently, instead of Mum and Dad. It was working quite well, I thought. It certainly got their attention. That's possibly because their real names are Sarah and Ben.

'*Don't* call me Paula,' she snapped. And then she yabbered on and on, and the lottery results came on the telly. And I listened with half an ear because I had a ticket. In my school bag. I couldn't be arsed to go and find it, because I knew you never win these things.

'I've had enough,' said Paula. 'You're just taking the piss the whole time.'

'Thirty-four!' said the announcer. My bra size. Or my nana's house number, as I told the press.

'Yeah, right,' I said.

'You treat this place like you're staying at the Ritz and you've got a load of personal slaves. You treat my purse like a hole in the wall machine.'

'Number seventeen!' said the announcer. My friend Shazia's house number. It sounded right. Yes. Seventeen.

'You're foul to poor Natasha.'

'It's character-building for her,' I muttered. In the background the ball marked 23 rolled down the tube. Twenty-three. My dream age.

No more education and free as a bird.

'Other girls don't treat their parents like you do. Other girls are nice to their mothers.'

'Mmmm . . . *really?*' I asked. Forty-one rolled into place. Paula's next birthday. And she thought I didn't care.

Four numbers. Four numbers correct. That's got to be good, I thought. That's got to mean something. Maybe I'll win a couple of hundred. But I needed to check . . . find the ticket. . .

So I said, 'Look, Paula, could you shut off the chit-chat for a mo?'

That's when she started screaming. She slammed her Burgundy down on the glass coffee table – could've been a bloodbath – and shrieked, 'That's it! I've had enough! Apologise!'

I hardly noticed. I sat frozen, eyes glued to the telly, watching three little balls roll into place.

Thirteen. Raf's birthday. A personal triumph of detective work to find that out – Raf wasn't the sort for birthday celebrations. When it all became public I had to pretend that I'd chosen it because we used to live at Flat thirteen when I was a kid.

'Number eight!' Jack's birthday. September eighth. I was sure I had eight.

Seven. My lucky number ever since I joined the Brownies on my seventh birthday and decided that it was the happiest day of my life. Kind of ironic because the Brownies housed a secret terror cell that made my life hell for the next two years. They were the Pixies and they hated little Gnomes.

'You're just ignoring me! You've got no respect!' she was bellowing, while I stopped thinking about the poxy Pixies and started checking and rechecking the numbers frantically in my mind. Oh my God. Oh my *God*. Oh *my* God. Oh. . .

'Umm, Paula. . .' I said, cautiously.

By now she was yelling and pointing, telling me she'd Had Enough, Could Take No More. And I couldn't find the words to tell her what might have happened, and I couldn't stand the embarrassment if it turned out that I'd got the numbers wrong. What if I'd picked Poor Little Natasha's birthday instead of Jack's? What if I'd forgotten my own bra size?

So I said, 'Fine. All right. I'm going, I'm going.'

And I grabbed my denim jacket and pulled on my fake Uggs and picked up my school bag.

And I left home – me and my potentially golden ticket.

Chapter 2

Apparently ninety per cent of female lottery winners keep their ticket in their bra until they can get it validated.

Outside, I scrabbled around in my school bag for the ticket. The Ticket. Of course I couldn't find it. My fingers grabbed at random objects – passion fruit lip balm, a furry unwrapped tampon, fossilised satsuma peel, crusty used tissues – until I remembered that I'd folded it into my purse. I pulled it out and squinted at the numbers in the dusty orange glow of the street light. But I couldn't think what I'd seen on the telly. Numbers swirled around my head . . . eight . . . twenty-three . . . fifteen? Forty-four? Twelve?

If I had. . . If it was. . . A huge flat of my own with a home cinema and a games room, an Apple Mac. A car and a driver until I was seventeen and passed my test. Driving lessons. I could skip GCSEs, AS levels, A levels, uni. Fast forward to the age of twenty-three. Oh my God. Oh my God.

I'd never really known what I was going to do with my life. I used to panic whenever I thought about the future. Latimer's Loaves was waiting for me, and I'd kind of accepted that I'd probably go and do a degree in Business Studies (yawn), but sometimes I dreamt of rebelling, doing my own thing.

The problem was, I didn't really know what my own thing was. Should I travel . . . or run a stall at Camden Market . . . or do a degree in Film Studies? I mean, it all sounded vaguely interesting and way cooler than baking cakes, but not definite enough to actually make a choice and say, 'That's me. I'm a traveller,' or, 'I sell vintage clothes,' or, 'I study old movies'.

Now, maybe, just maybe I was free! Forget baking, forget decision-making. I was a multi-millionaire! I didn't *have* to do anything ever again!

Possibly.

I turned around. I needed to go back in. Check my numbers. Surely Mum would understand . . . be OK?

But what if I'd got it wrong? What if this was the biggest disappointment ever? She might even be sympathetic . . . comforting . . . nice. I couldn't bear it. No. She threw me out, she chucked out my ticket too. Wouldn't that look great in the papers?

I was still holding the ticket in my sweaty hand. What if I got mugged? What if I lost it? So I stuffed it in the safest place I could think of, my bra – which was a personal favourite, a great bargain from Primark, turquoise satin with bubblegum pink ribbon trim and massive uplift. The ticket was scratchy next to my skin.

I started trudging down the hill, working out where to seek refuge. Which lucky friend should I share the moment with? Jack and Shaz were the obvious ones to pick from. But Jack was planning a night out with the lads – it'd have to be Shaz. Friday was mosque day, but maybe she could clear a few aunties out of the way for me.

It was hard to know what to text, though. In the end I put: *Hi. Can I come round? Might have won lottery.*

A text pinged back right away. It read: *More than £100??? Enuff 4 yr jacket? Now not gd, big family dinner. c u 2moro?*

Personally, if my best friend had hinted at a lottery win in a text I'd have thrown in a *squee* or two, a smiley and a load of *!!!!!!!!!* But Shaz wasn't like that. She utterly despised girliness. I think that's why I liked her so much. She was different from the crowd.

Tithe Green was a pretty normal, boring London suburb. All the interesting shops and stuff in London were in places where rich people lived – Hampstead, Notting Hill – and we got left with the tedious old rubbish. The shops ranged along the Broadway were really dull – charity shops, a hairdresser's, a café, the Hard as Nails salon and our shop, Latimer's Loaves.

A little way down the hill there was a sign reading 'Internet Café', which had appeared about a month before in what used to be a clothes shop called Lalla's Treasures. Mum almost bought a cardigan there once, until she realised it cost one hundred and fifty pounds.

Dad was pleased when the internet place opened, because Lalla had given up on her business six months before, and moved to Madagascar to do animal conservation.

'It's not exactly upmarket,' he said, 'and I'm not sure how long it'll last – I mean, surely most people don't need anything more than Wi-Fi – but it's better than leaving it untenanted. Nothing kills a high street faster than shuttered windows.'

'Nothing kills a high street faster than a huge shopping mall opening up less than three miles away,' pointed out my mum.

Dad shrugged. 'We've got a very loyal clientele,' he said. 'People who've been coming to Latimer's Loaves for sixty years.'

'That's what I mean,' said Mum.

Anyway, normally I'd have had no special interest in some internet café, but a few days before, on the way home from school, I'd seen Raf going in there. Perhaps it was a regular hang-out for him. Unlikely, but worth a look.

You really wouldn't expect to see Raf there. He lived in a massive house in Melbourne Avenue – I'd secretly trailed him home from school one day – Tithe Green's most expensive road. He probably had a huge bedroom kitted out with a Mac and flat-screen wall-mounted TV and a state of the art iPod deck.

He'd joined our school earlier in the year – weirdly, halfway through GCSEs – and no one knew what to make of him. The boys thought he was a snob who'd been expelled from some private school.

'Drugs, probably,' said Jack. 'He always has shadows under his eyes, and they've got that sort of blank look.'

We girls had a different idea altogether. We thought he was classy, mysterious and drop dead gorgeous, not to mention stylishly elegant yet totally masculine – not an easy combination to pull off.

We were all obsessed with paranormal romance books, films and television series. We wanted our own tasty vampire or cuddly werewolf – especially a sensitive, poetry-reading, emo type. Normal boys just didn't match up. They were just too . . . well . . . normal.

When Raf turned up – tall, with a tense, thin body, and dark hair falling over his hard, grey eyes – the female half of year eleven buzzed with excitement. There was something about him . . . something different.

'Gay,' said Jack, dismissively, but we sensed magic. We sniffed supernatural. We watched the way he avoided eye contact, sat alone at lunch, and we recognised the signs. Raf was an angel. Or a vampire. Something special, anyway.

I mean, he wasn't even on Facebook. He'd been spotted going into the old cemetery. Clearly there was something paranormal about him.

Girls plotted to become his Science partner – not that we actually have partners in Science in the UK, it must be a special American thing – and spat with envy when Mr Pugh seated him next to lucky, lucky me. Every Science lesson I got an incredible adrenaline rush – normally school was so boring that I spent my hours there in a hypnotic trance. But I hadn't achieved anything. We hardly ever did practical stuff in pairs. I don't think the people who wrote the National Curriculum even *thought* about the romantic potential of Double Science GCSE.

In America, according to loads of books I'd read, people could have whole long conversations while they're supposed to be doing experiments. In England we have to keep our eyes on the whiteboard and our ears tuned to the teacher. No wonder we're a complete national mess. I think I'd managed to speak to Raf twice in class, and both times I got told off by Mr Pugh. I did spend a lot of time looking sideways at Raf's lush, dark eyelashes and gunmetal eyes, the way his long fingers cradled a test tube. I'd found out his birthday by peeking at the class register. October thirteenth. But that day he was as reserved as ever.

All the other girls shivered and giggled whenever he spoke, hoping he'd reveal his hidden powers. I tried to remain calm and confident when we had to discuss things in class. But we'd never moved beyond the strictly scientific. He didn't seem to talk. And so far he hadn't bitten anyone.

I didn't really believe the paranormal theories, but I dreamed of being the one who got close to him. I saw him as an outsider, a bit like me. I mean, I had Jack and Shazia and loads of other friends (four hundred and thirty-five on Facebook) but I always felt kind of lonely. I didn't know why.

Six months in, I was almost ready to give up. I'd tried everything – a different perfume every Science lesson, a request for help with homework, offering him gum. . . I'd had nothing back, except the odd semi-smile. But persistence is my middle name – not really, it's actually Jade – and I never, ever give up. I think that's one of the things that Paula found so wearing about me.

It was worth scanning the dingy café – not a café at all, really, just some dusty booths and screens, a machine for hot drinks and a fridge for cold ones. No Raf. But it still seemed like a good idea to check my numbers online, give up the lottery dream in private.

I could see two guys – one looking at Facebook,

the other playing online poker. I tapped Poker Guy on the shoulder. He turned, annoyed.

'Who do I pay?' I demanded.

He grunted, eyes still on the screen. 'Boy. Over there.'

And then I saw Raf, behind the counter at the back of the café, staring down at a book. Staring rather than reading, I'd say – his eyes had that blank, empty look. Lost, lonely eyes. Sad eyes. Eyes that only the right girl could make happy. That would be me, obviously.

I charged over, momentarily forgetting the ticket nestling in my B-cup.

'Hey, Raf, hello,' I gushed. 'Fancy seeing you here.' And then, when he looked up at me, grave and unresponsive, I added, 'Errr. . . It's me, Lia. From school.'

My stupidity coaxed a tiny smile out of him. The cutest smile. His lips kind of crinkled, and his eyes warmed up.

'I know who you are,' he said. 'Do you want to use the internet? Two pounds an hour.'

'Oh. Umm. Yes please.' I rooted around my bag for the cash. 'Do you work here, then?'

'Yes,' he said. There was a pause. 'Evenings, mostly,' he added.

Sometimes it's hard to stop things coming out of your mouth before you think whether you should say them. This was one of those moments.

'Really? Why?' I was looking at his clothes – plain, simple, jeans and a black T-shirt, but indefinably well-cut and, you just knew it, expensive.

I wouldn't have thought you'd need to, I thought, but I didn't say it. But it was as though he could read my mind. The warmth drained out of his eyes.

His face was still and somehow closed. All traces of the smile disappeared.

'It's my job,' he said, cold as a corpse, handing me a token. 'Over there.' And he pointed to a monitor as far away from him as the little café could provide, and turned his eyes back to his book – a big, dark, leatherbound volume, I noticed.

Huh. Moody or what? Oh well. I had other things to think about. Although, glancing back at him, I briefly reconsidered the paranormal theory. He looked so out of place behind the counter. Like he was in focus and everything else was blurred. As though he didn't belong in this grubby café . . . this city . . . this planet at all.

Anyway, I put the token in the slot and the computer sprang to life. I found the lottery site, the wonderful people who might have a lot of money for me. I didn't know the amount at that point. I didn't know if I'd won a penny or a pound or enough to cure malaria in the whole of South-east Asia. Or nothing at all. That seemed the most likely option.

I extracted the ticket from its hiding place. The guy at the next screen, Mr Poker Face, gave me a strange look when he saw me groping my own chest, but I shot him a killer glare and he quickly turned back to his cards. I clicked on the link . . . the Double Rollover link. And there they were. Five numbers. My ticket shook in my hand. One winner, it said. One winner in the whole of the UK. Jackpot £8,005,342.

And the numbers.

Thirty-four.

Seventeen.

Twenty-three.

Forty-one.

Thirteen.

Eight.

Seven.

I was burning hot, and I felt kind of sick. The numbers blurred as I frantically checked and re-checked. . .

Thirty-four. Seventeen. Twenty-three. Forty-one.

Thirteen. Eight. Seven.

Oh my God. Oh my God.

The next thing I knew, I was clasped in Raf's arms.

Chapter 3

Think carefully about how you break your news to friends and family. Take some time to think out your own plans first.

I gasped. I blinked. And just for a minute the amazing feeling of Raf wrapped around me, his smell – coffee, soap – the softness of his shirt, the hardness of his chest, distracted me. We felt so good together . . . my curves, his angles. We . . . he. . . What the hell was going on?

'Oh my God!' I shrieked, pushing him away. 'What are you doing? My ticket! My ticket! Where is it!'

'This ticket?' asked Mr Poker Million, waving a familiar piece of paper at me, clutched in his porky fingers. 'Is it yours?'

'Yes! Yes!' I screamed, grabbing it out of his hand and stuffing it back into my bra, realising too late that several buttons had popped open and everyone in the room was staring at my chest.

Raf took a step backwards. 'Are you all right now?' he asked.

Hallelujah! He sounded really caring and concerned. Why hadn't I thought of collapsing in Science months before?

'You passed out . . . I think . . . your head was on the table. . . Obviously I wouldn't have . . . otherwise . . . Take some deep breaths. Where's that water?'

Facebook-checker had a plastic cup of warm *eau de tap* in his hand. Raf passed it to me, and I took a tiny sip. Then I thought about the numbers . . . the ticket . . . eight frigging million . . . and I swallowed the wrong way and water poured from my nose. I scrabbled for a tissue.

'Are you OK?' asked Raf, while I coughed and spluttered. He still looked concerned. Caring. Gorgeous. Only slightly repelled.

I clutched at his hand. 'Raf! Raf! I've won the lottery!'

'The lottery?'

He *had* to come from another planet. 'Yes . . . you know . . . the lottery. Double Rollover. Numbers. Money.'

'You've won . . . how much have you won?'
He couldn't have looked more serious.

I started laughing hysterically. 'I've won . . . oh
my God, Raf. . . I've won millions . . . like eight million
. . . millions. . .' And I threw myself at him, spinning
him round, giggling like a maniac. It took a minute to
realise that he was trying to pull free. I stopped, hand
to mouth, still laughing, but with tears in my eyes as
well. 'I'm sorry . . . it's so exciting. . . I'm just . . . I can't
think straight. . .' I was squeaking like a piglet.

'It is exciting,' he said, 'I'm really happy for you.'
God, his voice was flat. 'You should ring your family,'
he added. 'They're going to be thrilled.'

I was crying properly now. The other guys were
backing away, picking up their stuff.

'I can't ring them,' I wailed. 'My mum just
chucked me out. She doesn't want to know me. She
hates me, Raf.'

Raf looked horrified. I couldn't tell if he was
appalled that I'd spilled my guts – Jack would've
been – or at Paula's brutal behaviour (as well he
might be). He turned to the men.

'We're closing,' he said. 'You've got to leave
right now.'

Poker Face was halfway out of the door already,

but the other guy decided to argue.

'It's a late night café,' he said. 'I've still got forty minutes that I've paid for. You've got no right – I'll report you to the owner.'

Raf glared at him. For a moment his face looked – I don't know – frightening. Powerful. Like someone who could kill with a glance.

Then he shook his head, stuck his hand in his pocket and pulled out a crumpled fiver.

'Sorry,' he said. 'Look . . . compensation. It's an unforeseen emergency.'

And the guy pocketed the note, picked up his bag and walked out. Raf locked the door, and pulled down the blind.

I'd just about stopped crying, but I was still at the choking, hiccupping stage.

He handed me a clean tissue, and put his arm around me.

'It'll be fine,' he said, his voice soft and soothing . . . almost hypnotic. I remembered that film where Robert Redford tames foaming wild fillies by snuffling in their ears. *The Horse Whisperer*, it's called, and it always makes my mum cry. I wished Raf would snuffle in my ears.

I blew my nose. 'Sorry. You must think I'm mad.'

He reached out his hand, almost as though he didn't know what he was doing, and tucked a strand of my curly hair behind my ear. His hand brushed against my cheek.

'No,' he said, 'of course not. Not mad. You've had a shock. But Lia, this is something really special. Your life will never be the same again. Some row with your mum – that's nothing, it won't matter, I'm sure.'

His hand was still touching my hair. His other arm was soft on my shoulders. I held my breath. He was so close I could feel his breath on my skin. He leaned even closer . . . gazing with those silver-grey eyes . . . magical eyes. . . Oh. My. God. Was he going to kiss me?

Then someone hammered at the door, and Raf jumped away from me, like I was poison.

The door burst open. A man with his own key – a furious man shouting, 'What the hell are you playing at? What's going on? Why is the door locked?'

He looked like Raf, this man – the same dark hair and grey eyes, but older and burlier, face covered with stubble, the same dark shadows under his eyes, same pale skin. A much older brother? A really young father? He was in his thirties, I reckoned. Head of the werewolf pack, clearly, and furious enough to morph any minute.

I shivered. He'd noticed me.

'Aha. Right. I see. You've got a *girlfriend* here. Well, no wonder you forgot that the opening hours are actually until 2 am.'

His voice was softly amused – mocking even. I hated him instantly. Raf looked away, his fists clenched tight. For a moment I thought he was going to explode into violence.

'You don't know *everything*, Jasper,' he said. 'Actually, you don't know *anything* about me.'

Their eyes locked for a furious ten seconds. Then Jasper said, slowly and deliberately, 'I know what I'm worried about,' and Raf looked away.

Of course I was desperate to hear more. But it seemed a bit mean not to help Raf out.

'It was my fault,' I said, 'not Raf's. I fainted. He was going to walk me home. But it's OK, I can go by myself.'

'No, no, no,' said Jasper, suddenly super-friendly. 'It's fine. Forgive me. I overreacted. Raf – I'll see you at home later.'

'Maybe,' said Raf.

'Definitely,' said Jasper.

Raf sighed. 'Yes, *OK*. . .' he said, his voice little

more than a hiss. And he shrugged on his jacket, unlocked the door and said, 'Come on, Lia, let's go.'

We walked along the Broadway . . . past Latimer's Loaves, past the Hard as Nails manicure bar, past the Post Office. My mind was churning – Raf! The money! Raf! Eight million! OMG! OMG!

Raf suddenly seemed to remember that I was there. 'I'm sorry,' he said. 'You must think I'm rude. Are you all right with going home? Maybe you should call your friend? Shazia? I've seen you with her.'

He'd been watching me. Raf'd been watching me. He knew who I was friends with. I didn't think that was stalker-ish behaviour – and who was I to complain if it was, considering how I'd trailed him virtually to his doorstep? I thought it was sweet.

He knows who my friends are, I thought. Wow. . . Eight million pounds! Eight million pounds!

The annoying thing was that the hugeness of the jackpot was slightly diminishing the enormity of being with Raf, and vice versa. I needed to concentrate on both things and my mind was skittering like a spider on speed.

'No . . . Shazia's busy,' I said. 'Don't worry about me. I'll just go home, I suppose.'

'What about that guy, Jack?' he asked, 'He's—'

'Nah,' I interrupted. 'He's busy too.'

'It can't be too bad at home. They'll be so happy when they hear your news. And it's late. They'll be worried about you.'

I wanted to spend time with him, but I felt like such a wimp . . . a damsel in distress, needing an escort home.

'I'll be fine,' I told him.

But he shook his head. 'You fainted. It could happen again. And those guys, they saw your ticket and where you . . . umm . . . where you keep it. I'll walk with you, it's fine. You live up on Windermere Road, don't you?'

He knew where I lived. How? OK, that did seem a little strange. Could he have followed *me* one day? Surely not. I mean, what a coincidence. Also, although it was a completely normal, sane thing for me to have done, in a cool boy it would seem demented. I glanced sideways at him. He was frowning.

Actually, it was kind of helpful to be obsessing about Raf as we walked uphill to my road. It stopped my mind churning around, thinking, eight million! Eight million! Every now and again an *eight million!* would break through and once I let out a little squeak. Raf didn't say anything. His default silence was infuriating. At last I had a chance to talk to him and he wasn't making it easy at all.

We walked past the big, posh houses, and got to our end of the street – the line of modern maisonettes that someone had squeezed onto an empty plot in the 1970s. I always felt that our house was a bit embarrassed to be living near such impressive neighbours. Well, never mind. I was soon going to be looking at luxury penthouses in Hampstead or Primrose Hill, maybe. . . Yes, Primrose Hill, to be closer to Camden Market, with all the lovely shops and stalls. I'd be able to buy anything I wanted. One of those pretty cupcake-pink houses. Oh my God.

I dragged my mind back from clothes and jewellery and an amazing, bright purple velvet sofa that I'd seen last time I'd been to Camden. In two minutes time we'd be at my house. I had to find something to say to Raf.

'Look – that guy, shutting up the café – was it OK?' I asked. 'I'm not going to lose you your job or something? He sounded pretty angry.'

'It's OK,' he said. 'Jasper loses his temper really easily. He's just a bit . . . a bit tired, that's all.'

'Jasper?'

'My half-brother. He owns the café. I have to work for him.'

'Oh,' I said. 'Why? My dad owns the bakery but I don't work for him.'

He shrugged. 'I just do.'

I was going to ask more but the door opened. Grrr. My dad must've been looking out of the window. He was wearing his dressing gown, pale-faced and unshaven. God, how embarrassing. He should know to keep out of the way, looking like that. Just because it was midnight, there was no reason to show himself in public looking like a zomboid hospital patient.

'Where on earth have you been?' he asked. 'Your mum's been so worried about you. . . She's gone out in the car to see if she could spot you.'

What the hell? 'She threw *me* out,' I said, furious again. 'She told me to leave. Did she tell you that, *huh*? Oh no, I suppose it was all *my* fault.'

'She said you were rude and obnoxious.'

'She's a cow! She's a liar!'

'Well, come in now, anyway. You'll have to apologise when she gets back.'

'I'd rather *die*!'

Raf gave a little cough. 'Err. . . Good evening, Mr Latimer.' He offered my dad his hand and, after a tiny, amazed pause, my dad shook it. 'My name is Rafael Forrest. I'm at school with Lia and I manage the internet café on the Broadway.'

I loved the way he said his name. Raff-ay-el, overlaid with some sort of sexy foreign accent.

'*Do* you? Impressive, that, if you're still at school,' said Dad, King of Sarcasm.

'I work nights,' said Raf.

'Well, I have to say, we were all glad to see that unit open again.'

'Thanks,' said Raf, politely. 'You run Latimer's Loaves, don't you?'

'Been in my family since 1834,' said my dad, clearly delighted to find someone who was possibly interested. 'Opened by my great-great-grandfather. We've been hit recently by the credit crunch . . . and the mall . . . and all those low-carb diets, but yes, it's a great little business.'

I glanced at Raf to see if his eyes were glazed with boredom. Instead he looked bizarrely interested.

'It must be a challenge to work out how to compete,' he said.

My dad perked up immediately. 'Well, we small businesses must stick together,' he said. 'I've got a few plans—'

'I *fainted*!' I interrupted. 'I *collapsed*!' I was slightly overdramatic, to head off Dad's lengthy explanation of the benefits of setting up a Tithe Green Retailers' Association.

'Lia had some exciting news,' said Raf. 'It was too much for her.'

'She fainted? That's not like you, Lia. She's as strong as an ox,' Dad beamed proudly.

'I'd better be getting back,' said Raf. 'Bye, Lia, see you at school.' And he walked off, fast, into the shadows of the night, no doubt imagining me as a sturdy, bovine, cud-chewing beast.

'Well, Lia, found yourself a guardian angel then?' said Dad with, I swear, an actual sneer. I felt like he'd tied my guts into a knot.

'Raf was actually *worried* about my safety. He actually walked me home because I *fainted*. Not that *you* care.'

Dad scratched his head. 'Had you been drinking? Surely not, with that very well-mannered young man – not your style, I'd have thought, but wonders never cease.'

My parents were convinced that it could only be a matter of time before I started binge-drinking and smoking skunk. They often predicted that I'd be starring on one of those awful reality TV shows where normal British teenagers are shipped off to boot camp in Oregon. They have to hike round the wilderness with horrible, militaristic American hippies, and are forced to share their feelings until they crack up and start wailing over letters from home and saying they were wrong and bad and they love their mummies and daddies so much. Parent porn, Jack and I call it.

'Shut up,' I said automatically, although I was also a bit stunned by Raf's general . . . poise, you could call it. He had the manners of someone who'd been around a long time . . . a vampire, perhaps . . . but the face . . . the stern, serious beauty of him. . .

Fallen angel. Or just angel, as apparently the fallen ones are really unpleasant. Had to be. He'd told me that everything would be all right with my family once they heard my news. Maybe he was giving me some sort of Angelic Message.

'Well,' said my dad, 'you're going to have to apologise to your mum. She's very upset, says you were rude to her.'

'She was rude to *me*.'

'C'mon, Lia. Think about it. Keep the peace. She's been worrying about you.'

'Oh, yeah, right,' I said.

'What's this exciting news, then? Talent-spotted by a modelling agency? Decided to do some work for your GCSEs? Hit me with it.'

He was always so busy being funny, my dad, that I couldn't remember the last time I'd had a proper conversation with him.

'Ha, ha, very amusing. No, I've won the lottery.'

Dad laughed. How he laughed. He started wheezing and had to blow his nose on a tatty old hankie.

'You're as good as Harry Hill,' he said, playfully ruffling my curls. 'Won the lottery, eh? How much? A tenner?'

'Nope. Eight million,' I muttered, head down.

'Eight million? Eight *million*? Ha, ha . . . pull the other one.'

I fished around for the ticket. 'Here you go. You can check if you want.'

'You're not serious, are you? How can we check?'

'Internet,' I said, but he chortled to himself and said, 'I must be getting soft in the head. You can't trick me, young lady.'

'It's true . . . it is,' I said. 'I'll prove it. I'll ring them.'

He flopped down on the sofa and watched as I pulled out the ticket, found my mobile phone, checked the credit on it. There was a bit, but not enough for a long conversation. I held out my hand for his. He handed it over, saying with a big grin, 'When you've got your eight million you can pay me back.'

I got my ticket out and turned it over and found the number you have to call if you think you've won. Some woman with a strong Liverpool accent answered.

'Hello, I think I've won your jackpot. The Double Rollover. Eight million.'

Dad shook his head.

'Just putting you through.'

I waited. Dad waited.

'Hello,' said another voice, with an equally strong Scouse flavour.

'Hello,' I said. 'I've won, I think. I've got all the numbers.'

'Can you give me your name?'

'Lia. L-I-A. Lia Latimer. L-A-T-I-M-E-R.'

'Hello, Lia, I'm Ruth. Can I take your number?'

I gave her my mobile.

'Can you read me the numbers on your ticket?'

'Thirty-four,' I said. 'Seventeen. Twenty-three. Forty-one. Thirteen. Eight. Seven.'

Dad pretended he was the lottery company

representative. He mimed writing down the numbers, checking them carefully. . .

'Well, those numbers are all correct,' said Ruth. 'We'll get a Winner's Adviser to call you.'

'Oh!' I said. 'Wow!' I was *squee*ing like a WAG. 'Oh! Wow! It's real! I really have . . . are you sure?'

Dad grinned, rolled his eyes and waved his finger in a circle. 'You can't wind me up,' he said.

Ruth said something about security checks and validation, and asked for my address. I was trembling as I spelled it out.

Dad said, 'Who is it then? Shaz? Jack? That boy Ralph?'

Ruth asked where I'd bought the ticket. I gave her the address of the newsagent at the bottom of Jack's road.

Dad yawned and said, 'That's enough, Lia. I'm going back to bed.'

'Hang on a minute,' I said to Ruth. 'Can you just talk to my dad? He thinks I'm joking.'

'Hand him over.'

So I did. Dad took the phone. And I stood and watched as he refused to believe her . . . told her she was joking . . . accused her of being Shaz . . . listened . . . shook his head . . . looked at the ticket . . . wandered over to his laptop . . . and finally, voice choking, said, 'Oh Lord. It's not a wind-up at all, is it?'

And then he handed me back the phone, collapsed onto the sofa, and drank a big gulp of Mum's Burgundy.

Ruth told me to write my name and address on the back of my ticket. 'Someone's going to ring you back,' she said.

She told me all sorts of stuff about security arrangements and documents and all the time my heart was thumping so loud I could hardly hear her. I sat down next to Dad. I didn't want to faint again, without Raf there to catch me.

'And then what?' I asked. 'When do I get the money?'

And she explained that they had to check the ticket, and make an appointment, and they'd come to our house and sort things out. I shouldn't tell too many people yet, and quite soon, all being well, I'd be having the whole winner experience.

The Whole Winner Experience. Woo hoo. I liked the sound of that.

And then she said, 'Goodbye, Lia,' and I said, 'Goodbye, Ruth,' and I didn't quite know what I was going to say to Dad because he was still just sitting there, with his head in his hands, murmuring softly, 'Eight million. Eight bloody million. Oh God. Eight million.'

Then the front door slammed and I heard Natasha chattering away about some lame movie, and Mum fussing about shoes being left in the hall for people to fall over, and Dad rushed out to meet them.

'Sarah!' he said, 'Sarah! You'll never guess . . . you'll never believe it.'

'*What?*' said my mum. 'Has Lia rung? Is she at Shazia's?'

'It's . . . it's . . . Lia . . . eight million. . . Sarah, we've won! We've won the lottery!'

That's what he said. 'We've won the lottery!'

And I stood there and thought, who said anything about 'we'?

Chapter 4

*Winning the lottery may have a strange effect
on the people close to you.*

It's amazing how a few million pounds clears the air
after a family row.

Mum rushed at me, like a jackal scenting a crippled
antelope, and gave me a hug. I stiffened, corpse-like,
as she enveloped me in clouds of Chanel Coco
Mademoiselle.

'One thing I'll say about you, Lia, my darling, is
that you do things in style,' she burbled, giving me a
big slurpy kiss on the cheek. I pulled away.

'Urgh. Paula . . . keep your bodily fluids to yourself.'

Natasha was leaping up and down. 'Oh my God!'
she shrieked, right in my ear. 'Oh my God! Lia, you
are amazing! You're the best! Oh my God, Lia!
Can we go shopping tomorrow? And singing lessons,
Lia, can I have singing lessons?'

Huh. I might have known. Natasha had been desperate for stardom since she was ten. Mum and Dad had totally mishandled the situation by stringing her along, instead of telling her the truth – she croaked like a reptile. I'd done my best to straighten out her expectations – I thought it was only fair – but no one understood the subtle difference between being mean and my cruel-to-be-kind strategy, designed to shelter my little sis from humiliation and disappointment. As I often pointed out, she should have thanked me for my honesty.

I opened my mouth to tell them to forget it. This was my money. I was buying a flat, leaving home, starting out on my independent family-free twenty-three-year-old life, a blissful seven years early.

And then I shut it again. I don't think I'd ever seen everyone look so happy about something that I'd done. Sort of done. Normally they looked angry, upset and/or disappointed.

I thought of Raf's Angelic Message. I'd bide my time.

I gave Natasha a hug. 'Yes, you can have singing lessons,' I said. 'Best teacher you can find. And we'll go shopping. You can get those shoes . . . you know

41

. . . those silver ones. I'm going to make some phone calls.'

Upstairs in our tiny bedroom, I lay on my bed. I imagined my new penthouse flat. A huge double bed. A satin bedcover . . . dark purple, maybe, with pale lilac cushions. Or maybe silver? A TV screen . . . a computer room . . . a sound system. A walk-in wardrobe. My music as loud as I wanted. I'd get to pick what went on the television. Privacy. Control. Independence.

There didn't seem to be a downside. If I got lonely I'd just ask some friends round. I might even ask Raf . . . which led me on to thinking about his strong arms around me, his serious grey eyes, his strange formal manners, the way he leant towards me. Could he really be some sort of supernatural being? Surely not . . . and yet. . .

I pulled out my phone. Where were my friends right now? I had the biggest news of all time and there was no one here to celebrate. I could hear corks popping downstairs, Natasha shrieking, Mum laughing. I called Jack. No answer. Huh.

A gaggle of giggling neighbours had invaded the kitchen, drinking cava with Dad, while Mum was yelling down the phone to Nana Betty in Cardiff.

Mum's voice goes super-Welsh when she's talking to her mum or sisters, so she sounds like a camp Rugby centre-half.

'No, Mam, Lia's won it . . . yes . . . Double Rollover. . . No . . . Lia.'

Nana Betty's a bit deaf.

'No, Mam,' bellowed my mum. 'We won't let her fritter it all away on drugs.'

Audrey from next door was laughing so much that she had to dash to the loo.

Mum handed the phone to me. 'She wants to talk to you,' she said.

'Hi Nana!'

'Lia!' yelled Nana, all the way from Cardiff. 'Congratulations, my darling! How do you feel?'

'Oh, I don't know.' I really didn't. 'Excited, I suppose. Shocked. I don't know what I'm going to do next!'

'It'll be fine, you have fun,' she said. 'Just keep away from drugs and naughty boys, Lia, and you'll be fine. Just muddle through, that's what I always say.'

Nana Betty has two mottoes, Just Muddle Through and Aim for the Top. My mum said once that if everyone followed Nana's advice, the world would probably end.

'OK, Nana. Can I buy you a present?'

Nana shrieked with laughter. 'Don't be silly, I'm an old lady. I've got everything I need. You spend it on yourself, darling, and Natasha. Money is wasted on the old. You need it when you're young, your life ahead of you.'

'Oh, thanks, Nana.'

'How's the boyfriend, Lia? Say hello to Jack for me.'

'He's just my friend, Nana, you know that.'

'He's made for you, my darling. Listen to your nana. A lovely young man like that doesn't come along every day.'

There was no point arguing with her. My nana's been gaga about Jack ever since he plunged into an early puberty and emerged at fourteen, six foot tall, muscled, blond, blue-eyed and with completely flawless skin.

'If only I were sixty years younger,' Nana would sigh, loud enough for him to hear. She was possibly the world's oldest wannabe cougar. Jack loved it, and flirted outrageously with her. But then Jack's such a lad that he'd probably cop off with a seventy-year-old, given half a chance.

'OK, Nana, love you,' I said, and handed the phone back to Mum. I took a gulp of cava. The bubbles hit the back of my throat and made me sneeze.

My mum put the phone down. 'She's very happy for you,' she told me, 'and she hopes you won't spend it all before you've found yourself a good husband. Her words.'

And then some more neighbours arrived and Dad opened another bottle and we started googling how much things cost. . . Houses (Mum) . . . cars (Dad) . . . holidays (everyone) . . . clothes, shoes, jewellery, electrical equipment, singing lessons. . .

'Eight million's not really enough in London,' said Dad, after we'd looked at a few ads for mansions backing onto Hampstead Heath. 'Why couldn't you win twenty million? Or forty, just to be safe.'

'Oh my God, Graham, how greedy are you?' I said. 'Anyway, it's my money, actually, not yours. I'll be choosing the properties, thank you very much.'

Mum and Dad glanced at each other. 'Same old Lia,' murmured Mum.

I shot her a filthy look. I might have won eight million pounds, but I hadn't forgotten that she'd thrown me out. At least I could buy my own leather jackets from now on . . . except that if they cut off my allowance that wouldn't really be *fair*.

Natasha was fiddling with the Wii, putting on her

karaoke program. Typical. She comes over as sweet and shy, but really she's a show-off, my little sister. A secret show-off. Only I realise.

She was singing some song about dreams coming true – one of those rubbish *X Factor* hits – and gradually all the neighbours fell quiet. Mum and Dad were hugging each other, watching Natasha as her voice soared towards those high notes. I winced. Couldn't they hear how tinny she sounded?

Obviously not, because everyone started clapping.

'I'm going to bed,' I said. 'Night, everyone.'

'I'm coming too,' said Nat. 'Wait for me.'

One massive advantage of buying my own place was going to be having my very own bedroom. Natasha and I had shared a room ever since she was one and I was three – I wasn't too delighted to have my space invaded then, and I hadn't got used to it over the ensuing thirteen years.

But the problem with Natasha is that she's so blinking nice, sweet and well-meaning, that perfectly reasonable sibling rivalry makes you feel like a Nazi.

She was lying on her bed, surrounded by fluffy animals, writing her diary. 'Natasha's a very *young* fourteen,' my mum used to say. She thought it was sweet, whereas I realised that Natters needed to ditch the cutesy girliness fast if she was ever going to be a social success at school.

'Oh my God, Lia! I don't know how I'm ever going to be able to sleep again!'

'It's me that's won, not you,' I pointed out. 'I can do my own excitement, thank you very much.'

My friend Shaz would've told me off for being a grumpy bitch. But Nat just stared at me, a little bit puzzled, and I felt like I'd clubbed a baby seal. So I said, 'Anyway, I've got something to tell you.'

Because, actually, Natasha and I got on OK when we were all on our own. Things went wrong when we were involved in delicate negotiations with the parental enemies, or when she embarrassed me in front of my mates, or insisted on singing at family parties. You get the picture.

I described how Raf put his arm around me, how he smoothed away my hair.

'He was leaning in towards me,' I said. 'I definitely think that maybe he likes me.'

'Oh, Lia!' she said. 'That's amazing. Oh my God. He's gorgeous. It's like everything's happened for you at once. Like a fairytale!'

There was not a shred of bitterness in her voice. Maybe she was thinking of her silver sandals, or maybe it was the singing lessons, or maybe she was better at covering up envy than I would have been.

All my life I'd felt like Natasha and I were in a competition, scoring points off each other. All my life I'd been watching out that she never got more of anything than I did.

And now I'd won. Definitely won. Undoubtedly won. I was eight million pounds ahead.

So why did I feel uneasy? Why did I wish she'd won as well?

Chapter 5

Fifty pounds is a reasonable amount of cash to carry with you.

I left it until 10 am to go round to Jack's, but of course he was still in bed when I got there.

'You'll have to come back later,' said his mum, trying to shut the door on me.

I pushed past her. 'That's OK, Donna; I'll go and wake him up.'

I could feel her disapproving eyes drilling into the back of my head as I bounced up the stairs. Not my biggest fan. She'd always thought I was a bad influence on her darling son, and blamed me for every time we got into trouble, even though it was Jack's idea to let off the fire alarm in year six, and it was him who put Cuddles the school guinea pig in Miss Fay's desk drawer.

It was me who told him about her rodent phobia, though.

At first Donna was suspicious of me because I wore jeans and liked running around and shouting and 'behaving like a boy'. When I turned fourteen and discovered hair products to turn my frizz into curls, and started wearing mascara and lip gloss, she changed her tune. Now I was 'too tarty'. Not a suitable friend for her precious baby, anyway.

Who cared? I bounced into Jack's room – where the boy wonder was curled up asleep, bare legs poking out from under his Tottenham Hotspur duvet – and sat down heavily on his calves.

'Oi!' he said, sleepily, blinking at me. There was a distinctive whiff in the air. Stale deodorant mingled with freshly-delivered fart. I was sure Raf's room never ponged like that. It'd be full of fresh air and classy aftershave. I wondered if I'd ever get to smell it.

'Whoa. Hey, Lia. Here for an early morning encounter with Little Jack? It's just that I think we'll have to get rid of my mum first, somehow.'

His voice was loud enough for Donna to hear, bustling around on the landing. She gave a loud snort and slammed the door to her bedroom.

'Shut up, you moron,' I said. 'Dream on.'

'Oh go on, Lia. Just a quickie. You know you

want to. Otherwise, what are you doing here?'

'I've got something big to tell you!'

Jack looked puzzled. And then slightly concerned. 'Bloody hell, Lia, if you've messed up. . .'

I thumped him.

'I have won the lottery. I am now worth eight million pounds. If I wanted to, I could buy all the houses in this street.'

'Bollocks,' said Jack. 'You have absolutely no idea about house prices. You should talk to my cousin Eddie – he's an estate agent in Hemel Hempstead.'

'Shut up about Eddie. The point is not house prices. The point is that I have won the lottery.'

Watching Jack grasp an idea is like chucking a coin into a deep wishing well. There's a long pause, then *plop*, *splash* and little ripples as comprehension dawns.

'Jesus Christ! Bloody hell!' Jack ran through his long vocabulary of swear words at increasing volume, and launched himself across the duvet to give me a bear hug, just as Donna stormed through the door.

'Jack! Mind your language! And what's going on here?'

'Nothing, Ma, although technically you have no right to ask that question given that I am sixteen and this is the privacy of my bedroom. If I choose to entertain a girl here, you'll just have to lump it.'

'But it won't be me,' I said, shrugging him off. 'Jack, I'm going to call Shaz, see if she can meet up down the Broadway Café. Half an hour?'

Shaz was busy, so it was just Jack and me having breakfast at Tithe Green's main eating place, which used to be a greasy spoon before it got a manager with ideas and wipeable Cath Kidston tablecloths.

'Right,' he said, spooning sugar into his tea. 'Tell me.'

'I told you. I won eight million pounds. And a bit more.'

'On that ticket? The one we bought the other day?'

'Yup.'

Jack had this big goofy grin that you mostly saw when he scored a goal or when it was time for Food Tech, his favourite subject. Or when he was thinking about sex. So he was quite a smiley boy, really, because his life revolved around food, football and fantasy. His dual ambitions were to play for Tottenham and to win *MasterChef*.

'Of course, ideally I'll do both and then it'd have to be *Celebrity MasterChef*,' he told me once. 'But that's OK.'

'Bloody hell, eight million, that's so cool,' he said, as his plate of bacon, eggs and sausage arrived.

'Breakfast's on me,' I said, generously, spreading strawberry jam onto a croissant that had been crafted by my dad's fair hands just a few hours earlier – the café was one of Dad's best customers.

'Too right it is. Breakfast's on you forever.'

'Who says?'

'I say. I bought the ticket, after all. I'm your manager.'

'Err . . . who said I need a manager?'

'I did. Buyer of the ticket.'

'Jack. You couldn't manage a bus queue.'

'I'm the captain of the A team, Lia. Proof of my leadership potential.'

'The A team that lost to the B team two weeks ago,' I pointed out. He stuck his tongue out at me.

'Told you it was a good present,' he said.

'You didn't know it was going to be worth eight million! You were buying me the world's meanest birthday present.'

'God. Typical. I buy you a present worth eight sodding million pounds and you're still not satisfied. *And* I said I was going to get you a DVD. Won't bother now. Huh. *Women*.'

'Jack! What are you *like*?'

He bit into his fried egg, and yolk exploded over his chin. We were still laughing when I spotted a skinny, dark-haired guy standing by the counter, studying the takeaway menu. Argh! Raf!

I rushed up to the counter, supposedly to find serviettes for Jack, but actually – 'Oh! Wow! Hi Raf. Fancy seeing you in here. I thought you had a café of your own.'

Raf looked terrible. Huge dark shadows under his eyes. His hand, as he picked up his latte to go, shook slightly.

'Hey Lia,' he said. 'Ummm. I . . . errr. . . '

'Come and sit with us,' I said.

'Oh.' Awkward silence.

'That'll be fifty pence extra if you're having it in,' said Janice, the café manager.

Raf looked as thrown as if she'd asked him for fifty thousand pounds. He dug deep into his pockets.

'Here you go,' I said, tossing a coin to Janice. I knew she'd catch it because she plays netball with my mum. Bit sad, really, middle-aged women playing a game they should have grown out of when they were my age, but my mum didn't really get why I thought she should do aqua aerobics, or badminton, or something else a bit more age-appropriate.

Raf followed me to our table. 'Look who's here,' I said.

'Who?' Jack was busily buttering toast.

'Raf, you know Raf. From my Science group.'

The air seemed to congeal, like the egg on Jack's chin.

'Oh yes,' said Jack, narrowing his eyes. 'We've met.' He put on a posh accent. 'Hello *Rafe*.'

I chucked him a wodge of serviettes. 'It's not Rafe. It's Raf. Grow up.'

'It was a goal,' said Raf. 'You know it was.'

'Should've been a red card.'

'The referee's decision is final.'

'Cheat.'

'Bad loser.'

'Thug. I saw Olly's leg after you crashed into him. Call that a tackle? Maybe you thought we were playing *rugger*.'

I flapped my hands at them.

'Shut up! I've won the lottery! That's more important than football.'

'That depends,' said Jack, 'whether you're talking about a decision that was downright daylight robbery.'

Raf shrugged. 'We still won.'

I gave up, finished my croissant, drained my mug.

'I am going to go and spend large amounts of money,' I said, although I wasn't quite sure where this money was going to materialise from.

'Wanker,' said Jack. 'Posh twit.'

Raf just sneered.

'And then I am going to investigate holidays for after GCSEs. Ibiza, I thought. Or Crete. I thought a group of us could go. I would like to invite both of you. But I can't do that if you're going to fight all the time.'

That shut them up. Raf had a strange look in his eyes. As though he was trying to focus on something small, a long way away.

'Crete is nice,' he said, softly. 'I've been there. . . I think you'd like it.'

'You're forgetting one thing, Lia,' said Jack.

'What?'

'What about Shazia? Her dad's never going to let her go on holiday with all of us, is he? How're you going to buy him off, Lia?'

Oh. This was a problem. Shaz's dad used to be quite normal about religion – i.e. not very interested

– but then a few years ago he started going to the mosque a lot more and ratcheting up the Islamic rules they kept at home. He was always threatening to move Shaz to an all-girls school, and about a year ago she started wearing a headscarf. We never really talked about it. Shaz was mega-sensitive about Islamophobia – she was constantly lecturing Jack because his dad read the *Daily Express* – but I'd always assumed that she found it a real pain. You can't imagine someone as stroppy as Shaz wanting to hide under a scarf. I had no doubts that when she was eighteen she'd just do her own thing.

'I'll have to sort it out somehow,' I said. 'Maybe we can pretend it's a girls-only trip. Or go to a Muslim country – Morocco, maybe, or Turkey.'

'Dubai,' said Raf, dreamily. 'The world's only six star hotel is in Dubai.'

'You're going to be spending Lia's money for her, are you?' asked Jack. 'Because, as her manager, I can tell you that if she's going to fork out for a six star hotel, the guest list will be strictly limited. Just Lia and me – and Shaz, if we can persuade her.'

Raf finished his latte and stood up. 'I'd better be going. Bye, Lia.'

I watched him walk away. 'Thanks a *lot*, Jack. I've

been trying to get to know him all year, and you have
to be completely obnoxious.'

'You have?' Jack speared his last rasher of bacon,
and plunged it into his mouth. He'd have to learn
some table manners if we were going to hang out at
six star hotels. Although I'm not sure if they'd even
serve a Full English in Dubai.

'Don't waste your time with him, Lia. He's
clearly gay.'

'No he's *not*.'

'He *so* is.'

'You're just a homophobe. And he's *not*.'

'So you fancy him?'

'That's my business.'

'Yeah, right, Lia. Don't bring him on our holiday.
Anyway I'm going. Thanks for breakfast.'

Jack gave me an eggy kiss on the cheek and left. I
went to the counter, asked for the bill, which came to
£15.75 – the prices went up with the polka-dot
tablecloths – and pulled out my purse.

Nothing there.

I might be a multi-millionaire, but I was just as
skint as I had been the night before.

Chapter 6

How good are you at making decisions?
Because you'll need to improve. . .

'The most important question for you to think about,' said Gilda, 'is whether you go public or not.'

Gilda was my Winner's Adviser. She was about Mum's age but a bit curvier, and she had a nice friendly smile. Plus she had eight million pounds for me. I liked her right away.

Anyway, when she started going on about publicity I was kind of surprised. Surely the most important question was how I was going to break it to my family that my money was mine. Only mine. And then there was the question of how to move things on with Raf, after our promising start. If only Jack hadn't put him off. Maybe I could pop round later and find out. . .

Also, how quickly could I move out of this shabby maisonette, and into my own plush apartment?

Could I leave school right away? Was that leather jacket still on the stall? And should I pick chestnut highlights or go the whole hog and opt for the Japanese straightening treatment, to eliminate my messy curls forever? Obviously that wasn't the *most* important question, but it was what Natasha and I had spent forty minutes discussing that morning, with Shaz texting in her thoughts from her granny's house in Wembley.

We'd done the boring bit where I handed over the ticket and my birth certificate and my passport and Gilda scanned them and checked them and sent them all off on her laptop to head office.

My Personal Banker, 'Call me Kevin', arrived (tall, younger than my dad, looked a little bit like Daniel Craig. Mum and I gave him extra-big smiles). Kevin handed over my cheque book and bank details, and a debit card.

And then Gilda pressed a few buttons and *kerching!* – a slow *kerching*, admittedly, Gilda said the money could take up to forty-eight hours to arrive. (How? Why?) But eight million pounds was coming my way.

I felt exactly the same, and yet completely different. I was a sixteen-year-old schoolgirl, I was a multi-millionairess. I could buy anything I wanted, go anywhere in the world – but I still had History coursework which was due in at the end of the week. If I'd suddenly discovered that I could fly it wouldn't have surprised me. Anything was possible. Now this had happened, so could anything else.

'There you go, Lia,' said my dad, who still wasn't looking all that well. He was pale, and beads of sweat stood out on his top lip. 'You'll never have to come running up the hill to bum money off me to pay your café bill again.'

'Ha, ha,' I said.

'We'll be looking in your purse for a spare tenner,' said Mum.

'Hands off!' I said.

'Have you thought at all about anonymity, Lia?' asked Gilda. 'If you decide to go public, then we need to organise a press conference quite soon. We wouldn't want the news to get out and you wake up to find the world's press on your doorstep.'

'Lia definitely wants to stay anonymous,' said Mum, stirring her tea. 'She's much too young to cope with all the attention. We'll keep things very quiet. Just tell a few friends and family.'

'Yeah, right, Paula,' I said. She'd been on the phone all morning.

Gilda said, 'Paula? I thought your name was Sarah,' and Mum said, 'Oh, a family joke! Lia's always kidding around,' with a totally false, merry, little laugh.

Gilda was back on to anonymity. 'How possible do you think it will be to keep Lia anonymous?' she asked. 'We tend to find that if one or two people know, then sooner or later – but usually sooner – the winner gets a call from a journalist.'

'We'll just tell them to go away,' said Dad. 'Lia's only sixteen.'

'What if I want to go public?' I asked – not that I had any real opinion on the matter.

'We'd hold a press conference, give the press a chance to get the story and hopefully they'd lose interest quite quickly,' said Gilda. 'It's a difficult choice.'

'It'll be fine,' said Mum, 'as long as you don't do anything to fuel the fire, as it were. You'll have to really behave yourself, Lia, if you're in the public eye.' She looked thoughtful, a hint of a smile on her face.

'What do you mean, fuel the fire?' I asked suspiciously.

'Oh, you know, unwise behaviour,' said Mum. 'I've read about lottery winners going off the rails.

Drugs . . . dodgy boyfriends . . . you know the kind of thing. Big headlines. Lots of fuss.'

'Oh, that's very unusual,' said Gilda. 'Most of our winners are nice, normal people, just like you.'

OMG. I was in danger of becoming a celebrity. Oh my God. Any secret I had would be unearthed. *Heat* magazine would circle my zits – not that I suffer badly, but everyone has the occasional bad skin day. I'd be chased by crowds of paparazzi. Publicity was a seriously bad idea.

'I'm going to stay anonymous,' I said, glaring at Mum.

'Some people don't tell a soul,' said Gilda. 'They want everything kept absolutely secret. I saw a couple a few years ago, they had three children, all grown-up and living in their own homes, bringing up their own families. Didn't want them to know. One woman – I went round to her house and she kept on looking out of the window. Checking her watch. After a bit I asked her what the matter was. "I'm just looking out for my husband," she said. "Don't want him finding out about this."'

Mum laughed. 'Talk about tight-fisted,' she said. 'You'd never have got away with that, Lia. Mind you, I can't see why anyone would want to.'

I examined the bracelet that Natasha'd given me for my birthday.

'You might enjoy the publicity,' said Mum. 'I bet we could get you into magazines, try modelling, that kind of thing.' She'd obviously appointed herself as my PR adviser. Trust her to try and take over.

My mum knows all about press conferences because she works for a PR agency. She spends her life calling journalists and trying to get them interested in her lame clients who are never real celebrities, just people who've done boring stuff. Naturally, she doesn't earn megabucks. I kept telling her she needed to represent cooler people – Lady Gaga, for example – but she never listened.

'Well, I still think anonymity would be better,' said Dad.

My phone buzzed. I'd turned off the sound, but it'd been jumping and vibrating all morning, like a bumblebee caught in a glass.

Gilda said, 'How many people already know, Lia? Is this going to be a secret you can really keep?'

'Err . . . I'm not sure,' I said feebly.

'Are you on Facebook, Lia? How many friends have you told?'

Whoops. I hadn't got around to posting it on

Facebook. But loads of people had left comments on my wall, and Natasha had already created a page called, 'My sister's won the lottery.' Fifty-seven random kids liked it already. Oh-oh. . .

Mum said, 'We told some of the neighbours . . . and Lia's told some friends. There were people in that internet café, weren't there, Lia? And I suppose Natasha might tell a few of her friends. And so will Jack and Shazia – you know, really, Ben, Lia, we'll have to have a press conference. As soon as possible, really.'

So Gilda and Mum started talking about the arrangements, and Dad sighed and said, 'It seems a shame,' and I sat there trying not to vomit. Trying not to panic. Working out how I'd avoid unfortunate headlines. Could I do it? I'd have to.

The press conference was set for the next day. Mum booked us in at the hairdressers, although I was desperate to get down to Camden and make sure I nabbed the leather jacket before anyone else did. In the end, Shazia offered to go for me. What a friend! I generously gave her twenty pounds to spend on herself.

She turned up with it at the salon, as we sat there being wrapped in aluminium foil – chestnut highlights! Yay! I flew out of my seat to hug her.

'Wow! Thanks Shaz! It's fabulous!' I tried it on and twirled round the salon.

'Perhaps you could come and sit down, we're only half done,' said the hairdresser.

'Oh, whoops, sorry,' I said.

'You don't think you're wearing that to the press conference, do you?' said my mum.

I wanted to see what Shaz had bought for herself. 'Of course,' I said, coldly. 'Oooh, Shaz, that headscarf is gorgeous. I like the shiny stripes.'

'And what else were you thinking of wearing?' asked Mum, dangerously cool.

'Well, there's my mint green top . . . you know, the one I got from Cancer Research for three pounds fifty and chopped the sleeves off. And then there's that denim skirt – the really short one that I customised with the tartan. . .'

That skirt was two pounds fifty – Help the Aged. Honestly, I didn't see why anyone would ever spend more. If you know what you're doing with vintage, you never have that awkward moment when you turn up at a party and you're wearing the same H&M dress as the class anorexic, but three sizes bigger. Plus you're saving the planet *and* helping good causes.

Win, win, win.

Mum sniffed. 'You want to appear on TV and in all the papers wearing second-hand clothes?' she said. 'Clothes stripped off *corpses*? Old ladies' leavings? That disgusting jacket, which stinks and is probably contaminated with *fleas*?'

To be totally honest, the jacket did have a funny whiff about it. I hadn't realised at the open-air market stall. It clashed badly with the pong of the hair dye. But there was no need for her to trash my style.

'What's wrong with my clothes? You're just jealous because I look so good and you're so old and boring and conventional.'

Natasha and Shaz made eye contact in the mirror.

'Lia didn't mean that,' said Natters soothingly, while Shaz said, 'I think your hair looks great, Mrs Latimer,' even though Mum was at the clips-and-foil-strip stage and looked like an armoured hedgehog.

'Time to come to the basin, dear,' said the hairdresser. Mum got up. 'Tell you what,' she said, 'let's just have a little trip to Harvey Nicks this afternoon. If you really want to wear charity shop clothes after that, be my guest.'

I couldn't be bothered to fight. I was too busy

scrolling through hundreds of texts on my new iPhone – first purchase, naturally. The whole school seemed to know my news. I had messages from everyone.

Everyone except Raf.

Surely, if he liked me, he'd have texted . . . asked me out? I knew he had my number because I'd put it into his phone on some flimsy pretext to do with Science homework. He'd never contacted me. What was his game? Did he even have a game?

How could I win eight million pounds and not get the boy of my dreams?

I was brooding about Raf all the way to Knightsbridge. But I forgot him as soon as we went into Harvey Nichols. I'd never been anywhere quite like it.

Normally I hated shopping in ordinary shops. But this was no ordinary shop. It was stylish, mega-expensive, the kind of place where you might see a celebrity buying knickers. Just walking through the departments – quiet as a museum – made my outfit feel shabby and old. The assistants smiled, but their eyes judged us – Nat's bulging jeans, Mum's Zara trouser suit, my smelly jacket. My confidence was stripped away. I felt angry – how dare they? – but also ashamed. 'We're not poor!' I wanted to yell. 'I've won millions of pounds!'

Then Mum had a word with one of the assistants, explained about the lottery and the press conference. And everything changed.

We had a massive changing room, just for us. We had orange juice and little biscuits. A lady – the personal shopper – brought us stuff to try on. Shoes . . . bags . . . even underwear. And the clothes . . . the clothes. . .

I'd always scoffed at designer clothes before. I couldn't understand why people would pay thousands of pounds for a pair of trousers. But trying them on – a pair of Chloé trousers, a top from Dolce and Gabbana – the gorgeous, silky feel of them, the way they fitted, the way they looked. It was seductive. It was fun. It even felt like my mum and me . . . we were getting on.

I actually liked the final outfit she picked out for me – a flouncy red skirt (Dolce and Gabbana) and a little black jacket (Frost French).

I even drummed up a little bit of enthusiasm when she tried on a desperately dull beige suit and minced around the changing room saying, 'I think this is Euro-chic personified, don't you, girls? The kind of thing that Carla Bruni would wear if her daughter won the lottery.'

Obviously, I could have pointed out that Carla Bruni is a supermodel as well as being the French president's wife, and looks as much like my mum as Natasha looks like Naomi Campbell, no offence.

But I just said, 'Paula, that's *so* your colour. It really matches your foundation,' which made her narrow her eyes and say, 'Perhaps I'll try it in the taupe.'

There was something about being somewhere so different from anything in our ordinary life. It softened us. It made Mum clap her hands when I did a twirl in my skirt and say, 'Oh Lia, darling, you look beautiful.' It made me grin right back, when normally I'd have grimaced and insisted on principle that the outfit was rank and there was no way I'd be seen dead in it.

I wondered if it was just money that was making us feel like this, if shopping trips and a nicer house and exotic holidays would magic away all the arguments, all the hurt. It didn't seem to me that life could be that simple, that buy-able. But here we were, getting on, laughing together, picking out the best outfits for each other.

Mum paid for the clothes, but I promised to pay her credit card bill. £1,013. I felt like Bill Gates in my incredible generosity. Then we met up with Dad and admired his new Paul Smith jacket. And we had supper in one of those sushi bars where the food travels round the counter on a little train and you work out how much you've spent by looking at the coloured rim of the plate.

We'd been there once before, for my fifteenth birthday, and then we were under strict instructions about how many plates we could take, and which colours to choose. But today we could have anything we wanted. A plate of sashimi went by, and Paula grabbed it. A plate of California rolls – snaffled by Natasha. Prawns. Crab. The train went on and on and round and round.

We were all laughing and chatting and talking about Gilda and the press conference.

'We can finally expand the bakery,' said my dad. 'That was always your grandad's dream, Lia.'

'And houses,' said Mum. 'How about a nice, big house with a conservatory? A huge garden? An en suite for everyone?'

'Do you think if I have singing lessons, I can get good enough to audition for *Britain's Got Talent*?' said Natasha.

I suppose I could have told them all about my plans for a flat of my own and leaving school and being independent, but it didn't seem like the right moment.

Maybe, I thought, we're going to be a happy family now, a smiling, laughing, rich, happy family. It only took eight million pounds. Easy-peasy.

Maybe being a lottery winner would change me too. Maybe I'd start being a nice person – someone who didn't wind everyone up, who curbed her urge to tease her sister, whose dad took her seriously, whose mum actually liked her. I knew money couldn't buy health or happiness, but becoming a multi-millionaire had to change me . . . didn't it?

The train rumbled round and round and we kept on taking things, but the plates were always full and the food just kept on coming. And that's when I realised that my life from now on was going to be like a sushi train – with infinite choices, on and on, forever and ever, round and round, more and more.

It made me a little bit queasy.

Chapter 7

Becoming a celebrity is a whole lot easier than you'd imagine.

'Over here, Lia!'

'This way, darling!'

'That's great. . . Lifting the glasses in the air. . . Lovely!'

There were three camera crews at the press conference, plus loads of photographers and reporters. The room was hot and stuffy, and the journalists smelled of sweat and cigarettes. Luckily I'd double-sprayed with deodorant beforehand. But I could feel my face going a bit pink.

People want to be famous so they can get rich. It's a well-known fact. Look at all those idiots lining up to be on reality shows. No one becomes a celebrity because they're rich already. What would be the point?

But then I remembered Paris Hilton. She's an heiress. She has pots of cash. Why did she want to be a celebrity? Did she have a choice? She'd really got famous because of that sex video on the internet. My toes curled inside my new Manolo Blahniks.

But I forgot poor old Paris immediately the press conference began.

There's something about being asked lots of questions, with a roomful of people desperate to hear your answers. It makes you feel special. It makes you feel important. It makes you feel like you're really grown-up . . . fully-formed . . . someone who has the answers.

'How does it feel being one of the youngest winners ever?'

'Oh, it feels good. Yes. Very good. Exciting.'

'Are you going to stay at school, Lia?'

'Umm, well I have to. GCSEs. I don't know what will happen after that.'

That was my tactful way of telling the world that I was leaving school as soon as possible. Luckily no one noticed.

'What are you going to do with your money, Lia?'

'Oh. . . I haven't decided. I'll buy my sister some singing lessons so she can go on *Britain's Got Talent*.'

They loved that answer. There was a ripple of approval through the room. The cameras flashed. Natasha gave a whoop from the back of the room. She had to stand there because the lottery publicity people said that minors weren't allowed in pictures. All the approval, all the attention was coming my way. For the first time since she was born, I wasn't having to share with my sister.

I liked that approval. I wanted more of it.

'I'm going to buy my mum and dad a holiday to say thank you for everything they've done for me,' I said. 'I'm going to take all my friends shopping. I'm going to give a load to charity.'

'Have you got a boyfriend, Lia?'

I got an instant flashback to Raf's strong arms wrapped around me – and I flushed and giggled and said, 'No one special,' completely unconvincingly.

When we watched it later on Sky News, my mum shot me a piercing glance and said, 'What was that about, Lia? Jack?'

'Paula! What are you like? Oh my God. Can't I even have a male friend without you thinking we're at it? You have *such* a dirty mind!'

They only showed a few minutes on the news. But the questions went on and on.

'How did you pick your numbers, Lia?'

'How much pocket money did your parents give you before your win?'

'Do you work at your dad's shop, Lia?'

'Tell us about buying your ticket . . . had you ever bought one before?'

I took a big gulp of lemonade when they asked that question – Natters and I both had tall glasses full up with Sprite.

'I can't give you alcohol when you're under eighteen,' said Gilda, as she filled up my flute.

'I was with my friend at the newsagent – he bought it for me,' I said carefully. 'It was the week after my birthday and he hadn't got me a present.'

Oh, they loved that. They were like a roomful of puppies who'd been tossed a ball. Tails wagging, feet scampering. They were all over it.

Which friend? What's his name? What did he think of your win? Are you going to share the money with him? Is it the best birthday present you've ever had?

This was such a stupid question – from the *Daily Star* – that I momentarily dropped my saintly-sweet façade.

'Duh, *yes*,' I said. And then, quickly, 'Err . . . although, if I hadn't actually won anything, he'd still owe me a proper present.'

They all laughed. And then someone said, 'Are you going to get him a proper present now?' and I nodded and grinned and gulped down some more lemonade.

I rang Jack as soon as we got home, when everyone was busy sorting through the takeaway menus because Paula said she was too excited to cook.

'Hey,' I said. 'Umm, Jack, at the press conference I told them, I told them you'd bought me the ticket, right?'

'I know you did,' he said, and he didn't sound too happy. 'We had a couple of reporters come round. Wanted to interview me about how it felt buying someone a present worth eight million pounds.'

'Oh my God, Jack, what did you say?'

He laughed, 'Well, naturally I told them that I bought it for you in exchange for a steamy night of unbridled passion.'

'Oh my God! You didn't!'

'No, of course I didn't. Chillax, Lia, I'm not a complete dickhead. I just said I hadn't got you a birthday present yet so I bought the ticket. And that I'm really pleased for you, and that's it.'

'Oh . . . good. . .'

'My mum was really narked, though, said I should've bought my own ticket.'

'Yeah, but, Jack, it was the numbers that mattered, not the ticket as such.'

'You want to tell that to my mum?'

'Umm, no. Look, Jack, I'm going to buy you a present. To say thanks for the ticket.'

'Really? Like something expensive?' His voice went all croaky. 'Like . . . a *motorbike*?'

I wondered how much a motorbike cost. Loads, I bet. And Jack couldn't even get a licence until he was seventeen.

'Yeah, of course. A motorbike. A car as well, if you want.'

Jack's whoop of joy nearly blew my ear off.

'Yay! I love you Lia!'

And that feeling I had in the room full of journalists, that special, grown-up, approved feeling swept over me again. I was doing the right thing. I was sharing my luck. I was Lia, the lucky, kind, generous one. Jack loved me. I loved him.

As a friend, of course.

Or at least I did, until we got the papers the next day and I saw how he'd totally stolen my moment.

'He bought his friend a lottery ticket . . . and she

won a fortune' was the headline in the *Daily Telegraph*. 'The £8m Sweet Sixteen present' in the *Daily Mail*. 'How Lia got lucky – on a ticket from a friend' in the *Express*.

It was the same in almost every paper. Only the *Sun* didn't go big on Jack, but had, 'Lia the baker's daughter wins a load of bread,' which wasn't much better. Oh, and the *Independent* had an opinion piece on page five. 'Should the lottery experiment end?' it asked. 'Is it right that a schoolgirl wins eight million pounds when the NHS can't fund vital operations?' which made me feel really guilty for about two nanoseconds.

The pictures of me weren't too hideous. The designer outfit did make my legs look nice and long, and the jacket showed off the way my chest had exploded over the last year . . . but in quite a subtle way. I'd had a blow-dry beforehand so my newly-chestnutted curls had that crispy shine; and Natters had done a great job on my make-up. My dark eyes looked bigger than usual, and my mouth a bit smaller.

It was kind of annoying to see that Jack actually had more quotes than I did, and the papers had made him the hero of the story – particularly as he'd said stuff like, 'I'm really glad for Lia that she's won,' and, 'It's totally up to her if she wants to give me anything.' But it could have been far worse, I knew.

The next few days were crazy. Suddenly I was a media star. Mum and I were on breakfast telly. We met Lorraine Kelly, Christine Bleakeley, Adrian Chiles. Lorraine's just as nice as she looks. Adrian's just as snarky.

I was interviewed in the *Daily Mail*, the *Daily Telegraph*, on Radio 1. They all asked if Jack would be interviewed too, but his mum refused.

Jack texted me. *She's really angry. Keeping head down.*

Never mind, I thought. I'd talk to Gilda. Maybe when I bought Jack his motorbike, she could arrange another press conference. Jack's mum'd be happy then. Jack would be happy too.

And everyone would see how nice I was.

Chapter 8

Getting lots of attention is like drinking too much. You get a bit silly. Your judgement goes out of the window. You may want to appoint a sensible friend to monitor your actions in the first few weeks.

'It's a well-known fact,' said Shazia, brown eyes wide and serious, 'that winning the lottery ruins your life.'

'Oh right, thanks a *lot*, Shaz,' I said, buttering some toast – Dad's best sliced white – while she helped herself to an apple from the fruit bowl. Shaz had arrived freakishly early to walk to school with me – so early that I was still eating breakfast. Naturally she'd made herself at home.

'Don't look at me like that,' she said. 'I saw it on Channel Five. A documentary. One girl telling about how she'd been ripped off by all these guys. She was buying them cars, drugs, whatever. Then another woman said it had torn her family apart. Everyone was arguing over the money, saying it was unfair because she'd helped one child more than another.' She shook her head. 'I don't want that to happen to you, Lia.'

'That won't happen to Lia,' said Natasha.

'This girl, she said she'd broken up with her boyfriend six months after the win because he couldn't handle it, and she couldn't trust anyone else because she always thought they were after her money. So she was still single at thirty-five and really miserable about it.'

'Wimp,' I said. 'What was her problem? She could've just gone out with them on her terms, had her own place, done her own thing, never mind if she could trust them or not. She could've been thirty-five and having the time of her life.'

I loved saying stuff like that to Shazia. She was always really shocked.

'Lia!' said Shaz. 'That's not very romantic.'

'Well, Shaz, you were the one standing up for arranged marriages the other day. That's not exactly romantic, is it?'

Shaz looked a bit pink. 'It can be,' she said. 'My

auntie told me that when she met her fiancé, she had never felt anything like—'

But Natasha flapped her hands to shut her up and said, 'Shaz! Shaz! Lia's having a romance!'

'*What?*' said Shaz, sounding a lot more amazed than she should have. After all, I'd had three boyfriends before. Marcus Richardson and I went out twice in year nine, then he started trying to feel me up and I chucked him. I went out with Adam Norris for a whole month during year ten, and things were going quite nicely. We used to go to the cinema and hold hands, and I was quite hopeful that it'd get more serious. But then I went to France for the summer holidays and had a snog with a guy called Thierry (tongues and upper body groping) so I felt I ought to confess all to Adam, who was really upset and chucked me. And just as we thought we might be about to get back together again, his mum got a job in Moscow and they all moved there. You can't really make up with someone on Facebook, so after a bit I'd un-friended him.

Natasha spread Nutella onto her toast and said, 'Raf Forrest. You know, the mysterious one. All the girls in year ten think he's a vampire or an angel or something.'

'How stupid,' said Shaz, throwing her apple core into the bin. 'He's just an ordinary boy like anyone else.'

Shaz was about the only girl I knew who wasn't into the paranormal. She wanted to be an engineer, and she said that because she was into science she wasn't interested in anything supernatural. Strange, eh? Felicia Murray wanted to be a vet, and she'd seen all the *Twilight* films hundreds of times.

'He almost kissed Lia,' said Natasha.

I shushed her. Mum could burst into the room at any time. There was no way I wanted her knowing about my private life.

'He looked after her. She fainted when she found out about the lottery.'

'You *fainted*?' said Shaz in a horrified voice. I knew she thought I'd been a total wimp. Shaz would never faint, even if the school fell down.

'I was just a bit dizzy,' I said, 'it was hot in that café. Anyway, Raf was really nice and caring and walked me home.'

'Oh, there you go,' said Shaz, eyes brightening. 'You see. I told you. Men get a sniff of that money and they'll be flocking around you. I wouldn't trust him, Lia. It's not you he likes, it's the thought of your millions.'

'He's not like that,' I said, indignantly, but then Natasha spotted the time and shrieked with alarm and we had to run all the way down the hill to school. We still only just arrived as the gates were closing, racing through panting and giggling as they clanged shut behind us.

There'd been scandals and celebrities at our school before – Loren Anderson got pregnant in year nine, for example, and Jayson Fernandes was suspended for letting off a firework in the playground. Lily Marshall-Fisher got through the first auditions for *Britain's Got Talent* (she sings folk songs and her grandad plays the accordion) and Tommy Christie had a trial for the Arsenal youth team.

But no one had ever got anything like as much attention as me.

All day long, a tight crowd of people followed me. Everywhere I went people smiled at me, shrieked, said, 'Hello Lia!' very loudly, got out their mobiles and snapped my picture. I felt like HRH the Queen. Or even Cheryl Cole.

I'd held my own mini press conference in the classroom at break, in which I was infinitely more frank than I had been the day before. No, I was not going to bugger off to some private school. Yes, of course I was going to leave school as soon as I was legally able to. Yes, there was actually more than eight million pounds in my bank account. Yes, I had spent some already. At Harvey Nicks, actually.

People were asking Jack, 'Did you really buy her the ticket? Do you mind? Is she going to share the money with you?' I held my breath. He shrugged his big beefy shoulders, 'Nah. I'm a really generous friend. And Lia's going to buy me a motorbike.'

And then back to me. And there was no *way* that Jack was going to be the focus of attention. 'Yes, let's go shopping after school. Yes, anyone can come. The more the merrier! Spread the word! Yes, woo hoo, yay, we'll go to Top Shop. Yes, everyone's welcome. *Squee! Squee!* Yes.'

'Lia, can you sit down, please?' said Miss Turner, who taught us RE. 'You may have got lucky once this week, but that doesn't mean your luck is going to last.'

Kelly Anderson stuck her hand up. 'Miss! Do you think Lia's jackpot win is a gift from God? Or destiny? Or just random?'

'I have no idea,' said Miss Turner, 'which makes me a what, Kelly?'

Kelly looked baffled. 'A Buddhist, Miss?'

'An agnostic, Kelly. Let's all try and settle down now.'

At lunch we dodged the crowd, and found a quiet spot by the tennis courts. Just me and Shaz and Jack. It was a relief to be away from all those eyes and voices.

I lay on the grass and looked up at the sky and imagined my money as a huge stack of twenty pound notes, reaching up to the clouds. A mountain of shoes and bags and clothes and make-up. A pile of books and DVDs, laptops and iPods and . . . and . . . stuff. As much stuff as I wanted. Stuff for everyone I knew. New stuff every week. It was dazzling. It was incredible. I'd have to buy a huge house to put all the stuff I was going to buy in. I'd have to have a walk-in wardrobe . . . a personal dresser. . .

I could have anything I wanted. I could style my life any way I wanted it. I'd be like someone in a glossy magazine, showing all the special things in their life. Unique pictures and clothes and furniture. Objects that reminded them of holidays and adventures and people. You have to have money to have stuff like that. And if you don't, then somehow you're not as real.

It was warm in the sunshine, and I was sleepy and my mind was drifting. I could hear the murmur of voices. Shaz and Jack. I was always proud that they got on with each other, given how Shaz was kind of serious and sensible and wore a headscarf and all that, and Jack took nothing seriously at all. I was the missing link and I obviously did the job well, because without me I didn't think they'd have ever spoken to each other.

'You know,' Shaz was saying, 'he could be. . .'

'Leave it to me,' said Jack. 'I'll see him.'

I opened my eyes. 'What are you talking about?' I asked.

'Oh nothing,' said Jack lazily.

'Lia,' said Shaz, 'are you all right? You look a bit out of it.'

So I sat up and shook my curls to make sure there was no grass stuck in them, and said, 'Who, me? I'm fine. Fine. Never been better.'

Science was the last lesson of the day. I sprayed on some Impulse. I smeared Vaseline on my lips. I applied Mum's lash-lengthening mascara. I undid two buttons of my silky cream top (The Hospice Shop, three pounds). Thank goodness we didn't have a school uniform. I was ready. Bring on the lab partner!

I glanced over towards Raf as I slid into the seat next to his. I batted my lashes. But he looked away.

His nose wrinkled. My stomach clenched. No one had looked away from me all day. His hands were bunched into fists, knuckles white against the dark wood of the lab tops. He was definitely ignoring me. OMG. What had *happened*?

Mr Pugh was the first teacher of the day to congratulate me on my win.

'Marvellous! Wonderful! Fantastic!' he said. 'I hope your Maths teacher is going to work out the probability for you. . . Well, Lia, the sky's the limit. How are you going to make a mark with your money?'

'Ummm . . . I don't know,' was my feeble response.

Mr Pugh thumped his desk. 'Scientific research!' he roared. 'The call of the new! The possibilities! With that money, Lia, you could make a real difference! You could find cures to terrible diseases! You could find energy sources that would slow global warming!'

Oh God. 'Yes, but Mr Pugh, I'm not very good at Science,' I pointed out, even though he'd said so himself quite recently.

'Never mind, never mind, it doesn't matter,' he beamed – certainly not the impression he'd given at the last parent-teacher consultation evening. 'You can fund research, Lia. Do you know how difficult it is for scientists to get financial backing for their research? You must look into it. . . I'll give you some websites to look at after the lesson.'

The whole class was shaking with laughter. But Raf sat still as a statue in his seat. I stole a glimpse out of the corner of my eye. He had his head turned away, as though the sight of me revolted him.

What the hell was the matter with him? He'd almost kissed me . . . he'd possibly been stalking me – how *did* he know my address? He liked me, I was sure of it. What had happened between then and now? What had I done wrong?

Nothing. I'd done nothing wrong. Huh. If he was going to come over all Edward Cullen, then he could get stuffed. Stupid vampire stalker. Shaz was right. He *was* after my money . . . and now he'd realised he wasn't going to get any.

I couldn't quite work out how he'd come to that conclusion, but it didn't matter because he was correct. Obviously. Paranormal guys make really bad boyfriends, anyway, because they're so hung up on their own problems. Plus they might want to drink your blood.

I made sure all my stuff was ready in my bag so

I could leap out of my seat the minute the class was over. I stood up as soon as the bell rang, pushing my seat back and texting Shaz to tell her to meet me at the entrance. Shaz and Jack were in the top set, doing Triple Science, so I'd been able to carry on my unsuccessful pursuit of Raf away from the beady eyes of my critical friends.

I didn't even look at Raf until I'd made it to the classroom door. Then I allowed myself a little glimpse – a casual glance, taking in the whole room. He was still sitting at our desk, staring into space, making no attempt to put his books into his bag.

And then he brushed his hair away from his face and I saw it. A massive blue-purple bruise, circling Raf's puffy left eye.

Chapter 9

Keep an eye on the price tags.

There was nearly a riot going on at the school gates. A massive crowd was waiting for me, and there was a lot of shrieking – 'Lia! Lia!' – and shoving. Shazia was failing to organise the mob. The noise level increased one hundred per cent when I turned up.

Mr Bright, the school's site manager, told me to go back and wait in reception.

'I'm going to disperse the crowd,' he said. 'It may take quite a while. Next time you're issuing invitations, Lottery Girl, do it off school premises.'

So I was sitting in the school foyer, all by myself for the first time in days, enjoying the quiet stillness of the moment, when Raf came walking past.

He saw me. I know he did. But he looked away. How *dare* he?

'Oi!' I said. 'Raf!'

He ignored me completely and strode off down the corridor. I ran after him, and grabbed his arm.

'Hey!' I said. 'I was talking to you.'

He shook off my hand. He was deadly pale, and his eyes were wild.

'I can't talk to you,' he gasped, and slammed into the nearest door. The disabled toilet. Bugger. I stood as close to the door as I could, and I was sure I could hear something – a kind of moaning noise. . .

'Lia!' It was Shaz. 'Come on! Mr Bright's got rid of everyone and now it's just your sister and Daisy and Roo and a few others.'

'I'll just be a minute,' I said. Was he OK? Was he ill? Was there a full moon?

'What is it?' asked Shaz.

I gestured to the loo door and whispered, 'It's Raf . . . he's in there. . .'

'Oh, for heaven's sake, Lia,' snapped Shaz, not bothering to whisper at all. 'Get a grip.'

I followed her to the gates, where 'a few others' turned out to be about thirty girls from our year. Natasha was standing with three girls from her class – Sophie, Molly and Keira. I'd not seen them with her before, and just looking at their clothes and shiny-straight hair and accessories, I'd have said they were out of her league, friend-wise. But they all seemed to be laughing and chatting together like real true BFFs.

I raised my voice. 'OK, I'm going to the shopping centre and I'll buy one thing for everyone. But if you're not actually my friend' – I caught the eye of Georgia Gerrard – 'then you have to carry either my bag or the bag of one of my friends. Until we've finished buying everything that we want.'

'Who's actually on your friend list?' shouted Alicia, Georgia's sidekick.

'Well, not you, Aliss-ee-ya.'

'It's Aleesha,'

'I *know*, Aliss-ee-ya. You'll be carrying my sister's bag. Shaz, Daisy, Jasmine, Roo, Mimi . . . you can all get your bags carried too,' I said, eyes raking the crowd, desperate not to miss out anyone crucial.

'So, for one measly designer tee we have to act as personal slaves to losers like Shaz and Roo?' said Georgia. Bitch. I'd have said she was a racist bitch if she wasn't actually black. Although, I wouldn't have actually said it at all, because she would have beaten me up.

I opened my eyes wide. 'I don't see you offering to buy me anything, George. Fair's fair. . . And I won't get you one at all if you diss my friends. Piss off.'

But she was already on her way. 'Forget it, rich girl,' she flung over her shoulder. A chorus of *oooohs* followed her – but quite a few girls did as well.

In the end, there were twenty-one of us waiting for the bus – me, my twelve designated True Friends and eight bag-carriers. Three buses came and went, too full to squeeze us on. Girls were muttering. Girls were texting.

'It's not my fault,' I pointed out. 'I suppose we could get the Tube.'

Roo shivered. 'Oooh. Creepy.'

Getting the Tube meant walking through the old cemetery. The dark, overgrown, scary old cemetery, full of tumbledown grey headstones, ivy and rats. Sure, the path was lit, and well-used, and there was no need to explore further into the wild tangle of bushes and brambles. But we tended to avoid walking there alone. We knew there were ghosts lurking in the green shadows – not to mention perverts.

We'd be fine all in a big group, though, and I was turning towards the iron gates when Natasha pointed across the road. 'Look – a taxi firm. We can go in style.'

'Oh, *brilliant* idea, Nat,' I sighed – bloody hell, how

much would a fleet of taxis cost? – but she charged across the road and started interrogating Reza, the taxi company's owner.

'Four to a car . . . we'll need six cars. . .'

'No, we won't,' I said, and randomly picked out Lindsay Abbott, shouldering Roo's rucksack. 'Look, Lins, why don't you come shopping another time? I'll get you a T-shirt, OK?'

Lindsay looked pretty upset, but walked off anyway.

It still took about twenty minutes for Reza to summon five cars, by which time I was regretting ever agreeing to the whole trip. Plus Mum had texted me three times. Of course I didn't bother to find out what she was moaning about.

Out of the corner of my eye I noticed Raf trudging along the road, pale-faced, head down, still in human form, obviously. He passed the internet café without a glance at me, reached the iron gates of the cemetery and disappeared. Huh. We could've bumped into him at the Tube station. Stupid Natasha.

Reza made me pay up before we set off. Ninety pounds. He raised his eyebrows when I pulled out a brand new cheque book from the same bank that the Queen uses. Then Shazia picked up an old copy of the *Daily Mirror* and showed him my picture.

'Oh yes! Lottery Girl!' he said, gold teeth gleaming. 'At your service! You want regular taxi?'

'Maybe. . .' said Shaz. 'If you give her a discount now, she'll think about it.' And so he knocked ten pounds off the price.

'What a bargain!' said Shazia, squeezing into the back of a Ford Focus with Daisy and Roo, leaving the front seat free for me. It was nice of her, but I felt a bit like I was the mum and they were the kids, especially when I heard them giggling in the back.

I'd planned a quick swoop on Hollister and then maybe a slower stroll around Top Shop . . . New Look . . . Gap . . . H&M. But when we got to the mall, the crowd headed for the big department store. I tried to veer off into H&M but they all groaned.

'It's a bit boring in there,' said Shaz.

'We want to try on designer stuff,' said Roo.

I wasn't so interested. I'd had my fill of designer clothes the other day. I didn't really like buying stuff that was finished . . . that I couldn't customise. This shop was OK, but it wasn't anything like as special as Harvey Nicks. In fact, it was more my mum's kind of place . . . a bit middle-aged.

I picked out a few T-shirts, but nothing amazing

. . . the more I looked, the less exciting everything seemed. I wandered off into the handbag department, found a gorgeous patent leather shoulder bag, but when I looked at the price – £1,115 – I couldn't believe it. Surely no one ought to be able to afford a bag that expensive? How could it cost so much when other bags – almost as nice – were so much cheaper? Was it because the cheap stuff was made by slaves in sweatshops in India and China? Was it actually *better* to buy the really expensive bag?

I picked it up. I put it down. I picked it up again. I could feel a headache coming on.

My phone buzzed again, and without thinking, I answered it. Mum again. 'Where *are* you?' she demanded.

'Umm . . . at the shopping centre. I came with the girls after school. . . I thought I'd buy them something.'

It felt like a really bad idea right now, and nothing had actually happened. I couldn't stop thinking about Raf. Would he ever speak to me again? Who had given him the black eye? Where was he going? Was he OK?

'What? Kevin's due here at 6 pm. Your personal banker. Did you forget that you've got a meeting with him today?'

OMG, of course I had. 'Err . . . no. . . I'll be back by then. Sorry.'

I looked around for the girls. No one in sight. Then I spotted Shaz's stripy headscarf. By the time I reached her she was at the big communal changing room. Daisy was prancing around in a pink mini dress; Roo was taking her picture on her mobile phone. Natasha's mates had squeezed into white leather trousers. Everyone was laughing and posing and getting on, as if we'd all always been best friends forever.

So I picked out an armful of clothes and I joined in. It was a laugh to see the pictures that Roo took of me in a little black dress, and Shaz in sequins. It was jokes all the way when we wandered over to the shoe department and started wobbling around in six inch platforms, and doing the dance to Lady Gaga's latest video. And it was Natasha's brilliant idea to go and look around the make-up department and try all the most expensive brands.

So, when I looked at my watch and realised it was 5.30 pm, I didn't have the heart to search through their big piles of booty and get them to put the most expensive stuff back. I just handed over my debit card to the sales assistant, and smiled sweetly when she said, 'Oh my goodness! I saw you on the television! You're the Lottery Girl, aren't you?'

And I was in a bit of a daze as I punched my new pin code into the keypad. It was only when she handed me the receipt that I realised how much I'd spent.

Oh my God.

Seven thousand and seventy-two pounds, thirty-three pence.

What the hell would my mum say?

Chapter 10

Get to know your personal bank manager.
He or she can be very helpful.

'Think of your money as a forest,' said Kevin the Bank
Manager. 'It needs to be kept alive . . . replenished . . .
organised. You can't just chop down all the trees and
turn them into sawdust. However big the forest, that's
a wasteful way to behave.'

I tried to look serious and earnest. 'Mmmm,' I said.
'I see.'

'Think of it as a pet puppy,' he said. 'You can't just
ignore it. You have to feed it, take it out for walks.'

'I *was* taking it out for a walk,' I pointed out. 'I was
taking it for a walk to the shopping centre.'

'A fortune like yours doesn't look after itself,' he
said. 'If you go on seven-thousand-pound shopping
sprees every day, it won't last long.'

'It *will*,' I said. I'd worked it out in the taxi. 'I could go out and spend that much a thousand times.'

'So, you do that every day for three years and you've blown the lot,' he said. 'And if you add in a house and a few cars and holidays as well, then we're talking eighteen months. A year and a half to blow eight million pounds. Is that the plan?'

I'd spent the taxi journey home trying to think of ways to avoid mentioning the money I'd spent. And trying to work out exactly how it had come to so much. Obviously the shiny black bag had a lot to do with it. And I'd bought myself the black dress (£250) and some gorgeous red killer heels (£189.50). Shaz only had a long-sleeved top and some eyeshadow. But looking at the receipt I could see that someone had bought trousers for two hundred and fifty pounds, someone else had helped themselves to a T-shirt for forty pounds – forty pounds! – and there were tops, skirts, dresses, jackets – three hundred and fifty for a jacket! It must've been that leather one that Nat's friend Molly was trying on – jewellery, bags, shoes. . .

Natasha had gone to Molly's house to try everything on. She was pink with happiness as we left the mall, giving me a quick hug before she got into the cab.

'Thanks so much, Lia,' she said.

Her mates just waved their carrier bags at me. Talk about rude.

'Thank *you* very much too,' I said as their taxi disappeared, then bit my tongue. I sounded just like – *shudder* – my mum.

Mommy Dearest herself rushed into the hallway the minute I came into the house. I thought she'd start ranting and raving, demanding to know what I'd done, what I'd spent. Instead she was calm and pleasant, offering to make me a cup of tea. There was a funny gleam in her eye, though, and the suspicion of a smirk on her face.

'Kevin's had a call from his office,' she said, as I opened the door to the living room. 'I think you'll find he has all the details of your little shopping spree.'

And he did. Every detail.

'Are you aware you've spent nearly ten thousand pounds in less than a week?' he said, in total neutral mode.

'I know . . . you see, I went shopping with my friends, and I thought I was going to buy them all a T-shirt each, but they tried on loads of stuff, and then we had to leave in a hurry so I could get back and see you, and I didn't have a chance to sort out who was buying what.'

'Ah,' he said. 'So, indirectly, I was responsible for the amount spent?'

'Only sort of,' I said, generously. Mum would never have taken any share of the blame at all. I liked Kevin. It was going to be great, having my own personal bank manager.

'Well, Lia,' he said, 'in that case I need to make amends by discussing money management, before you have no money left to manage.'

And so he did. On and on. Investments and shares and interest rates and savings accounts. Spreading your risk. Government bonds. Independent financial advisers. I sipped my tea, and I nibbled at a biscuit and I nodded and smiled and said, 'Yes,' and 'No,' whenever it seemed to be required.

After a bit he sighed, and said, 'You're not listening to a word I'm saying, are you?' And that's when he started going on about forests and puppies.

'I've got loads of money,' I pointed out. I was wondering if I should get an actual puppy. I'd always fancied one, but mum said it wasn't possible, with everyone working and the cost of dog food. Now, though. . .

'I should be able to buy stuff for my friends if I want. Obviously I won't be doing it every day.'

'You're sure about that?' he said. 'Just a one-off? It's just that we do see some cases of lottery winners, youngsters like you, where people – friends, boyfriends – start to take advantage.'

'No one's going to take advantage of me,' I said. And then I remembered.

'Err . . . I will need a bit of cash quite soon. I said I'd buy a motorbike for my friend. And a car.'

'What sort of motorbike?'

'Erm . . . I'm not sure. He said something about a . . . a Ducati?'

Kevin whistled through his teeth. 'You're going to buy a top of the range motorbike for your boyfriend? And a car as well?'

'He's not my boyfriend. He's . . . it's just . . . he bought me the ticket. You know. As a present.'

'Ah yes,' said Kevin. 'There's no obligation, though, is there?'

'No, but . . . you know. . .'

'I do know,' he said. 'Anyway, looking to the future. Will you be investing some money in your family business? Is the plan that you will take over eventually?'

I sighed. When I was at primary school, having a dad who was the local baker was better than being a celebrity. How cool to have a dad who made everyone's birthday cakes! Who knew how to make doughnuts! I was the source of biscuits and fairy cakes. I made bread and buns and croissants. I might as well have had magical powers.

It was only when I hit puberty that I got embarrassed about having a father whose proudest moment was winning the regional championship for his jam tarts – and I realised that there could be more to my life than royal icing and custard slices.

Unfortunately I wasn't sure what that could be.

'I . . . I don't know,' I told Kevin. 'I mean, Dad always thought I would, but I wasn't sure.'

Mum and Dad hadn't said one word to me about the money and what my plans were. Dad had gone on getting up for work at 5 am every day. Mum was back in the office this week. Presumably they'd want to sit down and sort things out at some point.

'I took a look at it on my way here. A nice little shop. Your dad must be having a hard time in the current climate.'

'I suppose so . . . I don't know.' I squirmed inside at the thought of discussing Latimer's Loaves with Dad. What if he wanted me to sign on the dotted line, promise to take it over one day?

'You said at the press conference you wanted to buy singing lessons for your sister,' he said.

'Oh yes. . . I think she's sorting them out,' I said.

'Good,' he said. 'Lia, have you thought at all about what you want to do with your money? You'll need some ideas before you talk to the financial advisers. I'd strongly suggest that they set up a trust . . . keep the bulk of the capital safe until you are older.'

'I have got a plan,' I said, keeping an eye on the door. I didn't want Mum overhearing.

'I want to leave school. As soon as I can. And buy myself a really cool flat, and a car. I want to be independent and free and run my own life. I want to go on holiday with my friends, not my family. That's the plan.'

He had quite a nice face, Kevin, for an older man. He had big, pale blue eyes and blond hair, and only a few wrinkles around his eyes. They scrunched together as he smiled at me.

'And what will you do all day?' he asked. 'A little light shopping? Watching your enormous new television?'

'I don't know,' I said, although, yes, obviously, those would be important components of my dream life, along with planning holidays, meeting friends and reading magazines.

He sighed. 'Your financial adviser will be able to tell you how to achieve all that. You can invest your capital, make sure it generates a reasonable income. You'll need a solicitor to act for you when you're buying your flat. If the vendors get a sniff of a lottery winner they'll hoick up their prices.'

'Oh right,' I said.

'What do your parents think about this plan?' he asked.

'Well, they don't really. . . I haven't really. . . Can you not mention it yet. . .?'

'Everything we talk about is completely confidential,' he said. He scratched his head. 'But I'd suggest you share your plans with them. And think about what you're going to do with your life, in your smart new flat. Don't you think you might get bored?'

Bored? He must be joking. A life without Science and Maths and History? I'd never be bored again.

He opened his briefcase, and took out a leaflet.

'You might be interested in this. It's a weekend seminar for young people who've come into some money. Some are from wealthy families, some are lottery winners like you, some footballers, singers . . .

I think one of the Harry Potter actors attended one. It's about investment opportunities, but also the emotional implications of being so privileged. Some people feel very guilty. Integrating Wealth, it's called. Shall I see if you can go on the next one?'

A whole weekend with a load of rich kids, talking about money? I opened my mouth to say, 'No, thanks, I don't think so.' I needed a bit of normality back in my life. I wanted to go to Camden Market, hang out with Jack and Shaz . . . drop by the internet café . . . see if I could sort things out with Raf . . . I didn't want to think about investment plans, shopping sprees and designer handbags.

But I knew I really should do the sensible thing and sit down with Mum and Dad, to explain my plan to move out and leave school. I needed a delaying tactic. This could be the very thing.

'That sounds great,' I said, looking at the leaflet. 'Integrating Wealth. I think it's a really good idea. Can you sign me up for it?'

Chapter 11

*There may be some unexpected problems
in the early days.*

'Aaaah. Urgggh. Aaaaah.'

'Natasha!' I said, alarmed. 'Are you OK?' She sounded like she was dying.

I'd just come into the bedroom, fresh from a fashion shoot for *Teen Vogue*. Not as interesting as you'd expect, fashion shoots – there's a whole lot of standing around, being safety-pinned into ball-dresses. Natasha was standing by the window moaning like an asthmatic cow.

She turned around, 'I'm fine!' she said, bright and breezy. My heart ached for her. You kind of knew that whenever Natasha was happy it'd always end in tears. 'I was doing my vocal exercises for my singing coach. I have to do them twice a day.'

'Oh right,' I said. 'She's going for the croaking toad

sound, then? Natasha the Natterjack strikes again.'

The old ones are always the best. Nats threw her pillow at me, but there wasn't much force behind it.

'Natasha, I need to talk to you,' I said. I'd been so busy with press interviews and coursework that I'd hardly had a moment to think. Or even spend money. I was tempted to junk the homework, but then Mum and Dad would've got wind of my plans, and I wasn't quite ready for that huge explosion.

'Of course, Lia, what is it?'

'It's Raf. Nat, he's not been at school all week. I'm worried about him.'

'Why don't you phone him?'

'Because he was all funny last time we spoke. Like he didn't want to talk to me. And I've never called him. It would look weird.'

'Do you think it's something to do with his black eye?' asked Natasha.

One thing I'd say for my sister, she was a great listener. Shaz would've rolled her eyes and told me to stop thinking about boys and concentrate on my own concerns, such as homework.

I threw myself down on the bed.

'Well . . . thing is, Nat, what I was thinking, right. . . What if it was Jack?'

She gaped. 'Jack?'

'What if Jack belted Raf in the eye?'

'What, about the football match?' She looked dubious. 'I don't know . . . I mean, it was quite a long time ago.'

I struck my forehead. 'Duh! Nat! Not about football! About me!'

'About *you*? Why?' She didn't have to sound quite so disbelieving.

'Well, Shaz has this theory, you know, that Raf's after my money.'

'But he hasn't been near you! You said he was ignoring you!'

'Look, you don't have to rub it in. He's probably just working on his tactics. If he has tactics, which I don't actually believe he has, because I don't think he is after my money.'

'Well, why say he is after your money?'

'I'm not. I'm saying Shaz thinks he is. And she might have told Jack and Jack might have whacked Raf. As a lesson, to keep away from me.'

Natasha opened her mouth. A look of complete disbelief crossed her face. And then she closed her mouth again.

'It's possible,' she said. 'Lia, Molly and Keira asked

me to go shopping at Camden market with them, isn't that great?'

'I suppose so,' I said. 'Are you sure you want to be friends with them? They seemed a bit. . .'

'A bit what? They're lovely. They were really standing up for you, actually, when Georgia and Alicia were slagging you off at lunch yesterday.'

'You *what*?'

She clasped her hands over her mouth.

'Oh whoops, sorry, Lia. I wasn't going to say anything, it's nothing, really.'

'What were they saying?'

'Oh nothing. They were just reading that interview you did with *Bliss*, you know, and being a bit snarky.'

Huh. I decided not to ask any more. I really liked that *Bliss* article. I'd talked about my fantasy plans to set up an orphanage in South Africa, like Oprah.

'Well, they can be as snarky as they want, because I'm eight frigging million pounds richer than them,' I said, generously. And went back to thinking about my theory. Poor Raf. Stupid Jack.

The thought of two guys fighting over me was kind of . . . well, kind of exciting, particularly as they were the best-looking boys in the entire year.

Of course, I didn't especially fancy Jack, his

blue-eyed, blond, muscled look wasn't really my thing, but he was definitely on the fit side of the street.

Plus he'd been my best friend literally forever, so if we'd been in some rom-com movie we'd have ended up discovering we were secretly in love with each other. *I* knew the falling-in-love-with-your-best-friend myth was just Hollywood WTFery.

But did Jack realise? *That* was the question.

'Why don't you ask Jack?' said Natasha. 'He'd tell you, wouldn't he? If he'd hit Raf. I don't think he would, though. Jack's not like that.'

I gave her a quick glance. Natasha had always hero-worshipped Jack, something I'd hoped that I'd teased out of her.

'Or ask Raf,' she added.

Hmmm. I'd planned to see Jack anyway at the weekend. I could go and see Raf afterwards. Oh God. It was all going to be incredibly awkward and emotional and difficult.

I couldn't *wait*.

I got up. 'Thanks Nat, helpful as ever,' I said, and then sprinted fast for the bathroom, even though it was her turn on the rota. I heard her anguished squeaks just behind me as I slammed and bolted the door.

Next morning, Mum looked up from her coffee as I put my jacket on.

'Going out?' she said. 'I was thinking that we should have a chat, Lia. Talk about holidays, and, you know . . . plans. I've contacted a few estate agents, and I know your dad wants to speak to you about the business.'

'Yeah, of course,' I said, my heart sinking. 'Just not now, right?'

Normally she'd have told me I was being rude and ordered me to sit down. But this time she just smiled and stirred her coffee. I wasn't sure if I liked it. It was as if she'd had a lobotomy.

'The lottery press office called yesterday,' she said. 'They've had a few more media requests for you. The *Daily Express* want to do a photo-shoot and an interview, and maybe *The Times* as well. And *Hello!* magazine is interested too.'

I looked around. 'Here? *Hello!* want to do a photo-shoot in my lovely home here?'

'Hopefully we won't be here too much longer,' she said. 'The estate agents—'

'Look, I've got to go,' I said, hastily. 'Say yes to Gilda, and we can talk later, OK?'

I waited for the blast-off. But she just said,

'Don't worry, darling, we can talk any time.'

Odd. Very odd. I thought about it all the way to the café where I was meeting Shaz for breakfast before my bike-shopping spree with Jack. But as soon as I got there, I forgot all abut my mum. Shaz's eyes were bloodshot. She was blowing her nose.

'What's the *matter*?' I said, sitting down. 'Shaz! What's happened?'

Shaz sniffed, and reached under her chair and pulled out a plastic bag.

'I'm really sorry, Lia,' she said. 'I can't keep these.' And she handed back to me the floaty, long-sleeved top that she'd bought when we went shopping, and the pretty headscarf and bangles from Camden market.

'What? *Why*? Everything's perfectly modest' – I knew Shaz's dad's views on women's clothes and I never wore short skirts or low-cut tops at her house, which often put me off going there, to be honest – 'and they *really* suit you, Shaz. The colours are gorgeous.'

Her dark eyes brimmed with tears. 'My dad says I've got to give it back to you. He said if I wanted it I would have to pay you for it, but it's so expensive, Lia, and I don't think I can afford it.'

'But why? I've got loads of money.'

'In the Koran it says that you can't profit by gambling. I thought it was OK, because it was you gambling, not me, and Dad thought it was OK too, but he checked with the imam yesterday and he said' – she did a gigantic sniff – 'that I mustn't accept anything from you. Not a penny.'

The waitress brought us two hot chocolates and two croissants. We'd been coming here on weekend mornings for so long that we didn't even need to order.

'I don't believe it!' I said. 'That's crazy!'

Shaz shook her head gloomily. 'No, it makes sense, really,' she said. 'I understand it. But it makes things difficult. I'll have to be very careful that you don't ever pay for stuff for me – even this hot chocolate.'

'What about a present? Come on, Shaz, surely the Koran wouldn't want to stop me buying you a present? We're best friends! And I'm not even a Muslim.'

Shazia looked very grave. 'I know,' she said. 'My father said that if you were a Muslim sister then he would not permit me to be friends with you any more. But because you're not, he thinks it's all right. He's going to double-check with the imam.'

'Shaz! Your dad can't tell you who to be friends with!'

'It's not that he wants to dictate my friendships,' she said, 'but if you were a Muslim and you didn't see why gambling was wrong, then I probably wouldn't want to be friends with you anyway.'

'But it's not really *gambling*. It's the lottery! It makes loads of money for good causes!'

She shook her head. 'I thought that as well. But the imam says it's definitely gambling.'

There weren't many Muslim girls at my school – Shaz kind of stuck out with her headscarf. Most of them went to the girls' school round the corner. But Shaz was determined to go to the school with the Science specialism, and when we got friendly in year seven she was just totally normal. Then her dad started going to the mosque more often, and the headscarf appeared, and every now and again it was a bit of a problem, like when she couldn't have lunch during Ramadan.

But we'd never had a problem like this.

I got up to go. Shaz still looked really miserable, so I said, 'Why don't you come with us? Help us look at motorbikes?'

'Are you sure?'

'Yeah, it'll be really boring just listening to Jack droning on about engine power and stuff. And anyway, you're really good at Physics. You can advise us.'

'Oh well, OK,' she said, and she did look happier. I congratulated myself.

Jack lived at the other end of Tithe Green and the garage was miles away in Enfield, so we called a taxi. I sprang out to ring the doorbell, while Shaz texted Jack to get him to come down.

Unfortunately Jack's mum answered the door.

'Hello, Lia,' said Donna, face sour as a pint of week-old milk. 'What can I do for you? Perhaps you want to book a course of manicures, to match your mum's new acrylic nail extensions. She was telling me all about how you're going to buy them a holiday, get your sister singing lessons.'

Oh brilliant, thanks Mum. Donna owned the Hard as Nails Salon, right next to Latimer's Loaves. It sounded like mum had been in there, spending my money. Huh. I had better things to spend my money on than her artificial claws. I'd have to put a stop to that.

I wasn't quite sure how.

'Hello Mrs Hargreaves,' I said, really politely.

'Is Jack there? We arranged to pick him up and we've got a taxi waiting.'

'Oh you've got a taxi waiting, have you?' she said. 'Wouldn't want to spend all your money on keeping a taxi waiting. After all, we're still waiting to see what arrangement you're going to come to with our Jack.'

'Errr . . . what?'

She narrowed her eyes, so all I could see were her clumpy lashes.

'You know very well what I mean, Madam Lia. You need to play fair with my son.'

'But—' I said, and then Jack came thumping down the stairs, grabbed his jacket, said, 'Bye, Mum, come on, Lia,' and jumped in the back of the taxi with Shaz.

'Umm, goodbye,' I said.

She was looking at the taxi. 'You watch it,' she said. 'I know all about you, Miss Lia Latimer.'

'Errr . . . bye. . .' I said, and walked away. I was nervous – what could she mean? Oh God. I just hoped she'd be really pleased and surprised when she saw the amazing bike I was going to buy for Jack. So pleased and surprised that she'd forget anything else she might or might not be thinking.

You'd have thought it would be easy enough buying a motorbike, wouldn't you? Two wheels, handlebars, shiny bit in the middle. Jack was buzzing all the way in the cab, talking about the sleek, mean machine he was going to get. It was kind of annoying. He should have been a lot more grateful.

I was almost glad when we got to the garage and he immediately got into a fight with the salesman.

'I am not showing a boy of your age a sports bike,' he said. 'A 50cc, that's where you need to start. You're not even old enough for a provisional licence yet. Tell you what, son, why don't you come back when you're seventeen?'

'What happened to the customer always being right?' said Jack.

'I don't believe for one moment that you can afford a bike like that, and you certainly won't have the skill to ride it. Anyway, without a licence, I can't let you try it out.'

'I can afford it. My friend here's just won the lottery.'

He looked at me. 'Oh yes,' he said, 'read about you in the *Mail*. Going to save the world, aren't you?' When I nodded – what else could I do? – he said, 'Well, if you value your friend's life, you'll listen to me. I'm cutting my own throat here, but I wouldn't want to sign his death warrant.'

'Just let us have a look,' said Jack, 'now we're here.' And he looked at loads of models, and asked masses of questions, and before very long I'd got bored and found somewhere to sit and catch up with Facebook, while Shaz followed Jack around the showroom.

And the next thing I knew, Jack was back and asking me to write a large cheque.

'They'll deliver it,' he said, his face glowing. It reminded me of his sixth birthday party when his dad revealed that he'd secretly put up a Scalextric set in their attic. Jack was so excited then that he wet himself. I glanced anxiously at his jeans to check it hadn't happened again.

'It's just the best thing ever,' said Jack, and he insisted on dragging me over to the far corner of the showroom to see the bike – large, silver, kind of attractive, really. I wondered if I should buy one for me.

'It's not as powerful as the sports bikes, so I think it'll be OK, ' said Shaz, and the salesman said, 'Promise me, now, that you'll have proper lessons. I don't want your death on my conscience.'

So I wrote the cheque and Jack gave me a hug and a sloppy kiss on my cheek and then Shaz gestured to our taxi driver to drive round and pick us up. We'd decided to keep him waiting for us. We didn't want to be stuck in Enfield for a minute longer than we had to.

Jack celebrated all the way back to civilisation.

'This is the best day of my life!' he said. 'Lia, you are a complete and utter star. I can't believe I've got my own bike. Frank'll be so tanked when he sees it.'

Frank is Jack's oldest brother. Jack had spent his whole life trying to be better than Frank, a completely impossible ambition as Frank was twenty-two, gorgeous and played for Tottenham reserves.

'Calm down,' said Shaz, a little bit grumpily. I thought she must be feeling dreadful, seeing me spend so much on Jack when her dad had banned her from accepting anything from me. 'It's only a bike. And you'll need lessons and a licence before you can ride it.'

'Yeah, calm down Jack,' I said, not all that much less grumpily.

'It's so unfair that I have to wait until I'm seventeen to get a licence,' he said. 'If we were in America we could all drive *cars*. Sixteen. That's all you have to be to drive there.'

'And they all have their own cars,' I joined in. 'My dad said that even if I did have lessons and passed my test when I was seventeen, there was no way he could get me a car and pay extortionate insurance as well.'

Shaz and Jack were both laughing. 'Well, that's not his problem now, is it?' said Shaz.

'I suppose not,' I said. Obviously it was great, the possibility of getting a car as soon as I could legally drive. But somehow, all that I could imagine was me having to drive all my friends around. I glanced at Osman, my regular taxi driver – paunchy, grey-haired, chomping on his gum. Was I going to turn into him?

My life was going to be different from everyone else's. I'd never be able to moan about mean parents, or not having enough money to do stuff. It was like suddenly waking up and discovering that you were actually Bulgarian – actually, maybe Osman was Bulgarian, I wasn't quite sure. It wasn't a bad thing; it just meant you were a bit unusual.

I was looking forward to the Integrating Wealth weekend. It'd be good to meet other people who'd had a similar experience. Other Bulgarians.

Anyway, I hadn't forgotten my mission, to find out about Jack's brutal attack on Raf. How to do it, though?

'Did you see Raf's face the other day at school?' I said to Shaz. 'Someone had punched him.'

'I saw he had a bruise,' said Shaz. 'And he's not been in the rest of the week. Maybe he got mugged?'

'Maybe,' I said, glancing at Jack. He didn't seem to be listening, though. He was texting furiously.

'Jack, what do you think?' I asked, trying not to sound as though I were accusing him of anything. 'Did you see Raf's eye? Do you think he got mugged?'

'Who?' grunted Jack.

Shaz nudged him, 'Raf . . . you know . . . *Raf*.'

'Oh yeah, him. Billy-no-mates. Posh-boy Rafe. What about him?'

'His *eye*,' I said, meaningfully.

'What about his *eye*?' mimicked Jack.

'It was bruised. What do you think happened? Do you think he got mugged?'

'No idea,' said Jack, 'and couldn't care less. If someone punched him, it's no more than he deserved. Did I tell you what he did when we played their team? Useless ref should've red-carded him after ten minutes.'

'And he's got dodgy motives for chasing after you, Lia,' put in Shaz.

'Has he been chasing you, Lia?' said Jack, with what appeared to be no more than mild interest.

'Funny that, because I was sure he was gay.'

'He's only interested in one thing,' said Shazia. 'And it's not what you'd think, Jack.'

'Sure about that?' he smirked. I gave him a thump.

'Shut up, both of you!' I said.

'We've only got your interests at heart,' said Shaz, and Jack nodded and put on his most serious face and said, 'You listen to your elders and betters, young Lia. We know what's best for you.'

We dropped Jack off at his house – he had a football match – and Shazia got out too because she was going round to her cousin's house in the next street. She shoved a tenner into my hand for the taxi fare.

'No, Shaz, you don't have to—' I said, but she shook her head firmly and said, 'I do.'

We drove on to the Broadway and I paid the fare – £68.44. They charge a lot for waiting for you. It's almost never worth it. I wondered if I was compromising Shaz's soul by not telling her the full amount. But then, she only came with to do us a favour . . . and perhaps I shouldn't have kept the cab waiting. This was going to be super-complicated. I wondered if our friendship could take it. I really hoped so. I couldn't imagine life without Shaz at my side.

I swung into the internet café. It was much busier today, every booth was full. The customers were mostly sweaty men – the smell was appalling – but there were two groups of girls that I recognised from school. They'd obviously found out that Raf worked here – they were whispering and giggling as they pretended to look at Facebook. Alicia flicked me the finger. I ignored her.

Raf was behind the counter, dark head bent over a newspaper. My heart lurched. But when I got closer I realised it wasn't him at all. His brother Jasper flashed me a wolfish grin.

'Hello!' he said, pushing aside the newspaper, which, I noticed, was an old one with an interview that I'd done about 'Ten things I love'. 'You're Lia, aren't you? I'm sorry about the other night. Must have got the wrong end of the stick . . . didn't realise. . . You're here to see Rafael, yes? He'll be pleased to see you. I'll call him, get him to come down.'

I just grinned like an idiot and said, 'Oh, thanks, that'd be great,'

Jasper pulled out his mobile, called Raf's number. Called again. No reply. He frowned and opened the door at the back of the shop.

'Never keeps his phone on,' he said, 'although I've told him . . . I'll just . . . go and check. . .'

I wasn't sure what to do. I felt Alicia's eyes boring into the back of my head, and I followed Jasper to the doorway, which led to a flight of stairs. Jasper thundered up the stairs. I don't think he realised that I was behind him. Call me nosy – I just wanted to see a bit more of Raf's world.

At the top of the stairs, Jasper pulled a key out of his pocket and unlocked a door. It swung open, revealing an office . . . just like the one over my dad's shop, except dad's is clean and tidy and has carpet on the floor and pictures of us on his desk, and this was dusty and full of piles of paper and the lino was scarred and peeling.

And my Dad's office didn't have a mattress pushed against the corner of the room, with a body sprawled over it.

Raf's body.

Chapter 12

Sometimes your money will be a bit of a social embarrassment — like bad breath. It gets in the way of normal relationships.

'Jesus!' yelled Jasper and he rushed over to Raf. I stayed frozen with shock in the doorway. Jasper dropped to his knees, turning Raf over.

'Wake up! Wake up!' said Jasper urgently, shaking him roughly. Then he drew his hand back and whacked Raf in the face.

Oh my God. I was getting chest pains. I couldn't breathe. Was he dead? Was his brother abusing him?

Raf's whole body seemed to twitch, and his eyes opened. I stepped back swiftly, hiding behind the door.

'What's going on?' I heard him say, and then the rumble of Jasper's reply, but I missed anything else because I was quickly tiptoeing down the stairs, so shaken that I had to hold on to the wall to stop myself stumbling.

Once back in the café I couldn't decide what to do. Should I leave? Call the police . . . social services? Or stay and see what happened next?

'Hey Lia!' Oh God. Possibly the last people on earth I wanted to talk to. Alicia and Georgia.

'Hey,' I said, unenthusiastically.

'What are you doing here? Thought you'd have bought your own Apple Mac by now, rich girl.'

'None of your business,' I said.

'Come to buy yourself a boyfriend, have you?' sneered Georgia.

'Get lost, Georgia,'

'Because that's the only way someone'd look at you. If you paid them lots of money. And even then, they'd want to put a bag over your ugly face.'

I had a choice, really. I could ignore her or. . .

'You bitch!'

'Slag!'

'Stupid cow!'

'Minger!'

I felt someone touch my arm.

'Err. Lia. Jasper said you wanted to talk to me.'

Raf was standing next to me. He was pale, and

there was a red mark on his face, right next to the almost-faded bruise on his eye. But he was effortlessly stylish as usual. I didn't know anyone else who could make a T-shirt look so good.

I gave one last, furious glare at Georgia, and said, with as much dignity as I could muster, 'Oh yes, hey, Raf. I just wanted a word about . . . about something. Science coursework. You know, those experiments we had to do together.'

'Oh yeah, right,' he said, looking a bit puzzled – understandably, because I'd just invented the coursework. Georgia was looking baffled as well – it was unfortunate that she was actually in our Science group.

'Perhaps we could talk somewhere more private,' I said hastily.

Alicia and Georgia erupted into snorts and giggles. Raf ignored them and said, 'Yes, thanks Lia, I could do with some help with those experiments. Let's go into the office,' and walked fast to the back door.

I couldn't resist a triumphant glance at the girls as I followed him. No one was pretending to look at Facebook now. Several had their mouths open.

Jasper reached into the fridge behind him. 'What do you want, kids?' he said, 'Coke? Lemonade?'

'Coke, please,' I said, and Jasper tossed me a can. After a short pause, Raf helped himself to a Sprite, and led the way upstairs.

He pushed the office door open. 'It's a bit of a mess here, I'm sorry,' he said.

Looking round the room I spotted a couple of things I'd missed before. A rickety chest of drawers in the far corner, cream paint chipped and scarred. It looked like something out of a skip. A microwave, a toaster and a kettle. A plate, a fork. A towel, folded on the back of a chair. A stack of books against the wall.

The bedding on the mattress had been crumpled and creased. But now the duvet was pulled smooth, and some faded red cushions were arranged on it, in a slightly pointless attempt to make it look like it might be a sofa and not a manky old mattress.

Raf stood in the centre of the room, clutching his can. I noticed a little bit of toothpaste on his face. It'd make any other boy look like a dribbling nerd. On Raf it was just incredibly sweet and – when one thought about how close to his lips it was – very tasty.

He gestured at the mattress. 'That's all I've got to sit on here, I hope it's OK. Or you could have the chair.'

The office chair had a nasty brown stain on it.

I slid down onto the mattress, sitting with my back against the wall.

'This is fine,' I said. 'Very comfortable.'

'Yeah,' he said. 'I'm sorry.' There was a silence which went on just slightly too long. Awkward.

'I'm sorry, Raf,' I said, 'I didn't mean to disturb you. I just thought I'd come and see you, make sure . . . you know, no offence, from the other day.'

He sat down, not quite next to me, but near enough. 'That's all right,' he said. 'I might have come over as a bit . . . a bit rude. I'm sorry.'

Yes! Very promising! I was surreptitiously scanning the room for anything that would explain Raf's near-coma-like state before. No empty bottles or pills anywhere. I sniffed the air. Bleach underpinned by damp. Not even a whisper of pot.

Not that I really thought Raf was the sort of boy who'd indulge in drink or drugs. That'd be too normal and boring. No, more likely he was recovering from a night of running with the wolves. (Where would werewolves go in north London, anyway? Hampstead Heath? Or would they hang around dustbins like urban foxes?) Or *maybe* he was low on human blood to drink. I shivered and subtly shook my hair in his direction so he could smell my irresistibly edible scent.

'Are you . . . is everything all right, Raf?' I asked, with enormous and unusual tact.

He looked straight at me then, weighing me up with those hard, grey eyes. I felt as though he could see straight into my head.

'What do you mean?' he asked.

'I just wondered. I just . . . I was worried about you.'

He smiled then, almost laughed. 'You've just won millions of pounds on the lottery and you're worrying about me?' His voice was disbelieving.

'I saw that bruise . . . and you haven't been in school all week. I was worried about you. What's wrong with that?'

'Nothing,' he said. 'It's kind. You're a very nice person.'

I was blushing, I knew it. 'Oh, umm, thanks.' I said, and opened my can.

He opened his. We both took a swig. Awkward pause.

'I just thought, you know, that it would be better if we weren't friends,' he said, all in a rush.

'You did? *Why*?'

'Umm . . . errr . . . I always get things wrong when I try and explain. . . Oh God.' He gave me a cute, crooked smile. 'I'm sorry, Lia. It's complicated and I'm bad at putting words together. Your life has changed a lot overnight, and I suppose I just thought you wouldn't. . .' His voice trailed off. He tried again. 'It's just that you're . . . all those girls *stare* and I just thought. . . Jesus, what am I talking about? I don't know. Tell me about you. What's it like, winning all that money?'

So many people had asked me that over the past few weeks. But he was the first one I could really honestly answer. Everyone else was writing it down, or excited, or wanting stuff or giving advice or lecturing, or telling me about their feelings and problems with my money.

'It's odd,' I said. 'It's strange. I don't know who I am any more. I'm just the Lottery Girl, you know, not Lia Latimer any more. I mean, it's great, obviously, it's really exciting and it's fun and all that, but I feel it's changing everything in my life and I don't know where I am in all that.'

'Everything changes around you, just like that' – he snapped his fingers – 'and you don't know if you've changed as well.'

'The bank manager wants me to go on a weekend away for young people who've got lots of money.

Integrating Wealth, it's called. To understand about what it's like and how to cope and stuff.'

He took a sip of Sprite. 'Sounds like a good idea,' he said.

'I thought so . . . but now I don't know. What if they're all spoilt and posh and I don't fit in with them either?'

'It'll be fine,' he said. 'You belong with them.'

That seemed to kill that bit of the conversation dead. We both took big gulps of our drinks.

'Lia,' he said, 'you won't tell anyone I'm living here, will you? It's just that I think it's against regulations. It's meant to be an office, and they might stop me.'

He lived here? He actually lived in this dive? What about the big house on Melbourne Avenue?

'Umm, of course not,' I said, but he must have caught what I was thinking because he said, 'It's just really convenient, you know, when I've done late shifts. I really need the space . . . the quiet. I'm going to make it nicer, maybe paint the walls or something.'

'Yes but, couldn't you . . . what about . . . your family? Don't you live with them?'

'This is better. This was the best I could do. That's

why I was off last week; I had to sort out the furniture and stuff.'

I looked around. There must be a sink somewhere, and a loo, but did he even have a shower? And the microwave/kettle combo must be his kitchen.

He must have been desperate to come and live here, I thought, desperate to escape the big house I'd seen him go into. Come to think of it, it had looked a bit dark and eerie compared to the shiny cars and new paint jobs of the neighbours.

Maybe he really was a werewolf. Or a vampire.

Or maybe he had horrible, abusive, neglectful parents as well as a violent brother.

'Raf . . . are you . . . is everything OK?'

His smile was bigger and more confident. 'It's getting better. I've never really had my own home before. Actually, it's amazing. Do you ever get that feeling that you just want to be on your own?'

Was that a hint? I wasn't sure. But we were sitting quite close on the lumpy mattress. He was smiling – more relaxed than I'd ever seen him. . . I could see the fine hairs on the back of his hand.

Perhaps, I thought, he's like me. He's ready to be grown-up – say twenty-three – and independent, running his own life. He didn't wait until he had eight million pounds; he just got on and made it happen all by himself.

'Oh,' I said. 'Wow. Good for you. That's just what I want. That's just what I'm thinking, that's what I'm going to do. I'm going to have my own place.' And then I ground to a halt, because I was comparing my dream penthouse to this bare room and I thought I'd better shut up right away, before I said something he'd take as an insult.

'I'm sure you'll find somewhere that you'll like,' he said. 'Will you buy a flat? Or a big house for your whole family and you could just have your own bit of it?'

What was this . . . some kind of new Angelic Message? Raf seemed very keen on family togetherness, as long as it was *my* family and not his mysteriously awful one.

'A flat . . . I think. . .' I said. 'It's a bit difficult. I'm not sure how to tell my parents that I don't want to live with them. And the bank manager said I shouldn't look at properties, because they'll know I've won the lottery and they'll put the price up.'

Stupid, stupid Lia, I thought. I was actually getting somewhere and then I have to start blabbing on about myself and my money. On the other hand, what else did I have to talk about? My money had taken me over. I *was* my money.

'I could help – if you want,' he said, and then looked away, as though he were embarrassed, had stepped over some invisible line.

'Could you? How?'

'Well, I could talk to estate agents. Get the details of flats for you. Maybe go and look at some. And then we could look at them together and no one'd realise it was you because they'd think we were together . . . ummm . . . not that I'm suggesting. . .'

'You'd look at flats for me? That'd be great,' I said quickly. 'I could . . . I could pay you for your time, if you wanted?'

'You don't have to pay me,' he said.

Oh God, I'd done it again.

'Oh, I'm really sorry,' I said, 'I didn't realise you were a Muslim. But surely it's OK if I pay you for a job; I mean, it's not like a gift. Maybe you could ask the imam?'

'Ummm . . . what are you talking about? I'm not a Muslim.'

Oh God, how embarrassing. 'I'm really sorry. I didn't mean to offend you.'

Sometimes talking to Raf was like talking to an

139

alien. I could see him thinking through what we'd just said, trying to work it out . . . giving up, shrugging his shoulder. . .

'I'm not sure what . . . I've never been a Muslim. I used to be a Catholic and now I'm nothing.'

This seemed to me to be *exactly* what a fallen angel might say. Angels were Catholic, weren't they? Or was that saints? I wished I'd concentrated a bit more in RE.

'It's just that my friend Shaz. . . Oh well, never mind. Why can't I pay you? I mean . . . it seems so daft that I've got all this money and you won't take any. You could do this place up a bit.'

He smiled then, and I realised how rare and precious that smile was. 'To be honest, Lia, I could do with the money. But you don't need to pay me. I'd like to help you out.'

I reached out and touched his face, the side of his eye, still yellow and swollen.

'What happened?' I asked.

'This? Oh . . . my eye. It was just a stupid accident.'

I didn't believe a word of it.

'Come on, Raf, someone hit you. Who was it? Jack?'

'Your *boyfriend*?'

'Jack is *not* my boyfriend,' I growled.

'Oh,' he said. That smile broke through again. 'Oh. I thought he was.'

Somehow we'd moved closer together on the mattress. Somehow my arm was brushing against his shirt. Somehow our eyes had locked onto each other's. I could feel his breath against my skin. I was holding his shoulder, tipping my face up to meet his. . .

And kissing Raf was just as sweet and strange and special as I'd imagined.

Chapter 13

Set up a system for paying bills and household budgeting, so your spending doesn't get out of control.

The way our family finances used to work was really simple. Mum and Dad paid for everything.

Nat and I got a puny allowance – forty-five pounds a month for me, thirty-five pounds for her – which, half the time, never got paid. In theory we were meant to do chores or get jobs if we needed more cash. Actually, we'd just bum cash off whichever parent seemed to be in a better mood, always pointing out that we hadn't been paid our allowance. I usually reckoned to be able to push up my income to about thirty pounds a week.

As soon as I won the lottery, though, it all changed. Mum and Dad still paid the mortgage, and stuff like gas and electricity, but they started handing over credit card bills to me. And a lot of other ones too.

Anyway, that particular Sunday I was not interested in anything to do with money or even imagining my future in a Primrose Hill penthouse. I wanted to think about Raf's soft lips, and the way I gently slipped my arms around him, and how I applied more lip pressure . . . and touched the smooth skin of his back under his T-shirt . . . and what could have happened if his brother hadn't thumped on the door and yelled for him to take over downstairs. . .

'Really, it's not a great system,' said Mum, chucking me her Visa bill. 'We need to set up a direct debit or something. When are you seeing those financial advisers, Lia? You need to sort everything out properly.'

'Soon,' I said briskly, lying back on the sofa, closing my eyes and conjuring up Raf's big grey eyes . . . that toothpaste taste. . .

'Put a nest egg away for your future,' said Dad, 'and then perhaps we can talk about the bakery . . . the plans I've got. . .'

'And we can move house,' added Mum. 'It's ridiculous that you and Natasha are still sharing a room. You need your own space. Look at this one' –

she waved an estate agent's brochure at me – 'six en suites, a conservatory and a swimming pool. A swimming pool!'

Mmmm. . . Raf, all wet, and not wearing many clothes, me in a bikini, cuddling in the water . . . and my parents sitting on deckchairs, watching with vulture eyes and possibly binoculars and a video camera.

'What's the point of having a swimming pool in London?' I asked, glancing briefly at the Visa bill (£450 at John Lewis, £220 at Top Shop, £140 having her hair done). 'You'd only use it for two weeks a year. And six en suites? You can only use one at a time. Anyway, it's in Hertfordshire. That's not even London.'

'It's virtually London. It's in the green belt. In the countryside, darling. You could have a pony.'

'I don't *want* a pony.'

'You used to cry at night because you couldn't have one. Look, *this* house has a stables and a paddock.'

'Mum, I was seven and I'd just read some book about a girl with a pony. I don't want one now. And I certainly don't want to move out of London.'

'It's still on the Tube,'

'It's still frigging Nowheresville-in-the-Marsh.'

'There's another bill too, Lia. This one came

from Natasha's new singing teacher.'

I looked. I swear tears came to my eyes when I saw the amount.

'*Four hundred pounds*?'

'She's having two lessons a week. It's a wonderful opportunity.'

'Four hundred pounds a *month*. She can't—'

Natasha chose that moment to skip into the room. She was looking all happy and bouncy. Luckily she didn't hear the words 'even sing', because she was talking into her mobile. Mum glared at me. I turned my attention back to her Visa bill.

'Eighty quid getting your nails done? *Jesus*, Mum. Eighty quid! I'll do your nails for that.' Or would I? I didn't really need more money. Typical. A promising source of income opens up just too late to be useful.

'Don't be cheeky to your mother,'

'I'm not being cheeky. I'm paying her Visa bill, which comes to . . .' I turned to the second page, 'an unbelievable three thousand, six hundred pounds.'

Mum looked a bit shifty. Natasha had finished her call.

'Molly's invited me to stay over,' she said, eyes shining. 'Is that OK?'

'Who is this Molly?' asked Mum. 'Why don't you

bring her back here one day? I feel like I never see you any more, Natasha. You should have your friends to stay here.'

Natasha and I both snorted.

'Yeah, right, Mum, where are we going to put them?' I asked.

'Well, Lia, that's why we need to get on and look at a few houses. I know you girls will be much happier when you have your own space.'

It was the perfect opportunity.

'Thing is, I was thinking . . . I might buy myself my own flat.'

'Oh!' said Mum.

'Lia!' said Natasha.

'That's a great idea,' said Dad. 'The ideal investment. You could rent it out for a few years and move into it when you're older. Had you thought where you might look? Docklands?'

'Umm no. . . Primrose Hill, or Hampstead.'

'Very nice,' he said. 'Pricey, mind you, but you can afford it, Lia. And you can charge what you like in rent. You'll find some rich kid who'll want to live there.'

'Umm, well, actually, I want to live there.'

'Yes, when you're older. Maybe when you're eighteen, depending on where you go to university.

146

Buy something you can share with a few friends. Then they'll pay you rent.'

'Yes, well, maybe I won't go to university.'

Dad's face went all serious. 'Look, darling. I know we've always talked about you taking over the bakery. And I know I left school at sixteen and went straight to work with my dad. But you don't have to do that. Not now. Not now you've got all this money. We could get a manager. . .'

'No, I—'

'You don't have to worry about tuition fees or anything,' said Mum. 'I've been looking at some prospectuses for private schools; you could transfer for sixth form, Lia. Natasha, some of these schools specialise in Music – you'd get a great grounding.'

'Look,' I said, 'I'm not bothered about university. I want to leave school as soon as possible. Buy a flat. Live in it. That's it.'

'That's *it*?' Mum looked like I'd slapped her in the face. 'When were you thinking of moving into this flat?'

'Well, you know. Soon.'

'And then what? Parties every night? Spending all your money on God knows what . . . drugs . . . unsuitable boyfriends? I've seen stories in the newspapers about girls who win the lottery and go wild. You're sixteen, you have no idea what you're doing. I've been worrying ever since you won.'

I flung down the Visa bill.

'No you haven't. You've been spending *my* money. You want me to pay your bills for waltzing around getting acrylic nails and hair extensions and new shoes, while I'm stuck at school, bored stiff, learning about stuff I'm never going to need. And in the meantime all my money's going to be used up on your six en suites and giving the bakery a new kitchen.'

Silence. Then Natasha said nervously, 'Look, I'll take over at the bakery if you want.'

'With your Voice? Don't be silly, Natasha.' My mum's own voice was trembling.

'Lia, we won't take a penny from you if you don't want us to. But you know why we live in this house? So that we'd be in the catchment area for your school. We debated moving – somewhere further out, a bigger house . . . but we wanted to make sure of your places. And your dad needed to be near the shop, for his early starts, of course. We could've sold that bakery. We could've had a much easier life, but we wanted what was best for you.'

'Yes, right, but that was your decision. You chose that. Now I'm choosing this. You always just assumed I'd take over the bakery. I want to run my own life.'

Mum's face was grim. Dad just looked sad. I opened my mouth to take it back, say sorry, say I'd buy the six en suites, expand the bakery, but Mum got there first.

'I might have known you'd only think about yourself. Selfish, Lia, that's what you are. Completely selfish.'

'I am not!' I shouted, hoping no one could see the tears in my eyes.

'Your dad works his fingers to the bone for this family. I slave away in an office, writing a load of rubbish on behalf of useless losers to get them mentioned in publications that no one reads. Why do we do it? For you girls. How do you thank us? By throwing everything we've worked for in our faces.'

I was choking with fury.

'I'm not. Anyway, what about you? You're always horrible to me! You threw me out of the house – really late at night! You didn't care what happened to me! You've only been nice to me because you want my money!'

Natasha was crying. Dad put his arms around her.

'Don't worry, Nat,' he said. 'They don't mean it.'

'I do mean it!' I shrieked. 'She is just an evil cow, and I hate her, and I can't wait to get out of here and start spending *my* money on *me*.'

'Well,' said Mum, suddenly icy calm with a rasp to her voice just like Cruella de Vil. I wouldn't have been surprised to find a load of skinned Dalmatian puppies stashed in the freezer. 'You're going to have to wait a few years, madam. Like it or not, we're responsible for you until you're eighteen. There's no way I'm letting you shack up in some flat on your own.'

'Oh yeah?' I screamed, heading for the door. 'Try and stop me!'

Chapter 14

*It can be difficult to get anyone
to take your problems seriously.*

I went to Shazia, of course. The other options – rushing
to an estate agent, buying some penthouse on my
card, running away to Paris with Raf – seemed a little
complicated to organise right away.

She didn't mind me staying overnight, although
she insisted on texting Natasha so my family would
know where I was. I wanted to let them worry – well,
I wanted to let Mum worry – but in the end I agreed
with her that Dad didn't completely deserve to be
punished. After all, his main sin was to marry an evil,
grasping, selfish witch.

'Don't tell me about it now,' she said, mopping my
eyes and making me a hot chocolate. 'You might feel
better in the morning.'

But I didn't. We had the place to ourselves – her

dad was visiting family in Islamabad and her mum was at an all-night twin delivery (she's the head of our local flying midwife squad). I poured out the whole story. But Shazia, while sympathetic and great with cocoa and tissues, wasn't the perfect audience.

'Lia, you should show more respect for your parents,' she said, as we ate breakfast. We'd decided to skip the café, because my eyes were too pink to be seen in public.

'Why? They don't show any respect for *me*.'

'But they are your *parents*. Your parents, Lia. Their job is to care for you and help you make your decisions. Why do you want to move out anyway? You're only sixteen.'

'I want some space. I want to feel grown-up.'

'You'd have loads more space if you bought a new house for your family. You could buy it jointly. It doesn't have to be a present.'

'Yes, but I don't want them telling me what to do. And telling me I'm horrible and selfish.' I sniffed. 'Maybe I should be more selfish. If I look after myself, then no one has to worry about me.'

Shaz shook her head. 'You can't cut yourself off from your family. You need other people.'

I thought of Raf in his makeshift home. He'd understand me.

I scrubbed my eyes with a tissue. 'I was really happy too, before she spoiled it all, because of Raf. You know, Raf Forrest. He likes me, Shaz. He was so lovely. He kissed me.'

Stupid, stupid mistake.

'Oh my goodness, Lia, what are you like? You hardly know this boy. Now you're kissing him? I bet the pound signs lit up in his eyes.'

'I'm in love, Shazia!' I declared rashly, spreading my arms out wide to try and convey the total drama of the moment.

Shaz raised her eyebrows, shrugged her shoulders and said, 'I give up. You're completely mad. You've fallen for a handsome face.'

'Oh Shaz, there's *so* much more than that,' I said. 'We had a really amazing, intimate chat. He is just so gorgeous.'

'But you don't know anything *about* him,' said Shaz. 'You're in love with what? The way he touched you, the way he looked at you? Come on, Lia. What do you think of people in films who fall in love at first sight?'

'Yeah, but that's films, Shaz, this was really amazing.'

'Lia, you totally despise girls who think they are defined by a guy just because he deigns to look at them. Bella flipping Swan. You think they're mad and stupid, don't you? We've *always* agreed about that.'

'Well, I know, but this isn't love at first sight. I've been sitting next to him all year in Science.'

'And he's hardly said two words to you. He's given you the cold shoulder. Now, suddenly, he's staring into your eyes, getting you all worked up. What's the difference? Mmm, let me see. I can't think. Could it be eight million pounds?'

'Oh Shaz, come *on*.'

My phone rang. Natasha. I sent her the busy signal.

Shaz shook her head. 'Don't ask me to give you my approval, when I think you're doing the wrong thing,' she said. 'What kind of friend would I be then? Look, all I'm saying is, get to know him before you leap into anything. What do you know about his family? His home? What's he really like?'

'I'm not doing anything with his family,' I pointed out, to avoid admitting that Raf's brother was definitely abusive and totally gave me the creeps. 'And I've seen his home, actually.'

'Have you? Really?'

'Yes,' I said, and then I remembered it was meant

to be a big secret. 'But I can't tell you about it.'

'I give up,' said Shaz. 'I always thought you had a brain in your head. But now I'm wondering.'

'Oh, you don't understand. You study too hard, Shaz, it's not natural. When you fall for a boy, you'll see.'

Shaz's voice was a little shaky. 'I hope I'll be a bit more sensible than to fall for someone who doesn't share my values.'

'You'll probably let Mummy and Daddy pick someone out for you,' I said nastily.

'What's that supposed to mean?'

'Oh. Nothing. I mean, if that's what you want, that's fine. But I worry about you, Shaz. I mean, all this religion. You're letting it rule your life. Hiding under a headscarf. It's not very. . .'

Shazia slapped her hand down on the table. 'That's enough!'

My phone rang again. Mum. I switched it off.

'You – I thought you understood, Lia. I thought you respected me.'

'I do, it's just. . .'

'You don't get it, do you? I love Science, right, because it's about rules. It tells me how the world works. Islam is the same for me. It tells me what the rules of life are. How to behave. What good decisions look like. I can't always keep everything as I should do, but I try my best.'

'Oh. I didn't realise. You never said.'

'You never asked.'

Of course I didn't ask. We didn't sit around at school talking about religion and rules for life and stuff like that. We talked about celebrities and coursework, boys and shopping.

'You should've said.'

'You *could've* asked. I saw how shocked you were when I started covering my head. No one ever asked me why.'

'Oh. Well, it was a bit awkward.'

'Sometimes I wonder what we've got in common.'

'Oh well, thanks a lot, Shaz.'

'Look,' she said, 'I think – I don't know if I should say anything. . .'

'Don't hold back,' I said, trying not to sound bitter.

'It's just, I'm not sure you're handling all this very well. All the media stuff. People are getting upset.'

'People?'

'Girls at school. They're saying stuff.'

'What stuff?'

'Oh, you know . . . have you looked at Facebook recently?'

'Ummm . . . not in depth.'

I had about a hundred messages in my inbox and four hundred and sixty notifications. Every time I looked at Facebook I felt as though I were drowning.

She led me to the computer. She called up a page called 'Lia Latimer the Lottery Girl is a mean tight-fisted ugly slag'. There was a picture of me from *Hello!* simpering over a glass of lemonade – so many wall posts they made my eyes go blurry. And two thousand seven hundred and thirty-eight people had already liked it.

'Obviously most of them don't even know you,' said Shaz, while I sat in total shock, hands over my mouth, letting out little whimpers of distress, 'but some are from school. As far as I can tell, it was started by Lindsay Abbott – do you remember when she couldn't fit in the taxi when we went shopping? I think she's really narked that you never gave her a T-shirt like you said. And of course Georgia and Alicia never really liked you, anyway. Open your eyes. You'd better read it.'

It was horrendous. Totally random strangers calling me a jammy bitch, and about twenty wall posts from Lindsay and her friends moaning about the taxi thing. And saying rude stuff about my clothes and my hair and my body ('See Lia's got a nose job already – wonder how much that cost her?'). Why did people hate me? People who didn't even know me.

'Shaz, there must be something I can do. Complain to Facebook . . . get it taken down. . .'

'Possibly,' she said, 'but I doubt it. You're a bit of a public figure now.'

'Shaz! What can I do?'

'Well, you could try actually talking to people at school instead of spending all your time giving interviews.'

'You're not being very helpful,' I said. 'I'm beginning to think you actually agree with these people.'

Shazia sighed. 'I don't agree with them, Lia, I just think you've really changed. Even your clothes. You used to be a really fun, nice person. Now . . . I don't know. . . You're just coming over as a bit . . . a bit. . .'

'What?' I squeaked. 'Selfish? Spoilt? Thanks a *lot*, Shaz.'

Shaz's face never gives much away. She generally looks serious and sensible, but when I looked at her through my tears I realised that there was another side to Shaz, a self-righteous, judgemental side.

'Forget it!' I screamed at her, 'I thought you were my friend. But you're not interested in me at all!'

'No – Lia—' she said, but I was at the door.

'I'm going!' I said, 'I might just go and see if Raf wants to go away with me. We could go to Paris . . . or New York. . .'

She rolled her eyes. 'I'm not saying anything.'

'Good!' I slammed the door behind me.

I headed for the Broadway. Perhaps Raf would be at the café. Perhaps he'd be coming off his shift.

We could do anything. We could go to St Pancras and get on the Eurostar and spend the night in Paris. We could book into the Ritz. We could fly to New York. I was dizzy just imagining it all. There was nothing . . . nothing . . . stopping me doing whatever I wanted.

As long as that's what Raf wanted as well.

Chapter 15

Think before you act.

'Lia!' It was my dad's voice. His head was poking out of the door to Latimer's Loaves. 'Thank goodness. We were so worried about you. Come on in, sweetheart, and we'll have a chat.'

I shook my head. 'No.'

'Come on. Just with me. Not your mum. You and she are too similar, you know, two hot tempers.'

'Oh.'

'The girls are dying to see you. You haven't been in since your win.'

Oh great. Selfish old self-obsessed, self-centred Lia.

'OK then,' I said.

'Come and say hello to them,' he said, patting me on the shoulder. 'I'm just finishing up something in the office, I'll be with you in five minutes. We can have a cup of tea.'

He disappeared into the back of the shop and I took a shaky breath.

'Hello Lia!' chorused Rita and Norma. They were both pushing seventy, but they'd been called 'the girls' by my grandad, and they were still 'the girls' now, even though they both had hundreds of grandchildren and every time I went into the shop I heard all their stories about them. They reminded me of my grandad. He used to make gingerbread men with iced clothes, especially for me.

Latimer's Loaves had been part of my life forever – the shelves of jam tarts and currant buns, the iced fancies, cream cakes. Not a lot had changed over the years. Sugar and yeast smells of childhood to me, warm, homely, secure – and stifling.

I forced a big smile onto my face for the girls and Rita said, 'We're so excited for you, darling. What a wonderful stroke of luck. Winning the lottery! At sixteen!'

'Oh, thanks, Rita.'

'Are you having fun, sweetie?' asked Norma. 'We've been watching you on the telly . . . reading about you in the papers. We're all so proud.'

'Oh, err, thanks Norma. It's a bit weird.'

'Much better to win the lottery at your age, darling.

I buy a ticket every week, but what would I do with the money if I won?'

'I tell you what I'd do,' said Rita. 'A nice cruise. I've always wanted to go on a cruise. And then there's the family to think of. . .'

'Are you all right, darling?' said Norma. 'You look so pale.'

'Give her a gingerbread man,' said Rita. 'That's your favourite, darling.'

Rita always gave me a gingerbread man when I went into the shop. Over the years I'd devised many ways of avoiding eating them. But that day I bit right into his thigh. Pure comfort food.

'Thanks, Rita,' I said in a slightly muffled voice.

The door swung open.

'There you are!' said a loud voice. 'I thought I saw you coming in here.'

'Hello, Donna,' said Norma. 'Everything OK? What can we do for you?'

'I want a word with Lia, that's what,' said Donna.

'Hello, Mrs Hargreaves.' For some reason I felt nervous. I nibbled my gingerbread man's right arm and Rita beamed.

'Lia Latimer,' said Donna. 'At last. You can't avoid me any longer, you know.'

'I wasn't avoiding you,' I started to say, but a crumb hit the back of my throat and I started coughing.

'You've bought Jack a motorbike. A motorbike. How bloody dare you?'

'Umm . . . he wanted one. . .'

Her voice was really loud. 'Firstly, my brother fell off his motorbike when he was just about Jack's age and has never been the same again. I would never allow my boys to have one.'

'Oh!' She must mean Jack's Uncle Terry. I knew he wasn't right in the head. I never knew why.

'And secondly, Jack's morally entitled to half that money. He bought you that ticket.'

'Umm . . . it was a birthday present.' My eyes were full of tears from the stupid gingerbread crumbs.

A woman came into the shop, and asked Rita for a sliced wholemeal loaf. It didn't put Donna off one little bit.

'He bought you the ticket! Eight million pounds! And you try and fob him off with a motorcycle that'll probably kill him.'

'You bought Jack a *motorcycle*?' said my dad. I didn't even know he'd come downstairs.

'That's what he wanted,' I said. 'It's a really nice one.'

The wholemeal loaf lady showed no signs of leaving. Two more women had come in and were just standing there, blatantly listening.

'You're out of order!' said Jack's mum, her voice shrill and shaky. 'You're putting him in danger so he can't make a claim on your fortune!'

Rita and Norma shook their heads and clucked.

'That's not very nice, dearie,' said Norma. 'I think you need to calm down a bit.'

'There is no way that I am allowing him to keep that bike,' said Jack's mum. 'I'm sending it straight back, and you can give him a cheque instead. And for a sight more than twenty thousand pounds, thank you very much.'

'Now hang on a minute, Donna,' said my dad.

'Jack's got rights!' she said. 'Jack should have half that money, and you know it. We're going to sue you! We've got a lawyer! Call yourself a friend? You're just a selfish little slut!'

'That's enough, Donna,' said my dad. 'Why don't you leave now—'

'I am not a slut!' I spat. 'How dare you? I didn't have to give Jack one penny and I've just spent thousands of pounds giving him just what he wanted.'

'Not the first time,' she snarled, 'I've told you I don't like the way you hang round with my son. . .'

'Shut up!' I screeched, grabbing one of Rita's fruit Sponge Specials and hurling it at Donna's open mouth. It flew through the air – she screamed – and landed right on her chest. Cream and little lumps of pineapple slid down her crinkly cleavage.

'Lia!' said my dad. 'What have you done?'

Donna howled, 'I'll be talking to my lawyer!' and ran out of the shop.

'Get lost!' yelled Rita.

'You deserved it!' cried Norma.

And then I heard a cough. I turned around.

Oh no. No, no, no.

Raf was standing right behind my dad.

Chapter 16

A lot of people will be jealous of your good fortune. It's not easy — but it's not your fault either.

How could he just appear out of *nowhere*? And why, just at my moment of total humiliation? I gave a gigantic, yelping sob and rushed to the door, with my dad, the girls, several customers and Raf in pursuit.

They caught up with me halfway down the hill, just outside the fish shop.

'Lia!' said my dad. 'Come back . . . come back inside and we can talk about this sensibly. Don't worry about that stupid woman, she hasn't got a leg to stand on.'

I was desperately searching for a tissue, determined not to cry in public.

'It's the Lottery Girl!' said someone in the crowd.

'Disgusting behaviour,' said someone else.

166

'That poor woman, she had to go into Help the Aged to get wiped off.'

I sniffed, hiccupped and sneaked a cautious glance at Raf. I was expecting him to look completely disgusted at my appalling behaviour. His eyes were grave. But his mouth was definitely twitching.

'It was an accident,' said my dad. 'Norma! Rita! You've left the shop unmanned.'

Rita and Norma shrieked and scuttled off up the street.

'Didn't look like an accident to me,' said the woman. 'Assaulted with a fruit flan! I've never seen anything like it!'

Raf had his hand over his mouth now. I was trying not to look at him, but then my dad said, 'Actually, for your information, it was a Pineapple Sponge Special,' and I lost it altogether and started cackling with laughter, tears pouring down my face.

'Lia!' said my dad. 'Behave yourself!'

'I can't!' I spluttered.

'I'll talk to you later,' he said, stomping back up the hill. He turned back to look at Raf. 'I'll see you 5 am tomorrow,' he said. 'Welcome aboard. It's not usually like this.'

Raf managed to put on his most serious face and say, 'Thank you, Mr Latimer, I'll see you then.' But then he leaned against the fishmonger's window, laughing as much as I was.

'Oh my God. . .' he gasped. 'When you . . . and she. . . And then she had to be wiped off in Help the Aged. . .'

We were doubled up with laughter. I was just inching towards him, hoping I could somehow engineer a hug . . . a kiss . . . when someone tapped Raf on the shoulder.

He stopped laughing right away. Great. His big brother was standing there, alongside an older man. He had the same dark hair, mixed with silver, and his piercing eyes were blue-grey. He was dressed entirely in black, and his face was gaunt, grim and strangely attractive.

'So good to see you laugh, Rafael,' he said, in a deep, gloomy voice.

Raf looked as though he'd never laughed in his life. He was pale, sidling away from me.

'Hello Lia,' said Jasper. 'What's the big joke?'

'Nothing,' I said. The older man turned his eerie gaze to me.

'Lia Latimer?' he asked. 'The girl who won the

168

lottery. Well, well. I had no idea that you were a friend of Rafael's.'

'She's not,' said Jasper harshly. 'Why are you standing around here, Raf? You're meant to be at the café.'

What the hell? I waited for Raf to tell Jasper to piss off, to take my hand maybe, say that I was *more* than a friend. But he just glanced at me briefly, not even a smile, and almost ran down the road to the internet café.

'Raf was just having an interview for a job at Lia's dad's bakery,' said Jasper. 'Did he get it, Lia?'

I nodded. Aha! That was why Raf'd been there. My dad had been going on about taking on someone for the 5 am shift, so he wouldn't have to get up so early every day.

'Another job?' asked the older man. He sighed. 'Rafael's got more important things to do than work in some . . . some. . .' He waved a dismissive hand. 'Some suburban cake shop. It's a tragedy.'

'Never mind,' said Jasper. 'It's good for him.'

The man took my hand. His skin was cold and smooth as marble. 'Thank you, my dear,' he said, 'for making Rafael laugh.'

'Oh, no problem, my pleasure, any time,' I babbled,

completely mesmerised by his sapphire-blue eyes.

He didn't let my hand go. 'You have been given a rare opportunity,' he said, 'a chance to change lives. I would very much like to talk to you at some time—'

'But not now,' said Jasper. 'I'm sure Lia is very busy and needs to get going. Nice to see you, Lia. Come on, Nick.'

He let my hand drop. I could still feel the chill of his fingers.

'Another time, Miss Latimer,' he said. And they walked away, up the hill, past Hard as Nails, past Latimer's Loaves, in the direction of Melbourne Avenue. Huh. They must live in that huge house, while Raf was left to slave in the café and sleep on a mattress.

And then I remembered Donna and the cake and the way the pineapple lumps had clogged up her cleavage, and I rummaged for my phone. I suppose I'd better warn Jack about the tornado coming his way, find out exactly what Donna was planning.

But Jack didn't answer. I wondered about going round to his house, but the thought of seeing Donna – oh God, would I ever be able to go round there again?

No Shaz. No Jack. I had no choice. I headed home.

If Mum was horrible to me, I was buying a one way ticket to New York – but I had to get my passport from her filing system first.

Natasha was all alone. She took one look at me – tear-stained, cream-splattered – and said, 'What the hell? The phone hasn't stopped. Loads of papers wanting to talk to you.'

Oh my God. Oh my God. Donna hadn't gone to her lawyer or the police. She'd gone to the press.

'It was her, Nat, Jack's mum. She came into the shop. She was shouting at me, saying things. . . Nat, I threw a cake at her.'

'You did what?'

'I was really angry – she's such a *bitch*, Nat, she was saying horrible stuff.' My voice turned into a wail. 'And now she's going to tell the papers. . .'

'Oh, Lia!' Natasha threw her arms around me.

'And there's a page . . . a page on Facebook. . .'

Natasha's face gave her away.

'You knew! Why didn't you *tell* me?'

'I thought you knew . . . you've got the new iPhone. I didn't think you'd be that bothered. It's just a bit of teasing, Lia, that's what Molly and Keira said.'

'No one's making Facebook pages about *them*.'

'Yes, but you're like a celebrity now. That's what

171

happens.' Her voice was pleading. 'Don't be upset, Lia, we can make a fan page for you.'

'Oh yeah, great, who's going to sign up for that?'

There was a knock at the door. Natasha went and peeked out of the window.

'It's a reporter,' she said. 'And a photographer. What are you going to do?'

'I don't know! I don't know!'

The front door opened. Mum. Great gulpy sobs were building up inside me.

She was in her gym stuff and on her mobile. 'She did *what*?' she was saying. 'Donna said *what*? She threw *what* at Donna?'

She turned off her phone, and walked into the living room. I braced myself. I hadn't just disgraced myself, after all. I'd ruined the shop's reputation. Mum was going to explode any second – three . . . two . . . one. . .

But she just said, 'OK, girls, damage limitation exercise. I'm going upstairs to get changed, you get the kettle on. We're going to have ourselves a little press conference.'

Chapter 17

A good publicist is essential if you're dealing with the media.

There are times in your life when it really helps to have a mum who's in PR. I'd always wished she did something a bit more exciting or high-powered – Roo's mum, for example, is a marketing executive for Capital Radio and Roo gets loads of really cool freebies. And of course Shaz's mum is constantly rushing off in the middle of the night and delivering triplets who've got stuck.

My mum's job was so dull that I never had anything to boast about. But that day she was a total and utter star.

By the time she got changed, there were five reporters and three photographers standing on the pavement outside.

'If I know that Donna, she'll have given an exclusive to the highest bidder,' she said, 'which is good news for us, girls, because all the other papers will be out to trash her.'

She opened the door. 'Come on in!' she said. 'I bet you could do with a cup of tea.'

They all trooped up the front path and settled down in the living room while we ran around giving them tea and an entire packet of Jaffa Cakes.

And then Mum started. 'Of course, Lia's only sixteen,' she said. 'It's a lot to handle at that age. She's just a child, really. We're really proud of her, how she's handled it. She's only bought things for other people, you know, hardly anything for herself. She's taking it very seriously, going to go on a seminar soon which is about using your money responsibly. She asks me all the time about which good causes she should help.'

Lady Gaga would be *lucky* to get my mum as a publicist.

'Lia's trying to balance out all this media attention with her schoolwork. She's working very hard for her GCSEs. She's a very responsible and conscientious girl.'

I thought guiltily of my neglected coursework. I really ought to motor on with my slightly overdue History project.

'Any young girl might have lost her head momentarily if an older person was shouting at them, threatening them. Of course I don't approve of what she did, not for one moment. Lia will be writing to Mrs Hargreaves to apologise. And of course she should have asked Jack's parents' permission before buying him a motorbike. But you know how girls are . . . impetuous. A bit thoughtless. But she only wanted to make her friend happy and say thank you to him for buying her the ticket. She asked him what he wanted and he said a motorcycle. A really expensive, Italian motorcycle, wasn't it, Lia?'

The reporters munched their Jaffa Cakes, and scribbled in their notebooks.

'It's not surprising, really, if people are upset to see one girl with so much,' said Mum. 'But Lia's very responsible . . . very public-spirited. If it were up to her, she'd probably give it all away. We're spending time talking to her, making sure she ensures her own future is secure.'

She's laying it on too thick, I thought. But they seemed to like it.

'Why did you throw the cake at Jack's mum, Lia?' asked one reporter, reaching for a third Jaffa Cake.

'I really didn't mean to,' I said. 'I was helping my

dad in the shop . . . she came towards me. It was kind of an accident. I was panicking because she was shouting at me.'

I sounded sorry, I thought, and young and scared, and all the things Mum was making me out to be. We were a good team.

'Very upset, she was, according to her dad,' said Mum. 'You know, people forget how young teenagers are – they look like adults, but they're only children, really. Lia's having to grow up very quickly, in the public eye. I'm not excusing what she did – it was stupid and wrong – but she's only just sixteen.'

'Too young to play the lottery?' asked one reporter.

'Possibly,' said Mum. 'You have to be eighteen in the States, did you know that? And they don't give you the money all in one lump, but they pay it out over many years. Perhaps we could learn from that. Lia's going to be meeting with financial advisers soon, and that's the sort of arrangement I'd like her to put in place. It's a lot for a young girl to deal with.'

I just sat there and nodded and smiled.

Then Mum said, 'Actually, Lia's been doing a lot of good deeds, very quietly, no fuss at all.'

Had I?

'She's giving ten thousand pounds towards her school's sports hall.'

I was?

'And one of my husband's employees – Rita, she's called, Rita Boatang. Rita's got a grandson who's autistic. Severely autistic. Lia's going to pay for him to go to America to swim with dolphins. Apparently it could make a lot of difference. Lia's so thoughtful, she said immediately, "How can I help little Alfie, Mum?" We've been looking into it. Lia had actually gone into the shop to break the news to Rita, but Donna – Mrs Hargreaves – interrupted her.'

I was flushed with shame. Why hadn't I thought about Alfie? I'd known about him forever.

'That's brilliant,' said one of the reporters. 'Can we organise a follow-up with Rita and the boy?'

'Of course,' said Mum graciously.

'How much will the trip cost?'

'Around eight thousand pounds,' she said, smoothly.

'Errr . . . I'm really happy to be able to help Rita's family,' I said, sticking on a huge smile and wondering how much more of my money Mum thought I needed to spend to blot out Donna's story. Oh God, Donna's story. What was she going to say?

Then one of the reporters got a call from his news desk, who told him Donna had sold her story exclusively to the *Sunday Mirror*.

'Don't worry, though,' he said to Mum. 'We'll make her out to be the villain of the piece. You've got a lovely girl here.'

And then we posed for some pictures – 'Not too smiley,' Mum warned in a whisper – and they were gone.

I flung my arms round my mum. 'Paula, you were brilliant. You're the best. Oh my God. That was amazing.'

She was smiling and laughing and she gave me a kiss – I dodged – and she said, 'I appreciate the thanks, Lia, but if you call me Paula one more time, I will kill you. I mean it. If you really can't bring yourself to call me Mum, then you have my permission to call me Sarah. You've worn me down.'

'Oh . . . that's all right, Mum.' Call her Sarah? Was she mad?

'Now, you need to get on the phone to Jack. Make sure all's well with him. You don't want a big feud between you.'

But Jack wasn't answering his phone. Nor was Shaz. My stomach lurched.

'Maybe I should go round there.'

'Absolutely not,' said Mum. 'I think you need to keep your head down for a bit. Let the dust settle. You're behind with your coursework, aren't you? I think you can stay nice and quietly at home for a few days, catch up with your work. You've got the Integrated Wealth weekend coming up – you need to catch up with things. Maybe we could go on a day spa.'

'I can't go on a day spa if I'm pretending to be off sick.'

'I'll have a word with your head teacher,' she said. 'If you're giving ten thousand pounds to the sports hall, then I think he'll understand that you need a few days off.'

'Mum, I feel so bad about Alfie. I should've remembered him. I could've given them that money right away.'

She paused. She looked at me. 'I only just thought of him myself,' she said. 'It's funny, isn't it, how when big exciting things are happening to you, you don't remember other people.'

I tried Jack's number again. I tried Shaz. No answer. No answer. I didn't even think about trying Raf's number. I couldn't stop looking at that

Facebook page, the bitchy comments, the jokes about me.

I felt terrible. I felt utterly miserable and defeated and angry and in total despair.

Sort of.

Because if you've got eight million pounds, then even in your darkest moments you're still able to think, oh God, I'll have to go and live in San Francisco to escape this nightmare.

And you know you could, and you could have a great apartment and loads of cool clothes and do what you want.

It takes the edge off your misery. You know those long snakey things they use to teach you to swim? Being rich is like having a permanent noodle in the swimming pool of life.

And that's good – really, it's good. It's just hard to get used to when you're used to wallowing in despair.

Chapter 18

Good advice is hard to find.

Donna's face was all over the front page of the *Sunday Mirror*, frothed up, like she was about to have an old-fashioned shave.

'That's outrageous,' said my mum. 'They've mocked it up with a can of squirtable cream. We ought to ring the Press Complaints Commission.'

'Please don't,' I begged, quickly reading the *Mirror's* exclusive, which was all over pages one and three. It wasn't as terrible as I'd feared. Sure, she talked about suing me for half the money – 'My Jack's entitled to his share' – and accused me of trying to buy him off with a deathtrap motorbike – 'It's going straight back to the garage and if Lia's got any decency she'll hand the cash over to Jack.' And of course they made a big deal out of the cake. But that was all.

'It's not so bad,' said Mum, reading over my

shoulder. 'Anyone with half a brain could tell that picture's been mocked up. She looks a complete fool. And I think she's toned it down a bit, because she's still hoping you might make Jack an offer.'

'You mean she's not going to her lawyer?'

'I hope not. Anyway, look at us. We've totally outclassed her.'

I looked at the *Mail on Sunday*. Me, looking sweet and sorry. Rita's beaming face – she'd rung last night, incoherent with joy and gratitude. Little Alfie. Alfie's tearful mum.

'They've done a leader,' said Mum, turning to the opinion page. 'They say maybe sixteen is too young to be allowed to play the lottery, but Lia has a generous heart even if she is a bit impetuous.'

I was examining my phone for the twentieth time that morning. No word from Jack. Nothing from Shaz. I had no friends left in the whole world. There was a knock at the door.

I ran into the kitchen. 'Don't answer! I'm not talking to any more reporters.'

Natasha was at the window. 'It's not a reporter. Oh my God, Lia, it's him! It's Raf! What does he want? Why's he come here?'

'Let's find out, shall we?'

But Mum had got to the front door first. I could hear her interrogating Raf.

I attempted to push her gently to one side. She resisted.

'Err . . . thanks, Mum, but Raf's here to see me. We'll let you know if you're needed,' I said, really politely.

She ignored me. 'So, you're the lad who's going to be working in the bakery?' she asked him.

Raf stared at his trainers and said, 'Yes, just mornings.'

'And my husband tells me you're also working for your brother at night?'

'Yes, that's right,'

I had another go. 'Umm, Mum, I think Raf's here to see me, actually, aren't you Raf?'

Raf nodded gratefully.

'Never mind that,' said Mum, 'I'm concerned that you're taking on too much. A young boy like you, with two part-time jobs. When do you get your homework done?'

'Umm . . . at the café . . . it's not really a job which involves much work.'

'Hmm,' said Mum. 'I'm not at all sure that Ben should have taken you on. "It's too much for one boy," I said, when he told me about it. Two part-time jobs.

What do your parents have to say about it? When do you sleep?'

How could I stem the flood of inappropriate questions?

Raf shrugged. 'It's fine, really, Mrs Latimer.'

'So, that's OK,' I interrupted. 'Come on, Raf, we're going to be late.'

'What for?' said Mum, but I had already jumped into the fake Uggs – I badly needed to replace them with real ones – and grabbed my shiny new bag. I jostled past her.

'For the thing we're going to,' I said. 'Bye, Paula! See you later!'

'Don't call me Paula!' she yelled after me.

Halfway down to the Broadway I paused. I didn't want to revisit the scene of my crime. Plus what if I bumped into Jack . . . or Jack's mum?

'Where are we going?' I said.

Raf looked a bit confused. 'What are we late for?'

'We're not late for anything.'

'You said, "We're going to be late."'

'Yes, but that was just for Paula's benefit.'

'Who's Paula?'

'Paula's my mum.'

'In the papers they called her Sarah,' he said. Then

he kind of cleared his throat – *ahem* – and said, 'I did read some of the papers this morning. I thought you were wonderful.'

'Did you?'

'You're so confident and kind, and you do what you want, and you don't care what anyone thinks. . .'

Somehow my hand was holding his. Somehow I was standing right next to him. And he tipped his head down to meet mine and we kissed again . . . right in the middle of the street . . . and again and again and. . .

'Get a room!' someone yelled, and I looked over my shoulder. Dammit. That bitch Alicia.

Raf didn't seem to have heard her. He just stared down at me, his serious face breaking out into one of his rare smiles.

'I found some flats for you,' he said. 'We can go and look – if you'd like to. One in Hampstead, and one in Belsize Park.'

'Oh yes, I'd *love* to,' I said, and I whipped out my phone and summoned a taxi. It arrived about five seconds later, driven by Osman, my regular driver, grey and morose as ever.

'Reza's got me on permanent Lottery Girl standby,' he said, 'although he's told me to warn you that we're not having any food thrown around in our cabs. Lottery or no lottery. There are limits. Where to?'

Raf gave him the Hampstead address.

'They're having an open morning to show them. Newly renovated, and they're huge. I thought you might like to go, just have a look. It'll give you some ideas.'

'Humph,' said Osman. 'I hope it won't give you too many ideas. Reza's very happy with your account, Miss Lia, very happy indeed. We don't want you moving to Hampstead.'

'I'm just looking. Investments,' I said. 'This is actually a private conversation, Osman.' Honestly! Whose money was it, after all?

It's surprising how many people are interested in viewing a two million pound flat on a Sunday morning. The shiny new kitchen was full, everyone nosing around, trying out the waste disposal unit and investigating the built-in coffee machine. I didn't get the impression that most of them could whip out a cheque book and pay the full amount. Unlike me.

The estate agent turned a tap. 'Boiling water twenty-four/seven,' he said. 'You'll never have to use a kettle again. And it's really eco-efficient. Look, with these buttons here you can work the sound system for the whole flat.'

'OMG, that's incredible,' I said, but Raf had wandered off. I found him out on the balcony, gazing over the green leaves of Hampstead Heath.

'Sorry,' he said. 'I don't like crowds.'

'Are you OK?' He looked pale and tired.

'I am now.' He smiled at me. 'Do you like the flat? It's a bit too perfect for me.'

'Too perfect?' I loved the shiny, fresh, newness of everything.

'There's nothing to do to it. I'd want to find some old wreck of a place and make it nice. Make it into a home. It's too easy, moving into somewhere like this. It'd feel like you were living in a hotel.' He shivered.

'Are you cold?' I asked, moving closer.

'A bit, I suppose.'

My arms went around him, but then the door opened and the estate agent said, 'And here we have the roof terrace, stretching along the entire side of the building and with a built-in barbeque pit and fantastic views – I'm sure you'll all agree – of the Heath.'

I was dying to see the barbeque pit, but Raf said, 'Shall we go?' so I said, 'Yes, OK. I don't really think it's worth the price, is it?'

'Well, it probably is,' he said, 'but you're spending

a lot of money on gadgets that will break down. I mean, who really needs a built-in sound system?'

Out on the street, he glanced at my boots. 'Are you OK for a walk? Shall we go on the Heath? I want to get away from all those people.'

'The Heath gets pretty busy,' I said, but he shook his head.

'There are bits where you don't get many people. The main thing is to avoid that hill where people fly kites.'

'Oh, right,' I said. Parliament Hill had been one of my favourite places since I was tiny. I loved picking out the landmarks on the skyline – the Post Office Tower, Canary Wharf, the London Eye on a clear day. My grandad used to take me there to fly a kite.

'I think these boots are fine,' I said, 'and if they get muddy I can always buy some new ones.'

And then I blinked. He'd disappeared. Where the hell was he?

I turned around, scanning the street. No sign of Raf. But he'd been right next to me. . . Hadn't he?

'Here,' he said, appearing again from the door of a nearby shop. 'I'm sorry.' And he handed me a kite, a beautiful red kite with a green tail.

'Oh! But how . . . did you read my mind or something?'

'I didn't need to,' he said. 'Come on.'

And we ran all the way down the hill and onto the Heath, and we didn't stop running until we were halfway up the steep slope of Parliament Hill, when I got out of breath and had to collapse onto a bench, and it took us a bit of time to untangle ourselves and start walking again.

At the top of the hill – it was quite crowded, true – it was fresh and sunny, and you could see as far as Crystal Palace, and the wind was perfect for kite-flying. And Raf seemed to like watching me flying the kite, except I kept on turning round to look at him looking at me, which made the kite crash to the ground.

Then we walked and walked and he took me through the woods and into a little green patch, and there were no people and no dogs and everything was quiet and peaceful and there was only the rustling of the trees to disturb us. And he put his arm around me, and we cuddled up together and we didn't talk for a while.

'I love it here,' he said eventually. 'This is the kind of place that makes you want to be alive.'

I thought about this for a bit. Surely he meant 'glad to be alive'? That's what people say.

'Everything just goes away,' he said, 'and nothing matters.'

He was right. I wasn't worrying about Donna or Jack or Shaz or Mum or Dad or anything.

'What shall we do?' I asked him. 'We can do anything we want. Let's go and do something.'

His hand was stroking my cheek, very gently. 'Just here, just this is fine,' he said.

'I know, it's great, but we could do anything, Raf! We could go to the theatre, we can go and eat out, we could go shopping. What do you want to do?'

He laughed. 'I can't do anything much. That kite used up all my cash.'

'I'll pay! Come on, Raf, let's go and spend some money. Look, Shaz won't take any money from me. It's really awkward with Jack right now. So you'd really be doing me a favour.'

'Is it awkward with Jack because of his mum? Or because you think he's going to sue you?'

'Both,' I said. 'Everything. I can't explain. It's horrible when someone's your good friend and then you're not sure if you can trust them any more.'

'I wouldn't know,' he said, 'but don't worry about the money. He can't sue you. I looked it up on the internet. As long as it was only your name written on the back of the ticket and not his.'

'It was just my name. It was *my* ticket.' My eyes filled with tears. 'It was a present, Raf, that's all, just a present. If I hadn't won anything it would have just been a bit of rubbish in my bag, just a joke birthday present, just nothing. Nothing special.'

'It's OK, his mum is wasting her time,' he said. He kissed the top of my head, pressing his lips to my curls. His voice was a bit muffled. 'No name, no case.'

'Really?'

'I think so.'

'Gilda will know for sure.'

'Why don't you call her?' said Raf.

'Are you sure? OK.'

I pulled out my phone and called her.

'Lia!' said my Winners' Adviser. 'I've been trying you all morning. What on earth's been happening?'

'Oh, errr, nothing. Jack's mum was a bit upset. Gilda, can she sue me?'

'For throwing a pie at her? She could, I suppose, but she'd look very foolish.'

'No, for the money. She says Jack's entitled to half the money because he bought the ticket for me.'

'Well, again, she could try suing you, but her name

wasn't on the back of the ticket, and nor was Jack's. So I wouldn't worry too much.'

'Oh, phew,' I said.

'But Lia, perhaps we should have a chat about what's been going on. Throwing pies—'

'Oh, thanks Gilda, that's so much help. Bye for now,' I said hastily, switching off the phone.

I grabbed Raf's hand. 'You're right! Wow! Let's go and spend some money!'

Chapter 19

Expensive handbags are a liability.

Raf was rubbish at spending. Whatever I suggested, he looked awkward and offered a cheaper alternative.

In the end, I said firmly, 'No, I do not want to have a sandwich, or go to McDonalds.'

I dragged him into a Chinese and ordered dim sum before he could object.

He dithered a bit, but once he started eating he seemed to forget whatever it was that was bothering him. He was brilliant with chopsticks – so unlike Jack, who always demanded a fork – and he ate so much that I had to order some more.

'What shall we do next?' I said, pulling out my phone. 'Shall we see what's on tonight . . . music . . . theatre, even . . . clubs. . .'

'It's Sunday,' said Raf, reaching for the soy sauce. 'There won't be much.'

He was right. How annoying.

'Mmm . . . we could go and look at some shops, I suppose,' I said.

'OK, if you want to.'

He sounded about as enthusiastic as if I'd suggested a trip to the dentist for a quick bleach – not that his shining white teeth needed any cosmetic work, but I had been thinking about Americanising my slightly English gnashers.

'We don't have to if you don't want to,' I said. 'I thought you might like shopping.'

'Why? Me? No!' He looked as if I'd accused him of paedophilia.

'Well, I don't know. You just might. You look like you care about clothes.'

'I hate clothes shops, and everyone who works in them and shops in them, and everything to do with them,' he said.

'Yes, but the expensive ones, they're different. No queues, and people pick things out for you, and give you drinks and stuff.'

'Those are the worst,' he said gloomily. I'd taken his appetite away. He'd abandoned his chopsticks.

'If you don't like shops, then where do you get all your clothes from?' I asked. I could've said, Your

194

designer, expensive, stylish, beautiful clothes. Your brand name, labelled, cooler than cool, show-off clothes. Your rich and sexy clothes. Your. . .

'They were all just given to me,' he said. 'I didn't think you liked shops like that. You always wear stuff that looks like you've picked it up at a jumble sale or something and it doesn't matter, in fact it looks good, because you look good in everything.'

'Oh!' I wasn't sure whether this was a massive compliment or a huge insult. 'Well, it's true I've always been more into vintage in the past. It's only recently that I've been to a few of these designer shops, just for the experience you know. . .'

'If people knew how these shops rip them off, they wouldn't bother,' said Raf, stabbing a dumpling savagely with his chopstick. 'Look, it doesn't matter what I think. We can go shopping if you like.'

'It does matter what you think. Why do you say it doesn't matter? I want to do something you'd like.'

He shrugged. And then smiled. 'No one ever said that before.'

How strange was that? But the waiter came with the bill, and once I'd paid, it was kind of difficult to ask Raf what he meant. So instead I started quizzing him about the stuff he liked, discovering that he hardly ever watched television, his favourite film was something Swedish that I'd never heard of ('It's sort of bleakly uplifting.') He was reading a book called *War and Peace*, ('I was learning Russian at my last school and I got into Tolstoy. It's very good – really absorbing – but it's taking forever.') and he liked classical music although he didn't even play an instrument. Stuff like Liszt and Wagner and Beethoven.

'I know it's a bit strange,' he said. 'You probably think I'm an alien or something.'

'No, of course not,' I said, although the word *Vampire!* clanged in my head. 'My dad listens to Classic FM sometimes. I like all the film music.'

I decided to keep quiet about Stephenie Meyer, *Mean Girls*, *Desperate Housewives* and Katy Perry.

'Oh, right.' He was smiling.

'What? What did I say?'

'Nothing at all. Are you sure you don't think I'm an alien?'

'Of course not!'

'That's good. There's just a bit of me that's stuck in the nineteenth century, I think.'

'Oh, right, yes,' I said. 'I can see that.'

'I like history, and literature. Useless things, I know. I like places where everything's really old and quiet.'

'Why useless?'

'They're not going to earn me a living, are they?' His voice sounded sad, but when I looked at him, he was smiling at me.

We were walking aimlessly down the hill, and I realised we were heading for Camden market, and I didn't say anything because there's loads of other stuff going on at the market. It's not all clothes, and loads of it is vintage, and it sounded as though he approved of the concept of recycled clothes, even if he didn't fully appreciate them.

I tried to move the conversation on to even more personal stuff. Mind you, part of me liked the way he didn't give much away. Part of me wanted to keep hold of the idea that he was somehow magical, supernatural, mysterious.

But I'd been feeling a little bit worried that I was not as interested in other people as I should be.

'So . . . which school did you go to before?' I asked.

'Before what?'

'Before you came to our school, duh,' I said.

'Oh. Umm. I don't know. Lots of schools.'

'You don't know! You must know. Where did you learn Russian?'

'Just a school. You wouldn't know it,' he said

vaguely. 'We're heading for the market, aren't we? Have you got favourite stalls? Do you get all your vintage stuff there?'

I was ten minutes into a guide to the vintage sellers at Camden and the charity shops of Tithe Green – he asked loads of questions – when I realised he'd sent me off track.

'Raf, why don't you like talking about yourself?'

'What?'

'You don't. I want to know about you and you just change the subject.'

'Nothing to say.'

'But I want to know,'

'Nothing to know,' he said. 'Nothing good, anyway. Lia, are you going to expand the bakery? Your dad said he didn't know what was going to happen, he was waiting for you to make up your mind.'

'Oh God,' I said, 'it's so awkward. They just assume I'll take over one day and invest in it now, and I don't really know what I want to do. I'm not ready to make all these decisions yet.'

'Thing is,' he said, 'if you wait much longer, there might not be a bakery for you to take over.'

'You . . . you what?'

'It's got to be in trouble, your dad's shop.'

'Trouble? Why?'

'Well, there's the global economic crisis for a start, then there's all the competition – the new superstore – and the fact that, well, it hasn't really moved with the times, has it?'

What the hell had some global economic crisis got to do with my dad's bread shop in north London?

'That street has really suffered since the mall opened,' he continued. 'Jasper's going to find somewhere else for the internet café. That's why he hasn't invested in it all that much. He got the lease cheap, thought he'd try it out. But he says the Broadway's finished.'

'Oh. Where would he go?'

'He's not sure. Up north, maybe. He might even do something completely different.'

'But what about you?'

He shrugged again. 'I don't know. I'm kind of in the way.'

'Oh, God, Raf. . .'

'It's OK. He won't do anything until I've got through GCSEs,' he said. 'Then I can just leave school and, you know, whatever. . .'

'You mean you wouldn't do A levels?'

'I won't go to university. I just want to be

independent. So I don't need to rely on anyone else.'

I couldn't believe my ears. Raf did really well at school. He was obviously super-brainy – I mean, he liked classical music, for God's sake. *Beethoven*. He loved *history*. Why would he be bailing out at sixteen? OK, it's expensive to go to uni, but Raf's family lived in Melbourne Avenue, for heaven's sake, and anyway, they were always telling us at school that a degree was an investment, because otherwise we'd be stuck flipping burgers if we were lucky. And Raf was the most intellectual person I'd ever met. It seemed such a waste.

Then I remembered my plan for dumping education as soon as possible, and felt a bit confused. Guilty, even. I grasped his hand.

'I'm not going to uni either. I'm going to leave school as soon as I can.'

His face was impossible to read. 'That's your choice,' he said.

We were getting near to the market. I could feel that Camden buzz, the music, the smell – falafel, curry, beer. I got that familiar happy feeling.

'Hang on,' I said, 'I need to get some money.'

The streets were getting busier, and we pushed through a crowd to get to the cashpoint. Raf looked uncomfortable – I remembered he didn't like crowds – but he didn't complain. We'd just be here for half an hour or so, I told myself. Then maybe we'd go to the movies, or find a café, or go back to Raf's nice, private office, snuggle up on the mattress. . .

'Sorry!' Someone had barged right into me, just as I slipped my purse back into my bag. My purse with two hundred pounds in cash in it. My one-thousand-pound bag . . . my heavy bag which now felt strangely light. . . And it wasn't there! It wasn't there! Just the strap, dangling uselessly—

'Help!' I screamed. 'My bag! He's taken it!'

And the guy was running, with Raf right after him, and Raf grabbed his arm, and the thief swung out wildly and shoved Raf in the stomach, and Raf went staggering backwards, crashing into a stall selling jewellery, which smashed to the ground. Silver rings and crystal beads flew through the air.

And the guy was running again . . . getting away . . . but he'd dropped my bag and it was in some woman's arms and she handed it back to me.

'Oh my God, are you all right?' I shrieked, trying to pick up Raf and check my bag all at the same time.

He pulled himself off the ground. 'Sorry, Lia, I didn't get him . . . ouch . . . sorry about your stall. . .'

'You got him to drop the bag, though!' I couldn't hug him, because of the kite and the strapless bag (what a waste! That was the last time I bought a designer bag) but I was smiling at him, and he was smiling at me and his face was heading for mine.

And then he froze. His mouth never reached my lips. He was gazing over my shoulder, looking as though he wanted to throw up.

I turned around to see what had upset him. I recognised him immediately. The man with the blue eyes who'd been with Jasper. The one with the skull-thin face, the unsettling gaze, the strange, old-fashioned, deep voice.

'Jesus!' said Raf. 'Jesus *Christ*. What's he *doing*?'

I squinted. As far as I could see, the mystery man was talking to Charlie, owner of one of my favourite vintage stalls. The man handed over a dark bundle and Charlie was counting out twenty pound notes.

'Excuse me, Lia,' said Raf, his voice shaking slightly. 'I'll be back in a minute. Will you be OK?'

'How about giving me a hand?' said the jewellery stallholder, picking up earrings from the gutter.

But Raf was striding towards the man. And I was inching towards them too.

Chapter 20

Pedicures are better value than manicures —
except in the winter.

Day spas are useless for reducing your stress levels.
Don't believe magazines that tell you to pamper your
troubles away. It's like booking in – paying! – for a day
at a torture chamber.

Massage really hurts – they shove their thumbs
into your flesh, and stick burning hot stones on your
back. Plus they play vile, tinkly, New Age music.
I had to offer the masseuse extra money to replace it
with Florence and the Machine.

By the time she'd scrubbed and peeled my skin in
the cleansing facial, attacked my eyebrows with
red-hot wax and squeezed some blackheads, I was
pink and blotchy and even more stressed than I'd been
before I started.

Lying in the jacuzzi was fun, though, and the peace

and quiet gave me a chance to rerun Raf's weird conversation with the older man.

'You're not meant to be doing that!' said Raf. He turned to Charlie. 'Stop! Don't give him any money!'

'Rafael! What are you doing here? Go away!'

Charlie ignored Raf – 'Your boy, is it, Nick?' – and handed over a wodge of cash. The man – Nick – pocketed it.

'Give it to me,' hissed Raf.

'Oh, what's the harm? I have to make a living somehow. They can't stop me, you know.'

'No, but you know you mustn't . . . you shouldn't even *have* it. . .'

'Mind your own business, Rafael.'

'It is my business. I'm going to phone Jasper.'

Nick's voice was chilly. 'If you wish. You seem to have no free will, as far as he's concerned, anyway.'

Raf pulled out his phone. 'Dammit. No credit.'

That was my cue. 'You can use my iPhone if you want.'

Nick's face lit up. 'Hello! It's the fortunate Miss Latimer, is it not? How very nice to see you again. I'd been hoping to have a word with you.' And he took my hand and kissed it.

Raf could not have looked more furious if he'd

actually burst into tears and had a screaming tantrum in the middle of Camden market.

'Leave her alone!' he growled. Then he grabbed my hand and dragged me through the streets, hailed a black cab and virtually pushed me into it, giving the driver my home address.

It was only when the cab drove off that I realised that Raf hadn't got in with me. And I hadn't heard from him since.

Huh. I hadn't even begun to work it all out, and it was time for my pedicure. More hideous torture – she took a razor blade to the soles of my feet and the file set my teeth on edge.

But I did love my new metallic silver toe and fingernails, and I liked the way my eyebrows arched. I wasn't sure, though, that it was worth two hundred and fifty pounds per person, plus seventy-five pounds for the mud treatment and shiatsu.

'Feeling better?' said Mum, as we sipped green tea in the spa's café and relaxation room – which was kind of disappointing – just wicker sofas with white cushions, old copies of *Zest* and more plinky-plonky music. We'd ordered Superfood Health Salads. They didn't do chips.

'Not really,' I said. 'My masseuse was a sadist.'

'It was wonderful,' she said. Her face was all open pores and presumably so was mine. Great. I could feel zits bubbling up under my skin. 'It's such a healthy thing to do. You should have one every week – it's so important to break up the toxins in the body.'

'Oh yeah?'

'Apparently there's a wonderful woman at a very exclusive salon in Hampstead. She does everything, colonics, the works.'

'You'd *pay* someone to put a hose up your bottom and suck out the poo? That is the most disgusting thing I've ever heard!'

'Well, never mind the colonics, the massage is supposed to be the best in North London. Apparently Princess Diana used to go there.'

'She's been dead for *years*. You want to go there because they massaged someone who's dead. That is just *perverse*.'

'We could go together, a regular mother and daughter outing,' she said. 'I'm sure Princess Diana would have done that if she was still alive and if she'd had a daughter.'

'I don't think so,' I said.

'Oh, Lia,' she said. 'Why do you have to be *so* obnoxious *all* the time?'

What? *What?* It was my fault that I didn't want to do everything she wanted me to? It was my fault that she was fantasising about being like someone who's dead and didn't even have a daughter anyway? It was my fault that I didn't want to spend my money on every idea she had? Huh.

'I just said I don't think I want to go and have a massage every week,' I pointed out. 'I have got GCSEs coming up, you know. I have got coursework and revision to do.'

Just because I'd decided that qualifications didn't matter to me, didn't mean I was going to drop them altogether. In the parental battlefield, GCSEs were like a heavy iron shield, strong enough to withstand a hundred bombs and bullets. I'd spent the last two days catching up on coursework. We'd all agreed that we wouldn't discuss the future until I'd been on the Integrating Wealth weekend and met with the financial advisers, but I'd decided I might as well show willing on the exam front, to demonstrate my appreciation for Mum's brilliant PR skills, even if they had cost me eighteen thousand pounds.

To be honest, I was so relieved that Donna's story in the *Sunday Mirror* hadn't been half as bad as it could have been, that I was all prepared to be a model daughter and pupil. It was a pity that Mum kept raising the stakes by suggesting weekly massages.

'Well, I'm so pleased you're concentrating on your work,' she said. 'You could do anything, Lia, study in America even.' Her voice was wistful. 'You won't have to stay at home to save money, like I did. Most people my age were having the time of their lives, partying every night at university. I was stuck at home with your nana, head down, studying.'

'I thought studying was meant to be a good thing, according to you.'

'It is, it is, obviously . . . it's just that there's more to university than sitting at home with your mam.'

'Yeah, but then you came to London, didn't you, as soon as you got your degree, and it only took you a month to meet Dad.'

'That's right,' she said.

'Well, then. You met the love of your life, right away.'

'I know,' she said.

'You walked into the bakery to buy a doughnut and he looked up and he saw you and he said, "That's the girl I'm going to marry."'

'Yes,' she said. 'Very persistent, your dad.'

'I could go to New York and live there without even being a student,' I said.

'You certainly could.'

'I could just do some courses in Film and Philosophy and stuff. That'd be cool.'

'It would.'

'Or I could travel around, live in all sorts of places.'

'Yup,' she said. 'You could do that. But I think you'll find GCSEs are still worth having.'

I couldn't see why, but I sensed that might not be the best thing to say.

'Lia, darling,' said Mum, 'I wanted to ask you something.'

'What?' Alarm bells rang. Why was she calling me *darling*?

'Well it's just . . . I was thinking . . . I've been looking into. . .'

'What?'

'Cosmetic surgery.'

'What? *What*? Look, I know my nose is big, but it's bit much to suggest . . . bloody hell, Paula, how rude can you get?' I was shouting, I admit, but it's not every day that one's own mother wants to put her daughter under the knife to alter a perfectly functional nose that I'd spent years persuading myself looked just about OK.

'No . . . not you . . . your nose is lovely, Lia. What are you talking about? No, it's for me.'

'You? But your nose is *fine*.' It had to be. It was identical to mine.

'Not my nose. Lia, I really want a boob job.'

'A *what*? What do you *mean*?'

Mum was looking a bit flustered.

'It's just . . . two babies, you know, and then I lost weight. Well. They're like two little pitta breads. Just hanging there. I've thought for ages, if I could just plump them up. . .'

'There's nothing wrong with your boobs! That is so . . . urgh . . . yuck . . . I think I'm going to be *sick*.'

'Are you all right, dear?' said the woman running the spa café, who'd just appeared with our salads.

'I'm fine, thanks,' I said.

Mum was glaring at me. I waited for the woman to walk away and then I went on the attack again.

'They slice off the nipple, you know. They have to patch it on again. And sometimes the implants *burst*. And they'd stay all firm and smooth while the rest of you went all wrinkled and saggy. Imagine when you're seventy. I mean, that's not that long, really. I can't believe you want something like that – urgh, so *disgusting*. . .'

Mum took a forkful of her salad. 'It was just an idea,' she said. 'Never mind. Forget it.'

'Look, if you really want to . . . but Shaz and I watched this documentary on Channel Five and this woman, she went scuba-diving, right, and her implants literally *exploded*. . .'

'Never mind. It's not really worth it.'

'Look, you can have your new boobs, you know you can. Sorry, Mum.'

'That's OK,' she said. 'I wouldn't want them exploding.'

'Oh well, that was in Mexico. I'm sure they don't explode here.'

She sighed. 'No, you're right. At my age. What's the point?'

'You're only forty. You look pretty good, actually,' I said generously, although, honestly, if she was going the cosmetic surgery route, I'd have suggested starting with a quick burst of Botox on the frown-lines, no offence.

'And it costs thousands of pounds,' she said. 'Seven, to be precise.'

'Oh well that's *nothing*,' I said. 'Book yourself in. But you know, Mum, you're always telling us that you shouldn't just think about how you look. And there's *loads* more to you than the state of your boobs. You're a brilliant PR and you can be really nice and funny. You should have more self-esteem.'

She was looking at me, smiling, like I'd told her a joke.

'You are a funny one,'

'What do you mean?'

'Well, sometimes you're so self-centred and obnoxious, and sometimes you're so kind and generous.'

'Oh,' I said, baffled. 'I don't think I'm either, really. I just . . . I'm not used to having any money for anything.'

'I worry that you'll never have to work for anything,' she said, 'but then, your dad and I have had to work so hard for everything. It's great that you'll be free of that.'

'Oh . . . right. . .' I said. I could sense trouble coming, like you can feel a storm prickling the air, getting ready to crash and flash.

But she just smiled again and sipped her green tea and said, 'Do you know, Lia, winning this money could be the making of you.'

Chapter 21

When you're poor you think there are two sorts of people, rich and poor. When you've got money you realise that rich people are all different.

'My name is Lia,' I said, 'and money makes me feel . . . lucky. But also confused.'

'My name is Olivia,' said the blonde girl to my right. 'And money makes me feel fortunate. And also concerned.'

Everything about Olivia was perfect, from her honey-highlighted, glossy hair, to her long, long legs and her un-fake Uggs. I wondered what she was concerned about. The state of her nails? Whether she had lipstick on her teeth?

'My name is Sayeed,' said the next guy – Asian, Northern, frowning. 'Money makes me feel inspired.'

The blond guy next to me stifled a laugh. His name was Luke. The Honourable Luke Massingham, according to the list in our Integrating Wealth Weekend literature. Money made him feel warm and cuddly.

'Darryl,' said the next guy. Darryl Cook. Played for Manchester City. Rising star of English football. Jack'd be really impressed when I told him I'd spent a weekend with Darryl Cook. That's if Jack and I ever started talking again.

'Money makes me feel rewarded,' said Darryl. 'Also it makes me feel that I'm never going to be poor again. You can laugh,' he added, glaring at Sayeed, who stifled his smirk, 'but if you grew up on the estate where I did, you'd understand what I was talking about.'

'Excellent, excellent,' said Dr Flint. You may have heard of him. Dr Richard Flint, psychotherapist, writer, all-round expert on the psychological problems associated with wealth. Author of *The Discomfort of being Comfortable* and *Money Hurts*. He ran these Integrating Wealth weekends to help rich teens avoid the pitfalls ahead. Mum and dad weren't all that impressed when they found out I'd have to stay over at one of London's top hotels – 'Why can't you just get the Tube in?' said Mum. 'Or even a taxi? It's a complete waste of money.' Dr Flint insisted, though, that it was essential that we all stayed overnight, to allow us to contemplate our emotional journey with the minimum of distraction. Dad thought he was probably getting a percentage from the hotel.

I certainly wasn't complaining. My swish hotel room had a massive bed and was done in silver-grey and aubergine. I'd taken a load of photos on my phone so I could show them to my imaginary interior designer once I'd found my fantasy flat.

'I notice that most of you chose positive emotions to associate with your wealth,' Dr Flint said now, as we crumbled our croissants. This was our Breakfast Ice-breaker, and no sooner had we piled our plates with pastries than he'd insisted we start talking about our feelings. I sipped my orange juice and wondered if I'd said the wrong thing.

'That's good,' he said, 'but as you get older you may find the picture is not so rosy.' He turned his laptop so we could all see it. 'I'm just going to show you a short DVD.'

What a downer. Loads of dull-looking adults whinging on about how inheriting money made them feel unworthy.

'I felt that I didn't fit in any more,' said one bearded

wimp, with terrible clothes and a gorgeous house. 'I felt aimless; I had no purpose any more.'

I would have thought that an urgent style makeover would give him all the purpose he needed. But he moaned on for ages, and so did some earnest-looking woman, and the whole thing was designed to make you feel like having money was worse than being poor.

Only really rich people could think that, let's face it.

'Guilt can go hand in hand with a fortune,' said Dr Flint. 'Also lack of direction, loss of ambition, low self-esteem and general apathy. *Affluenza*, that's what some people call it. I prefer *Richpression*. But it's so hard to admit that most of us mask it from ourselves. We can't admit that there's a downside to being wealthy.'

I hadn't been feeling guilty at all in the past week. Upset, yes, and embarrassed. Worried about Jack. Neglected by Shaz who was spending all her time in the library. And obsessed with Raf...

But, guilt? No, since Alfie Lord's mum told the media that I was an angel from heaven, I hadn't felt guilty at all.

'Of course,' said Dr Flint, 'for those of you who have grown up knowing that you would inherit money, the situation is different from those who have come into money unexpectedly. Why don't you tell us, Luke, about your upbringing, and the attitude towards money?'

Luke had the kind of accent that you usually only hear from the Royal Family and in Hollywood films starring Hugh Grant. So posh it's almost Australian.

'Erm . . . I don't really know. . .' he said, running his hands through his floppy blond hair.

'Was there an assumption that you always had money to meet your needs? Did you ever hear anyone talking about money worries?'

'I really never thought about it,' said Luke. 'I was off to prep school at seven. . . Never spent much time with my parents in the holidays. . . They liked those hotels with kids' clubs, y'know, and the nanny always came with. . . Anyway, I've got a trust fund, right, and so have all my friends.'

'And how does that make you feel?'

Luke blinked his blue eyes. 'Ummm . . . good? I can't really imagine life without it.'

I wasn't exactly sure what a trust fund was, but everyone else seemed to know, so I didn't say anything.

'Pathetic,' snapped Sayeed, right behind me. 'My father was taking me into his shops from the day I was born. He was getting me ready to take over his empire, training me in the business. He made sure I could read a balance sheet when I was still at primary school. That's how to bring someone up to understand money. You, Luke, will waste so much money when you inherit it, just partying and playing around and not knowing the meaning of hard work. And as for you,' – he gestured towards Marcus, Darryl and me, the New Money kids – 'you'll probably be on benefits by the time you're twenty-five. Easy come, easy go.'

Oh! Ouch! 'My dad was taking me into his shop from the day I was born, actually,' I said, indignantly.

'OK, you'll be serving doughnuts behind the counter of your dad's one and only shop,' said Sayeed, with a sneer. His dad owned a chain of DIY stores across the north of England, and had diversified into property development. Sayeed was heir to the hardware millions. He acted like he was fifty-eight and he'd built up the business all by himself. We'd only been on the weekend for half an hour and I could already feel the group uniting against him.

'I ain't going to be on benefits at twenty-five,' said Darryl.

'When you're forty, then. Before, if you get injured, or dropped, or lose form. It's not exactly a long career, is it, football?'

Darryl snorted. 'Easy come, easy go, my arse,' he said. 'Let's face it, Sayeed mate, you never built up that business, did ya? The only people here because of our own talent and effort are Marcus and me.'

You might just about remember Marcus. He won *X Factor* a few years ago, but he only had the one hit. When we'd introduced ourselves, he'd told us all about how Simon Cowell had dropped him after his contract came to an end, and since then he'd had to get by on reality TV contracts.

'My agent's pushing me for *I'm a Celebrity, Get me Out of Here* next year,' he told us, 'but really, I'm here for advice on making the most of what I've got.'

Darryl was being a bit kind, really, saying that Marcus had got rich because of his talent. Actually, he won *X Factor* because everyone felt sorry for him. He wasn't that good-looking, had big, sad, brown eyes, had suffered from cancer when he was a child. Of course everyone voted for him.

And he wasn't that rich, either. He'd made about two million, plus he had a nice flat in Chelsea.

'But the service charges are murder,' he explained.

'Sometimes I think I'd better go back to Rotherham.'

'Good idea,' said Sayeed. 'My dad's got a new development there – we can sort you out with an apartment.'

'How about you, Lia?' said Dr Flint. 'This must have come as a bit of a shock to you.'

'It's great,' I said, 'I love it. I'm just beginning to get used to it.'

'No problems?' asked Dr Flint, looking at me over his glasses.

'One or two,' I said. 'People being jealous, mostly. Bitchy girls.'

Sayeed snorted loudly. 'Do you think we didn't see your friend's mum in the papers after you threw a pie in her face? You've had a bit of money for a few weeks and you're completely out of control.'

'Leave her alone,' said Olivia. 'Lia's incredibly generous. Did you see what she'd done for that little boy Alfie?' She turned to me, smiling. 'I wish I could do something like that. You must feel wonderful.'

'Why don't you?' I asked.

She looked a bit startled. 'Well, I would never meet anyone like that. And I don't think my parents would let me just write a cheque for eight thousand pounds.'

'I do what I want,' I said.

'This afternoon's session is about philanthropy,' said Dr Flint.

'That's giving to charity,' explained Sayeed loudly, looking at Darryl and Marcus.

'Do you want to get punched in the face or the stomach?' asked Darryl.

'Now, now,' said Dr Flint.

'Well, I'm really looking forward to that session,' said Olivia. 'I did use to feel guilty about being rich. Really guilty. And I couldn't talk to anyone about it because, you know, I thought they'd think I was mad.'

'Too right,' muttered Sayeed.

'All the girls at my school are from wealthy backgrounds and they just take it for granted that they're better than people at state schools, people who don't have our advantages. No one ever questions anything,' said Olivia. She'd gone a bit pink.

'Very good, Olivia,' said Dr Flint.

'And everyone's very competitive – you've got to get good grades, look good, be thinner than the other girls, but it's all for the sake of competition. There are about three girls who want to be doctors or whatever, and the rest are just going to live off their trust funds until they find rich husbands.'

I'd have to Google trust funds when I got back to my hotel room. Clearly they were good things to know about.

Darryl rolled his eyes. 'Where I come from, and where Marcus comes from, and Lia too – we haven't got time for stuff like this. We know we're lucky to have money. My mum's worked all her life, cleaning up other people's shit. She got paid less than the minimum wage. Hear that, rich boy? Now she's living in a bungalow in Alderley Edge and she's got a cleaner three times a week. Why should I feel guilty about that?'

'You could,' said Olivia. 'You could feel guilty because a footballer gets paid so much more than a cleaner.'

'Well I don't,' said Darryl.

Dr Flint intervened, started talking about self-esteem . . . relative values . . . finding purpose in life. . .

'Lia – what do you think?' asked Dr Flint.

'Errr . . . sorry?'

He looked pained. 'I was talking about the purpose of money. Can we find meaning in our affluence? All too often it strips away ambition and leaves people feeling empty.'

'Oh,' I thought about this. 'I don't feel empty. I'm

just a bit confused. I'm not sure that I ever really had any ambition to start with. Now, it's almost like I've got too many choices.'

Marcus said, 'I achieved everything I wanted to achieve in life when I won that final. Now . . . now I feel like my journey's over.' There was a tear running down his cheek.

'Now then,' said Dr Flint, shoving a box of tissues to him. 'That's exactly the kind of emotion we want to hunt out this weekend.' He made it sound like we were going on safari and our emotions were rare animals that we were going to shoot. *Wham!* That's a guilty tiger. *Bam!* A depressed antelope.

The whole thing was beginning to piss me off. After all, we'd paid plenty for this weekend – a cool one thousand five hundred pounds each – and the whole thing seemed to be a complete misery-fest.

'Look,' I said, 'we're all the same, actually. We've all got lucky. Some of us are lucky in our parents, and some are lucky with the sporting or musical genes and I just got lucky with some random numbers. But we all got lucky. There's no need to feel especially guilty about that. I mean, I never felt guilty before, but I was already lucky just by being born in the developed world. Even if you haven't got much money in Britain, you're probably better off than kids in other countries who don't get an education and have to work in sweatshops and their homes get flooded and stuff. It's not fair, sure, but it's not my fault. I don't have to feel guilty.'

And then I said it. Those words that I'd heard so often before. Mum's words. Dad's words. The most annoying words in the world.

'After all,' I said, 'life's not fair.'

Chapter 22

The world is full of worthy causes.
The problem is choosing who and where
and how much.

Mario lives in Colombia. He runs a barber shop. He supports his three younger brothers. A loan of one thousand five hundred dollars would buy him the equipment he needs to take on an assistant, grow his business.

Chantou lives in Cambodia. She's twenty-four and she supports two younger brothers and her disabled father. Two thousand dollars would help her buy rice to plant and a motorcycle to take goods to market.

Mario and Chantou were on a DVD all about different ways we could give, international ways – the amazing things we could do with what felt like relatively small amounts of money.

'Just one hundred and fifty dollars buys a water

pump,' said Martha, the woman running the Philanthropy session. 'That money could save countless lives in Africa and South-east Asia. Have you ever thought about what it's like living without a clean water supply? There are millions of people who do that, and children who die unnecessarily.'

I'd never thought about living without a clean water supply. I didn't even think I could live without hair products. Olivia's eyes were gleaming – I thought she was about to cry. I was thinking about Alfie Lord, swimming with the dolphins. His eight thousand pounds could have bought hundreds of water pumps. Mum's new boobs, our designer clothes – why didn't I realise? Why didn't I know about this?

Why did anyone in rich countries have anything at all, apart from the basics? Why didn't we all make do with loads less stuff and save the lives of thousands of suffering children?

On the other hand, Alfie was a suffering child. He really was. So why not give him a chance?

Martha was very into helping people help themselves. If we put money into micro-finance – loans to people like Mario and Chantou – then we were treating them as equal partners, she explained.

'I'd suggest finding a project or a country in which

to take a particular interest. It's incredible how satisfying it is when you see the difference you make to people's lives.'

Maybe that was what being rich was all about – becoming a global fairy godmother, helping other people. But what about my life? Where was my fairy godmother? Had she been and gone?

We had a session on trust funds, which turned out to be how people with loads of money in their families share it out to their kids. Luke had a whacking great trust fund. Olivia had one too.

'It's cool, yeah,' said Luke. 'I never need to get a job or anything.'

'So what are your plans when you finish Eton?' asked the guy leading the session, another one of these private banker types.

'I'm going to Ibiza for a while,' said Luke. 'Then I thought I might get a higher level scuba diving certificate . . . maybe travel a bit. . .'

What a loser, I thought. But I envied Luke's freedom. Because he'd always had money and a nice place to live – a stately home in Wiltshire – he didn't feel that he had to rush into buying a penthouse flat or tons of stuff for it. He could just drift around, go where he wanted, travel light.

He knew he'd never run out of cash.

Sayeed didn't want a trust fund. 'They make you weak,' he said. 'They make you soft. I want to earn my inheritance. My dad says that if I don't get into a top university, then he'll cut me out of his will.'

We gasped. Sayeed beamed.

'He's tough but fair, my dad,' he said. 'Not bad, is it? As an incentive, like?'

I imagined my dad saying, 'Get into a top university, Lia, or I'll refuse to let you take over Latimer's Loaves.' It wouldn't work at all; I'd be slacking on purpose.

What if he'd said, 'If you get into a top university, Lia, you don't have to take over Latimer's Loaves?' What if the lottery people had said, 'Get into a top university, Lia, or we'll take your jackpot away?'

It was all pointless thinking about it. It was too late. There was no incentive in the world that could make me work harder. No threat, no reward. I couldn't decide if that was good or not.

We learned about buying art, supporting film projects, helping put on West End shows.

'People who invest in the theatre are called angels,' said the banker running that particular session. 'It's a risky investment, but great if you're interested in plays and musicals, a really fun way to get involved.'

Having money opened doors to all sorts of exciting worlds, it seemed. It was just that it was the same door every time. The door marked 'money'.

By the time we got to our last session we were all exhausted. Olivia was enthusiastically reading through the literature on charitable giving. Sayeed and Darryl kept rushing off to take calls on their mobiles. Luke was flicking through a glossy magazine called *Tatler*.

'Oh look,' he said. 'That's my sister's twenty-first.'

Olivia and I scanned a page of grinning party-goers. All the girls looked like her, I realised. All the guys looked like Luke. They all had shiny, floppy hair and bright, white teeth and flawless skin. It was like an advert for a pedigree puppy farm.

Dr Flint made us sit in a circle. Time for emotions safari again. He homed in on Olivia.

'How have you enjoyed the day?'

'Oh, very much, it was inspiring,' she said. 'I'm going to research the projects Martha talked about, look into setting up a charitable foundation one day. I might even go on one of the fact-finding trips she talked about.'

'Fantastic!' said Dr Flint. 'Sayeed, how about you?'

'There were some investment possibilities that

sounded interesting,' said Sayeed. 'I might look into the art market.'

'Very good! Very good! You'll benefit a lot from learning about art,' said Dr Flint.

'Yes, some amazing profits to be made,' said Sayeed.

'How about you, Marcus?' said Dr Flint.

Marcus had his gloomiest face on – the sad puppy look that had persuaded Natasha to vote for him twenty-four times.

'It's over,' he said. 'I'm not rich like you lot. I've got nothing to build on. I got my win, got my contract and now it's all over. I've failed. I'm going to work through my money and then what? Celebrity has-been shows on TV.'

'Come on, Marcus,' I said. 'You've got a great voice. You did it once, you can do it again.'

Luke slapped him on his back. 'Come on, Marcus, you've come so far already.'

Darryl started singing. 'Don't. Look back. . .'

It was Marcus's signature tune. His one and only hit.

Olivia and I joined in. 'Don't worry about what's been and gone. . .'

Cue Marcus. He sniffed, rose to his feet and took over.

'You can do better . . . you can make your life

again. . . There's always hope. Hope. Hope!'

Olivia and I harmonised. Sayeed whistled. Darryl did a drumroll on the table in front of him and Dr Flint clapped the beat.

He did have a good voice. In a tiny room he sounded a lot better than he'd ever done on *X Factor*. By the time he finished the song he was in floods of tears. We were clapping and cheering.

'Great stuff, Marcus,' said Dr Flint. 'Does it help you to focus on your ambitions?'

'I'm going to get to number one again,' said Marcus. 'I'm going to show Simon Cowell where he went wrong. I'm never going back to Rotherham. I'm going to do all I can . . . everything it takes. . .'

We cheered again.

'How about you, Luke?' asked Dr Flint.

'Errr . . . gosh . . . I don't think I can compete with that. I suppose I could take school a bit more seriously. . . Like Sayeed says, find out a bit more about managing money . . . kick the weed habit. . .'

We cheered him, less enthusiastically.

'Darryl?'

'Obviously,' said Darryl, 'I want to play for the best premiership sides, play for my country, right, be a success on the field.'

We all got ready to cheer. He put up his hand to silence us.

'I want a lot more than that. I want to meet a girl who isn't a WAG. I want to finish my Open University degree. I want to have a life outside football that's waiting for me when my career is over. I want to look after my mum and my sister and my little boy.'

'Oh my God, you've got a little boy?' I said, while Olivia gasped, 'An Open University degree?'

'He's two.' Darryl's eyes shone, bright as his diamond stud earrings. 'Anton. We're not together any more, his mum and me, but she does a good job. I'm going to give him the best life I can. That's why I'm studying Economics. I want to make sure I'll never let him down. He's given me more purpose than anything else. . .'

Darryl already seemed to have more purpose in his life than fifty people put together. Maybe if I had a baby, I'd suddenly be filled with ambition and confidence, and I'd just know which decisions were best for me . . . for us.

A baby. Maybe. . .

'How about Lia?' asked Dr Flint.

'I'm really new to all this,' I said. 'A few weeks ago the only money worry I had was whether I could get my mum to give me twenty pounds. I just want to get used to thinking about money. It's been great meeting all of you today. I've really learned a lot.'

Everyone clapped this pathetic speech.

'Good stuff,' said Dr Flint. 'We don't all have all the answers all the time.'

I never seemed to have any of the answers, any of the time. Then I thought of Nana Betty's motto, Just Muddle Through. I was good at that.

After the last session we went and had dinner together in the hotel bar. I ate a burger and chips, and chatted to Marcus about what Simon Cowell was really like, and discussed Japanese hair straightening with Olivia – her friend had done it and hated her new flat-ironed look.

And then Darryl asked who wanted to go to a club, and we started debating whether I was too high-profile to pass for an eighteen-year-old. I'd drunk two glasses of red wine and I felt like I was twenty-three. My new life had arrived. I was sure I could blag it into a club.

Olivia and I went off to get changed. We were walking through the foyer, my mind on what to wear – that little dress I'd picked up from the seven-thousand-pound shopping trip, maybe, the shiny red shoes – when Olivia said, 'Oh my God! But . . . it can't be!'

A tall, slim figure, walking away from hotel reception turned towards us. I saw huge grey eyes. I saw a full mouth, a slightly crooked smile.

What the *hell* was Raf doing at *my* hotel?

I opened my mouth to ask. And then shut it again. Olivia – poised, confident Olivia – was babbling and giggling like . . . like my little sister Natasha. What a weird transformation.

'It's Rafael, isn't it? Rafael Forrest. I haven't seen you for years. You went off to Wingfield, didn't you? Freddie's at Eton, but I expect you know that. You do remember me, don't you? Olivia Templeton. Freddie Templeton's sister.'

Bloody hell. Even I'd heard of Wingfield. One of those fabulously posh boarding schools which is exactly like Hogwarts, only without the girls and the magic.

Raf hardly smiled. He barely glanced at me. 'Oh yes,' he said. 'That's right.'

My heart lurched around inside me, although that could also possibly have something to do with the two glasses of red wine.

'It's so strange to see you . . . I thought . . . ummm . . . this is Lia,' said Olivia. 'We're on a weekend course together. We're just going to get changed, go and hit a club. Do you want to come along?'

Raf shook his head. All trace of the smile had gone. 'No, thanks.'

Awkward silence. Olivia didn't seem to notice.

'Freddie loves Eton,' said Olivia. 'Plays a lot of sport, you know, same old Freddie. He won't *believe* I've bumped into you. I can't believe it either. Do you remember that time you came to stay one Easter holidays?'

'Yes,' said Raf. 'Yes. I remember.'

I was getting fed up with this. He was totally ignoring me. I'd been crushing on someone who was either incredibly rude or socially inept. And what was he doing here? He was a rude, socially inept, mad *stalker*.

'I'll just go on up and get changed,' I said to Olivia. 'I'll meet you back down here.'

'Oh, I'm coming as well,' she said. 'Bye, Raf, nice to see you again.'

His eyes sought me out again. What was he trying to tell me?

'Bye,' he said.

And we got into the lift.

I was fuming. What was going on? Why was

he here? Why was he ignoring me?

'Wow!' said Olivia. 'Well! Rafael Forrest! How strange was that?' She was shaking her head. 'I would hardly have recognised him. He was at prep school with my little brother Freddie – he's just a year younger than me – and he stayed with us one holiday. Last time I saw him, he had a mouth full of metal and truly appalling acne. But it was him, definitely. '

'I thought he was rude,' I said.

'When I knew him, he hardly said one word,' said Olivia. 'To be honest, he wasn't really Freddie's greatest friend – a bit of a loner, I think – but he always seemed to be stuck at school for most of the holidays, and the housemistress used to ring round, see who'd have him. He's a nice boy, my brother – you'll have to meet him.'

'I'd like that,' I said. A whole world was opening up in front of me, filled with Freddies from Eton and *X Factor* winners and going clubbing with Darryl, who was incredibly fit in all senses. Who needed some rude loser who lived in a grotty near-squat? Not me.

And then she said it. 'I must have been wrong.'

'Wrong about what?'

'Thing is, I'm sure I'd heard that Raf Forrest had died.'

Chapter 23

It can be pretty annoying sometimes to have had an experience that completely trumps absolutely everything else.

My entire body was shivering. I swear my internal organs turned to ice.

'You *what*?' I said.

'I thought he'd died. He collapsed at school, that's what I heard – there was some talk of drink or drugs – and then he died. No one ever saw him again. But that must've been completely wrong because there he was, absolutely fine.'

Oh my God! I could hardly believe my ears. As the lift door closed behind her it was as though a drum was beating: *Raf's dead . . . he's dead . . . Raf's dead.*

Vampire, angel, zombie (no, surely not), ghost. Ghost. Oh, Jesus.

I had to find out the truth.

As soon as I got to my room I texted him: *Why are you here? What's going on?*

No reply.

I texted again: *Why did you ignore me?*

No reply.

Argh. I called down to the front desk.

'Is there a tall, young guy in the lobby . . . dark hair . . . black jeans?'

The hotel receptionist ummed and aahed. 'I think so . . . would you like to speak to him? Excuse me, sir?'

'Hello?'

'Raf?' I hissed. 'Is that you? It's Lia. I'm in room five seven five.'

'Oh, right, Lia, sorry. . .'

'Five minutes,' I said, and put the phone down.

I timed him. He knocked at the door three minutes later.

I sprang to open it. 'What the hell?' I said. 'What's going on?'

He walked in, looked around. He seemed a bit spacey . . . almost as though he didn't know where he was or how he had got there. He was pale, sure, and there were dark shadows under his eyes, but dead? *Dead?* Surely not.

'Why did you ignore me when I was with Olivia?'

I asked. 'Why are you here?' There was a little scratchy lump in my throat.

He shrugged. 'I didn't know what to say. I wasn't expecting to see her. I've got something to tell you.'

'What do you mean, you didn't know what to say?'

'I needed to see you and she took me by surprise.'

'If you had something to tell me, why didn't you phone?'

He looked surprised. 'Oh. I don't know. I never really use my phone.'

Maybe he was a ghost from the nineteenth century? They didn't have mobiles then.

My phone rang. Olivia. 'We're all downstairs waiting for you. Are you going to be long?'

'You know, Olivia, I don't think I'll come,' I said. 'I'll probably never get into these clubs – too many people know me from the papers and the one thing they know about me is that I'm only sixteen. I might as well have had my age tattooed on my forehead. And anyway, I'm really tired. That was an intense day.'

'Are you sure? Oh well. See you in the morning.'

I turned back to Raf. How could I find out if he was dead or not? I had to touch him.

I walked slowly towards him. I put my hand on

his arm. He felt alive, all right, a bit chilly, but solid. I touched his face, stared into his eyes. He still had the end of the bruise, I noticed. Surely ghosts didn't bruise. He had a tiny blackhead just at the edge of his hairline. OK, obviously angels don't have blackheads.

'Lia,' he said, 'I wanted to explain. . .' And then he kissed me. If he were a vampire, then surely now would be the time. I closed my eyes, waited for the cold, sharp feeling of fangs sinking into my flesh, blood spurting. . .

But all I could feel was his mouth on mine, and his tongue, and his hands curving round my back and resting at the base of my spine.

And that's all it took to know *exactly* how I was going to test whether Raf was really alive or not.

After all, I felt twenty-three at least, and the hotel room was sleek and modern and stylish, like a magazine, like a penthouse flat, like a flash-forward to the rest of my life. And Raf was part of that. He was magically there with me. It was almost too exciting to be real.

We broke off from the kiss.

'I. . . Lia . . . I need to explain,' he said. 'The other day . . . Camden. . .' He looked around my room. The bed, with its perfect grey satin cover, shiny, white cotton sheets, the sofa, its purple cushions, the flat-screen TV. I remembered his lumpy mattress, his plans to paint the walls.

'I'm really glad you came to the hotel,' I said.

'I need to tell you—' he said, but I kissed him silent. His lips were soft and cold, and he reached his hand to my cheek, touching it so gently, it was as if he thought I wasn't real, and he wanted to make sure I wasn't about to disappear.

We kissed. We breathed. We kissed again. No fangs. No zombie rotten flesh. No angel wings – I ran my hands under his shirt to check that his back was smooth and feather-free.

'Do you want a drink?' I asked. 'There's a whole bar of stuff.'

We looked in the little fridge, with its miniature bottles of whiskey and rum and wine, its packets of Pringles and knobbly Toblerone. I love Toblerone, but it's a bugger to break up. What would a twenty-three-year-old drink? What would a ghost? I unscrewed a miniature bottle of Bacardi and sloshed it into a glass with some coke.

'I shouldn't—' said Raf, and then, 'Oh, what the hell. This is a dream, isn't it?' He broke up the Toblerone with one hand ('I've had a lot of practice,' he said, mysteriously.) He took another mini bottle of Bacardi, but he drank his neat. In one gulp. And then he was kissing me again, hot with rum, sweet with chocolate.

It didn't take long to move from kissing to touching. It soon became clear that we'd be much more comfortable lying down on the bed. I felt more relaxed than I'd ever felt before – the Bacardi? – but more awake too, tingling and brave. I was very, very sure what I wanted. I was more certain than I'd ever been about anything.

I wanted Raf, dead or alive. I wanted to get naked. I wanted to feel every bit of him next to every bit of me.

So I peeled off my top, and I pushed up his T-shirt, and as we touched, I felt his body shaking. As though he were scared. His eyes were closed. I felt a surge of incredible energy charging through me.

I could make a boy like Raf shiver with desire. I could solve the problems of the world.

I loved myself just then, as much as I wanted him. I loved the whole sexy grown-up feeling of being alone with the boy I'd been dreaming about, in our very own piece of my future. I loved the hotel room, the Bacardi, the way we moved together. I was in control enough to take risks. I was dictating my own adventure.

And we were in the bed, clinging together when we felt the chill of the sheets, and pushing, touching, stroking, closer and closer, skin to skin. We couldn't have been any closer. I felt I knew everything about him – his taste, his smell, the way his skin stretched as I stroked his hair away from his face, the sheer blissful joy on his face as he stared at me.

'You're beautiful,' he whispered. 'Lia. You're so beautiful.'

And there were no limits, nothing stopping us, no parents lurking or sisters in the same room, or brothers next door, or people at school. Completely alone together. Nothing to stop us exploring and touching and moving together. . .

'Lia,' he murmured, breathless in my ear. 'Lia . . . I haven't, you know . . . I'm not . . . prepared. I didn't think. I'm sorry. Oh, Lia. . .'

'Don't worry,' I said, shifting my pelvis, reaching down with my hand, showing him, touching him, guiding him. 'Don't worry. It's fine. Don't worry.'

And he didn't. And we did. And it was completely and absolutely and totally the most amazing experience of my life so far.

Apart from winning the lottery. Damn.

Chapter 24

You'll still have problems
that money can't solve.

Afterwards we cuddled up together, and I concentrated on the way my body felt, the slightly hazy, drunken way I wanted to laugh and laugh and the mad, loopy smile I knew was plastered all over my face. I could still feel the memory of him. Little echoes in the darkness.

Then I looked at Raf's face, his big eyes, his crooked smile. All the sadness had dissolved. He was lit up with happiness, like that moment when a Christmas tree turns from a scraggy fir with tinsel to the most beautiful thing in the world.

If he were a ghost, he'd certainly enjoyed feeling completely alive. But so close to his warm skin, his smell, his eyelashes, I could only think that Olivia had just got completely muddled up.

I dropped some words into the silence. 'That was kind of special.'

He grabbed my hand, kissed my palm. 'It was very special.'

I stretched. 'I feel really *alive*,' I said, experimentally.

He nuzzled my neck. 'I've never felt so alive.' His voice was slightly muffled.

I hugged him tighter, loving the warmth of his body, the soft touch of his skin, the sharp bones underneath, so strong but somehow so fragile.

'You should've told me you were going to be at the hotel,' I said.

'I didn't want to . . . you know . . . look like a stalker. . .' he said. 'But I needed to explain. That whole thing in Camden. I'm worried he's going to come and see you.'

'Who?'

'Him. Nick. My dad.'

'He's your *dad*?' I said, although I could have guessed if I'd thought about it.

He nodded. 'If he comes to see you, Lia, just ignore him. Don't listen to him. He's . . . he's . . . don't trust him. There are rules about how he is. He doesn't keep them.'

'Oh,' I said. I had no idea what he meant, but Raf's face was so bleak suddenly, that I needed to kiss him again.

'OK . . . Raf? Olivia said. . .' How to put it? 'Olivia said you were at school with her brother, Freddie, but. . .'

'Oh yeah, good old Freddie.'

He said the name – *Freddie* – as though he were spitting out a piece of rotten food.

'I thought he was your friend. She said you stayed at their house.'

'He wasn't my friend. They all had to have me to stay. It was like a rota. Like charity.'

He was moving away from me. I wanted to jump on him, pin him to the bed, hug him even tighter. I didn't, obviously, because that would have been a bit OTT.

Instead I gently stroked his face. 'Why didn't you spend holidays with your family?'

'I don't have a family,'

'Your dad? Jasper?'

He sighed. I could feel the breath lift his ribcage. He breathed! He was alive!

'I never even knew Jasper until a year ago. And my dad, he was always too busy. He used to take me to hotels sometimes. Hotels like this one. But mostly

I was left at school.'

'How could he leave you at *school*?'

'Boarding school. There are always some kids there for the holidays. But mostly it was because they were from Malaysia or somewhere else far away. Anyway, I was just used to it. Then I started getting invited to people's homes. I was pleased at first; it felt like . . . like I'd made some friends. But then I realised . . . someone said . . . that they'd been asked to have me. After that. . . It's difficult, you know, when you're not that friendly with someone during term time and suddenly you're in their house, having to meet their parents, talk to their sisters and brothers. It used to kill me, really. I'd feel like I'd lost the ability to speak.' He half sighed, half laughed. 'It still happens sometimes. I'm sorry.'

'Oh Raf, you've had a really difficult time.' I felt terrible for him. 'Your brother works you like a slave. I hate him.'

'He thinks it's good for me.'

'How can it be good for you?'

'That's what he says. He thinks I should keep busy. So I do.'

I didn't think so at all. 'I wish you'd told me this ages ago.'

'How could I? I only ever saw you at school, and you can't start talking about personal stuff in the middle of Science, can you? And you always had loads of friends around you. I really liked you; I really wanted to talk to you. I thought about asking you out, loads of times. But there was your boyfriend, Jack—'

'Jack is *not* my boyfriend,' I said.

'And your friend Shaz, she's a bit scary too. I could never see how to get you on your own. I even followed you home once, but I wasn't . . . I didn't. I didn't want to screw up so badly that you stopped being nice when we did see each other.' He swallowed.

'I think I really love you, Lia,' he said, almost under his breath.

When people talk about unprotected sex, they're warning you about babies and disease. When you have sex you're risking your health and your future. You could end up as a mother. You could end up dead.

You can save yourself from all that by using a condom.

But there's no condom you can use against the other sort of unprotected sex. The kind of sex you have when you don't know the person too well. You haven't protected yourself against their personality, your emotions. You don't know if they'll post videos on the internet, or rate your performance in a text to all their mates.

You don't know if you'll fall in love. You don't know if he's in love with you already.

Raf needed a whole load more than money could buy. He needed a whole load more than sex in a hotel room.

I wanted to ask Raf about what Olivia had said. Why had she thought he'd died? But he seemed so vulnerable, so easy to hurt. It seemed a crass and silly thing to say. I couldn't do it.

'Raf—' I said. But then my phone rang. And I didn't really want to finish my sentence so I answered it.

'Lia,' said my dad, 'you need to come home. It's Natasha. She's disappeared.'

Chapter 25

Money affects every situation,
but you never know exactly how.

'Has she run away before?' asked the policeman, sitting in our lounge.

'What makes you think she's run away now?' said my mum. 'Oh my God. I can't believe this. She's been abducted. My Natasha's been stolen. Oh God, she's been murdered. Why isn't she on the news? What are you playing at?'

'Calm down, we don't know that for sure, Sarah,' said my dad. They were sitting side by side on the sofa, clutching each other's hands. My mum had mascara smudged all over her face. My dad's face looked green and old.

'Natasha would never run away,' said Mum. 'She's quiet, Natasha. She's nothing like Lia. She's timid. She's not a risk-taker. She's very considerate as well.

She'd worry about our feelings.'

'Any boyfriends?' asked the policeman.

'Certainly not,' said Dad. 'She's very young for fourteen.'

I was texting and texting, phoning and phoning. Where was Natasha? Where was she?

Come on, come on, answer.

I pushed the buttons as hard as I could, as if by applying as much pressure as possible I could force Natasha to pick up.

'She's been seeing a lot of her friends, staying overnight,' said my mum. 'It's been chaotic here since Lia's win. It was just . . . this evening I suddenly realised I didn't know where she was. She hadn't rung me. And I called round the friends I knew – and a few others too – and no one knew where she was. And that's not like Natasha. You must admit, Lia, that's not like Natasha.'

'No one's seen her since her singing lesson this morning,' said Dad. 'I was expecting her to pop into the shop, but she didn't.'

'Oh Ben,' wailed my mum, dissolving into tears again. 'Where is she? Why didn't we realise? We're terrible parents. It's all my fault.'

I'd been back for an hour – had a quick shower,

stuffed my clothes in a bag, left a note for Olivia at reception, and jumped in a cab with Raf. I'd dropped him off in the Broadway. We hadn't said much in the cab – I was too busy talking to Mum on my mobile and ringing round any of Natasha's friends whose numbers I had, which wasn't that many because she never had many friends to start with, and I didn't clutter up my phone with their numbers.

Raf kissed me before he got out of the cab. 'If there's anything I can do, Lia, please just call,' he said. 'Really. Anything.'

'I will, thanks,' I said, and hunched over my phone again. I saw him walking off down the Broadway, saw the look on his face – so happy. Because of me.

I couldn't worry about him. I had enough to think about.

Natasha had come home from school as normal. Mum and Dad were going out to the cinema, had asked her if she wanted to come. She didn't. She'd gone out in the morning to her singing lesson.

'She was very quiet,' said Mum, 'but then, Nat's always quite quiet.'

And that was all they'd heard from her. She wasn't answering her phone. They'd called me and then the police.

'She's probably just met up with some friends and gone out with them and forgotten to charge her phone,' I said, although Natasha treated her phone as though it were a newborn baby and had never left it uncharged or out of credit. My attempts to reassure just backfired, though.

Mum wailed, 'Oh no . . . she couldn't even call for help. . .'

The policeman was looking through the list Mum had made of Natasha's friends. He asked me to take a look.

'You're at the same school, aren't you?' he said. 'Have you seen her hanging around with anyone in particular? Talking to any boys?'

I had a look. Mum's list was over-optimistically long. Everyone from Natasha's primary school class, even though she'd never really gelled with any of them. All the girls from her current class, ditto. Some of the boys.

I underlined the names of the girls who'd come shopping with us. Sophie, Molly and Keira.

'These are the ones she's been hanging around with,' I said. 'I don't like them much myself. We went shopping and I bought them stuff and they hardly said thank you.'

253

My mum spluttered through her tears. I passed her a tissue.

'God, Lia, I never thought I'd hear you say something like that,' she said.

'Huh . . . I'm being helpful, all right?' I said. 'I don't like these girls. They're users.'

'I've seen Natasha talking to a boy,' said my dad, suddenly. 'Young Raf. Came in for a job interview the other day. Chatting away to Natasha, he was, one day in the shop. Getting on like a house on fire.'

Raf? Natasha? *Chatting?* What the *hell?*

'Well, then,' said the policeman. 'Maybe she's with him. Do you have an address or phone number?'

I bit my lip. Of course, I could have told them where he'd spent the last few hours. But I didn't want to explain how I knew that. Anything to do with Raf needed to be kept as classified information until I'd had a chance to get my head around everything that had happened that night, which could take years.

Plus I wasn't as certain as Mum that Natasha had actually been kidnapped. Quite possibly, my baby sister was trying to grab a bit of the attention which had all been going my way. I sensed, though, that this was not an opinion that would go down well.

'He works at the internet café in the evenings,' said

my dad. 'Maybe he's there now. It's open late, isn't it? Maybe he'll know something.'

'It's 3.30 am,' said my mum. 'He's starting work for you next week every day at 5 am. What kind of a life does this poor boy have? Nothing but work, work, work. He won't be there now.'

I was really impressed at Mum's caring attitude towards Raf. She'd possibly be delighted if she knew how I was distracting him from his miserable life of constant low-paid toil. I was virtually a social worker.

'It's Saturday night,' said my dad. 'Maybe he does the Saturday night shift. He told me they get a lot of business then. I'm sure he'll be there. He's not working for me until Monday morning. And anyway, I've got his address. He wrote it down for me when I offered him the job. Here it is, five Melbourne Avenue.'

'What's a boy from Melbourne Avenue doing getting a job at a bakery?' said the policeman. 'It's millionaires' row, down there.'

'What did the singing teacher say?' I asked, to change the subject.

'Natasha was just the same as ever. Sang like an angel,' said Mum. 'She told her she should try for the *Britain's Got Talent* auditions. Natasha must've been over the moon.'

I opened my mouth to tell them about Marcus, and then closed it again. This wasn't the time.

The policeman put down his radio. 'We'll send someone over to talk to the boy in the café,' he said. 'Just see if he's there. He might know something. She might even be there. Don't you worry. Fourteen is a funny age. Sometimes the parents don't realise their kids are growing up. '

'You know Raf, don't you, Lia?' said Dad. 'What do you think? Has Natasha ever mentioned him?'

'Absolutely not,' I said.

'What else can you think of?' asked the policeman. 'Anyone with grudges against Natasha? Or the family? I know your daughter won the lottery recently, any problems arising?'

'Someone's kidnapped her, they're holding her to ransom,' said my mum, tears pouring down her face. 'Lia, we'll have to pay. Lia, you don't mind, do you? Poor Natasha . . . what if they hurt her? What if they mutilate her?'

I rushed to hug her. I couldn't bear to see her so upset.

'I'll pay anything,' I said. 'We'll get her back. Truly, Mum, it'll be all right. I know it will.'

'Donna's the only one with a grudge against us,'

said my dad slowly. 'And even Donna. I mean, the woman's demented, but she'd never hurt a child.'

'Who's Donna?' said the policeman.

Dad began to explain. And then the phone rang – the landline – making us all jump.

'Natasha!' said mum, but I grabbed it first.

'Hello?' I said, 'Nat?'

At first all I could hear was a scratchy noise, as though the telephone had been dropped. And then a muffled distant voice.

'If you want to see your sister again, it'll cost you. Get ready to pay up, bitch.'

Chapter 26

Some people will hate you, just because you have more than they do. Try not to take it personally.

It all got a lot more serious after that. A detective inspector turned up and questioned me about the phone call. He told us that they'd try and trace where it'd come from.

The policemen went and searched our bedroom, and pulled out Natasha's pathetic pink diary. They asked Mum and me to read it – see if anything jumped out at us. Dad was in the front room, talking to the detective inspector. Mum and I sat at the kitchen table, crying over pages and pages of Natasha's rounded, careful handwriting.

Lia's won £8 MILLION on the LOTTERY!!!!!!!!!!!!! It's the best thing that ever happened to our family!!!!!!!!

Lia says I can have singing lessons! OMG! This is the happiest day of my life!!!!!!!!! My sister is amazing!!!!!

Sleepover at Sophie's!!!!! So excited!!!!!

Mum and dad look so much happier. I think the shop will be safe now. I'm going to help dad out a bit more. Got to do my bit!!!!!

Marie says I sang really well today!!! Maybe she'll think I'm good enough for the Britain's Got Talent auditions! I've looked them up, they start next month.

Keira asked me to her party!!! Molly says I can borrow her black dress!!!

Plan for BGT: 1. LOSE WEIGHT! 2. BLONDE (?) EXTENSIONS (?) 3. Change name: Tasha? Stella? Sasha? Sasha Starr? Sasha Lamarr? 4. AUDITION SONG?????

Under any other circumstances I'd have been snorting with laughter and making a note to start calling Natters 'Slasher Lamarr' whenever I could. Or even Borat. But not that day.

Natasha's diary was plastered with emoticon stickers. Almost all of them were happy and smiley, ever since the day I hit the jackpot. Before that they were mostly sad, or frowning, or squiggle-mouth-confused.

'Don't cry, darling,' said Mum, holding my hand.

'We'll get her back. We will.'

'It's just . . . she's so sweet, Natasha. So nice. Look at this diary. She's too nice for real life. People are just going to hurt her, again and again. I can't bear it.'

Mum blew her nose. 'I know. She's not tough. She's not like you and me. She's like your dad. Always sees the best in everyone. It'd be so easy for someone to trick her . . . some boy, maybe . . . or worse. . . Oh, Lia.'

'These girls, these new friends. They don't really like her. They're not like Shaz or Jack, or my other friends. They just want her for my money.'

'She'd never see it, though,' said Mum. 'She's just so innocent.'

The first policeman came back into the room.

'We might be on to something with the boy, the boy at the bakery,' he said. 'He's disappeared too. His brother's very worried about him. Not seen him since Saturday morning. And the office at the top of the internet café – it's kitted out for someone to sleep there.'

'Oh my God!' Mum and I said.

'He'd been planning it,' said Mum. 'Planning to hold her prisoner. Oh God. Where are they? What's he done with her?'

'Look,' I said, 'I happen to know there's nothing

sinister about that room. Raf sleeps there. He doesn't like living with his brother, so he sleeps at the café. His brother treats him like a slave, he's got nothing.'

'He needs some money then,' said the policeman. 'Would you have recognised his voice?'

'Yes!' I said, although the line was so scratchy that it could have been Mickey Mouse at the end of the line and I wouldn't have realised.

'And anyway, I saw him this evening. He came to see me at the hotel. We're really good friends. We . . . err . . . had a coffee together.'

'Really?' said the policeman. 'Why didn't you mention this before?'

'Really?' said Mum, giving me a suspicious stare.

'Umm . . . yes. . . He's been helping me with my coursework. He's a really nice guy.'

He came to warn me, I thought. He came to warn me about his father. He said he wasn't to be trusted, that he was dangerous.

I couldn't form the words. I couldn't bear to think of Natasha . . . of Nick's skull-like face . . . of Raf. . . It couldn't be him. It couldn't be.

'What time was this coffee? When did he leave?' asked the policeman.

'He was creating his alibi!' said my mum.

'Err . . . not long ago, really. We shared a cab. I dropped him at the Broadway,' I said, mind racing. Surely Raf's dad wouldn't . . . surely . . . surely. . .

'He came to see me,' I said. 'He was really fine. And he didn't know about Natasha. He was totally shocked when I got your phone call, Mum.'

'He might be a very good actor,' said Mum. 'What do you mean, he came to see you in your hotel? What's been going on? We rang you at 2 am, Lia. 2 am. What were you doing with this boy?'

'*Nothing*,' I said. Could she be right? Was Raf acting? After all, I'd never had a clue what was going on with him. What if everything he'd said today was just made-up nonsense? What if he really was part of a gang of kidnappers and they'd sent him to seduce me . . . distract me . . . confuse me?

But he seemed so honest when he told me he loved me. That had to be a good thing – didn't it?

It was getting light. I looked at my watch. Six o'clock.

'I can't stand this,' I said, 'I need a friend here.'

'Jack?' asked Mum, but I shook my head. I'd have loved Jack to be here right now, but Jack meant Donna. I'd lost Jack forever. He was never going to forgive me for humiliating his mum.

'Shaz?' I said, 'Shaz . . . I'm really sorry to call so early. Really sorry,'

'It's OK,' she said, 'I was awake.'

'Look, can you come over, Shaz? Please? It's Natasha. She's disappeared.'

'Disappeared?'

'She might have been kidnapped.'

'Kidnapped! Lia! Is it on the news? What happened?'

'No one knows. We got a phone call.'

'I'm coming over. I'll be there really soon. It'll be OK, Lia, I know it will.'

When Shaz arrived, she hugged me tight. 'Let's go and talk upstairs,' she said. 'Tell me everything. I can't believe this.'

Our bedroom was a tip. If I'd known the police were going to search it, I'd have tidied up. They'd had a good nose through our stuff. Thank God I didn't keep anything particularly private in there. Natasha's Honey Bear was lying drunkenly on the floor. I picked him up. His goofy worn smile – she'd had him since she was six and I'd teased her about him a million times – made me cry again.

Shaz flew around the room, making beds, scooping up bracelets and earrings, folding, tidying, shutting cupboard doors and closing drawers. In less than ten minutes she had the room looking tidier than it had for years. Shaz could work miracles.

Then we sat on Nat's bed and I told her everything.

Well, not quite everything. One thing I knew about Shaz is that she wouldn't approve of sex with a boy who isn't quite your boyfriend in a hotel room. She wouldn't approve of sex with a boyfriend anywhere. She was incredibly strait-laced – like someone from the olden days.

So I told her that Raf had turned up, and we'd sat in the hotel foyer and had a coffee and talked.

And I told her about what he'd said, that he needed to warn me, that his dad was dangerous.

'Lia!' Shaz had finally lost her cool. Her eyes were shiny with tears. 'What did the police say when you told them? Are they looking for him?'

'I haven't told them – Shaz, I can't. What if it's nothing to do with Natasha? That's Raf's dad . . . I can't, *Shaz*.'

'Lia, you have no choice. No choice. What if he's abducted Natasha? What if he's holding her prisoner? The police need to know, Lia. They need to know everything.'

'Shaz . . . wait. . .'

'That phone call,' she said. 'What did they actually say?'

'"If you want to see your sister again, it'll cost you. Get ready to pay up, bitch."'I choked up, just saying it.

'That's a threat to kill,' said Shaz. 'They're saying they're going to kill her. What are you waiting for, Lia? Who are you protecting?'

'Oh God, you're right, you're right, come on, Shaz, come on. . .'

All I could see was Natasha's terrified face . . . Natasha in pain . . . Natasha crying. How could I have held back any information at all for even one second?

We galloped down the stairs, burst into the living room.

'I've got something to tell you!' I said. 'I think it's really important! I might know who's got Natasha!'

'Shush,' said Mum. I stopped, confused. Why was she telling me to shush?

Then I heard it.

Someone was opening the door. A key was turning in the lock.

'Natasha!' shrieked Mum and rushed into the hall.

The door swung open. My little sister stood on the doorstep, milk-white face, blood-red lipstick.

And her arm was around Raf's waist.

Chapter 27

You can't predict everything, but with money,
that doesn't matter as much.

I screamed, 'What the *hell*?' so loud it woke the neighbour's cat, and as Mum hugged Natasha tight, I beat my fists against Raf's chest. 'What were you doing with her? What's going on? Oh my *God*.'

'I'd like to ask you both some questions,' said the detective inspector.

'Are you all right, darling? Natasha? Where have you been?' said Mum frantically.

'I'm fine,' said Natasha faintly. Then she lurched forward and burped, holding her stomach. Everyone jumped backwards, but all that came out of her mouth was a clear liquid.

'Natasha!' shrieked Mum. Natasha retched again. This time the vomit was real and carroty, hitting Raf's black shirt and designer jeans.

'Oh my God,' said Mum, and dragged Nat into the downstairs loo.

'On second thoughts, I'll leave this to you, Jim,' said the detective inspector. 'I'll be off. Nice meeting you.'

The policeman said, 'That was Natasha, I take it? And Rafael? Too much partying?'

Raf was trying to clean the remains of Natasha's last supper off his jeans with a used tissue. 'I don't know . . . I just found her in the street.'

He was too busy removing vomit to notice the cynical expression on the policeman's face.

'And the phone call? Thought it'd be a laugh to waste police time and terrify Natasha's family? I think you've got some explaining to do.'

Shazia stepped forward and handed Raf a wet flannel and a clean white T-shirt, which she must have found on the ironing pile, because when he peeled off his own and put the new one on, it was slightly crumpled, a bit short and it had *Tithe Green Ladies' Netball Team* printed on the front. He still looked gorgeous, though.

I very nearly threw my arms around him, but there was far too much of an audience. Neighbours were beginning to emerge in their dressing gowns.

'I just found her. On the corner. She was sitting on

the pavement; she looked a bit . . . a bit out of it.'

'I'm fine,' said Natasha's muffled voice from the vicinity of the toilet.

'She needs water,' said Shaz. 'I'll get some.'

Mum and Dad and Shaz fussed around Natasha. They got her sitting down at the kitchen table, with Shaz mopping her brow and Mum and Dad asking her questions. The policeman went outside to phone his station. And it was just Raf and me left on the doorstep. I ignored the neighbours, grabbed his arm.

'Raf – Raf, what happened? You can tell me, Raf.'

'I . . . nothing . . . I mean, it was just like I said. I was walking up the road and I saw Natasha. She didn't look well. I thought she needed help.'

His voice trailed off. He looked around. The policeman was still on the phone, and we could hear raised voices from the kitchen. It sounded like Mum and Dad and Natasha were yelling at each other, which was quite strange, given that generally all family rows had me firmly at their centre.

'Raf – I—'

'Look, Lia, there's something I need to say. That's why I was coming to see you. . .'

Oh God. He was going to tell me about

his evil father. And then I'd have to tell the police.

'It's just. . . Look, I really don't want. . . I'm not sure how to. . .'

'Raf, I think I know. . .' I said.

'It's just that I should've, you know. Durex. And I did have . . . except I didn't want you to think . . . and I didn't assume, I just always . . . and there wasn't a right moment – and I'm sure I haven't, but I'll go and get checked if you want. And did you know about this thing called the morning after pill?'

Oh my God.

'It's OK,' I said gruffly. 'I'll take care of it. Don't worry.'

'I'm sorry. . .'

'That's OK.'

'Umm, Lia, I—'

But then Mum appeared again. I almost had a heart attack.

'We're going to have to take her to hospital,' she said. 'Something's not right.'

So unfair. Natasha starts shouting at them and they assume she's ill and has to be checked by a doctor. Whereas if I were to shout at them, they'd just roll their eyes and say, 'Typical, Lia.'

'Why?'

'She's slurring, her eyes are strange and she can't remember much. Just that she went round to a friend's house, there was a party somewhere, they all decided to go. That's all she remembers. That's not good, is it? We need to get her checked out.'

'I'm going,' said Raf.

'You're coming with me,' said the policeman. 'We're going to go back to that internet café and you're going to answer some questions.'

Raf's mouth dropped open. Anyone else would have looked gormless and moronic. He just looked like a stag caught by a hunter in a wood. A beautiful, huge-eyed stag. Is that a weird thing to imagine?

He barely glanced at me as he got into the police car. Then Mum, Dad and Natasha – a furious, tearful, stumbling, mascara-stained version of my sweet little sister – got in the car and drove off.

I waved at Mrs Little from number seventy-five. 'You can go inside now, the show's over!'

And then I slammed the front door shut. All alone. I breathed in, hearing the silence, trying to work out what to think about. Natasha? Raf? Raf's dad?

'How about the morning after pill, then?' said Shaz.

Argh! I jumped about a mile in the air.

'I couldn't help hearing what he said.' Her face was stony. 'Obviously, I wouldn't have said anything, except that I really feel you must do something, Lia, something sensible if you've done something. . .'

'Something stupid,' I finished her sentence for her. 'Why don't you mind your own business, Shaz?'

'I will – just as soon as you tell me what you're going to do.'

I could see she was almost bursting with the effort of not telling me what she thought.

'I'm going to do what I want to do, Shazia, not what you want me to do. Actually, it's not a problem.'

'Fine,' she said. 'Same old Lia. Does what she wants to do. Doesn't worry about her family. Doesn't worry about her friends.'

'You what?'

'Oh come on, Lia, you've been away with the fairies ever since you won the lottery. You spend all your time doing interviews and photo-shoots and mooning around about mystery boy. And all the time. . .'

'What?'

'Natasha. She's been getting into this new crowd. Molly and her mates. Did you notice? Did you check them out? They're all on that Facebook page, by the way.'

The Facebook page. My mind flinched away from even thinking about it.

'And then there's Jack. He bought you that ticket and all he's got is the press on his doorstep and aggravation from his mum.'

'I can't help it that his mum's a cow.'

'She's talking to a lawyer, wants to sue you for half the money.'

'She hasn't got a leg to stand on. Gilda told me that as long as it was my name and address on the back of that ticket, then no one else could have a claim on it.'

'Oh, so that's OK, is it?'

'Well . . . yes. . .'

'What about Jack, Lia? What about how he feels? He's meant to be your friend and you're not even talking to him. He bought you that ticket. You wouldn't have any jackpot without him.'

'I *am* talking to him. He just never answers his phone.'

'Oh really?

'Look, I had to let all the cake business die down. I don't want to fall out with Jack.'

'No,' she said. 'But people have been on the phone to him. Journalists.'

'*What?*'

272

'Trying to get him to dish the dirt.'

'What dirt?'

'You tell me, Lia. I feel like I don't know you any more.'

My hand reached out. I found the catch to the front door.

'What do you care, Shaz? I'm fed up with your . . . with your disapproval . . . judging me all the time.'

Shaz's eyes didn't flicker. 'Oh, I care, all right. But you don't notice that, do you, Lia? Well, I can tell you something. You're useless at secrets. Useless. I know there's something you and Jack are keeping from me. That day you bought the ticket – why didn't I come along?'

Just for one minute I thought I was going to hurl, like Natasha. The smell of vomit still lingered.

'You don't know anything about me,' I said, opening the door. 'You think you know everything, but you don't. You don't approve of me, OK, I get that, you don't approve of my money and my relationship with Raf—'

'Relationship!' she said contemptuously. 'Don't make me laugh.'

'But you don't know a thing about me and Jack, because there's nothing to know. We're just friends, that's all, we always have been and we always will be.'

'Sure about that?' she said.

'Yes, actually, yes I am. And how come you care so much, anyway? What's it to you— Oh! Oh my God! Shaz! You like him, don't you? You like Jack?'

'No, absolutely not,' said Shazia just a shade too firmly to convince me.

'Oh, come on . . . come *on*, Shaz. What's going on?'

'Nothing is going on, Lia. How could there be? First, the whole idea of Jack and me, it's ludicrous. Second . . . well, there's you, isn't there? There's always you.'

My mind was totally McFlurried.

'Shazia! Jack and I are just friends. Just really old friends. People think we're closer than we are, but that's just because we've been friends for so long. But you and him . . . does he know how you feel? Oh my God, he does! He does, doesn't he? And does he feel the same?'

She was trying hard to maintain her legendary calm, but Shaz's eyes shone with tears and her mouth was clamped tightly closed. She shook her head.

'You're talking *crap*.'

'But Shaz. . .' I took a deep breath. 'This is great. It's great, *really*. You and Jack – it's a bit weird, but actually, you'd be perfect together. Perfect. I'm really happy for you.'

I wasn't really sure if you could call the turmoil inside me 'happy' but it was a good target to aim for.

But Shaz's tears had won the battle.

'Don't be happy,' she blurted. 'Don't make up some romantic story. Because I know and Jack knows and you know, really, that there can never be anything between us.'

Chapter 28

*I've found it's best to hire somewhere
for parties, and bring in outside caterers.
Spend money on the things that people care
about and don't worry about every small detail
— there are people called party planners
who can do that for you.*

What does eight million pounds mean when you can't help out your best friend?

Shaz and I had a hug.

'It'll be OK, Shaz, I know it will,' I lied, and she went off home.

I sat and thought. About Jack and me, and Shazia and Jack, and Raf and me, and Jack again. And I didn't really get very far.

Then the phone rang. Mum, calling from the hospital.

'She's had a lot to drink,' she said. 'My Natasha.

I can't believe it.'

'She is fourteen, Mum.'

'Yes, exactly. She's fourteen. Not eighteen. Fourteen. She's been drinking spirits. Jesus.'

Mum's voice was all Welsh and wobbly. She was brought up very chapel, clean-living and teetotal and, although she's made up for it since, sometimes her roots start showing.

'They think she may have been given some drug. Some date rape drug. I can't believe it, Lia. Who would do something like that?'

'Oh my God! Has she been raped? Mum!'

'No, no, darling, nothing like that. They've examined her, she's fine. But she's been knocked out by something, and they're doing more tests to find out why. We'll be here a few more hours at least. Will you be OK?'

'I'll be fine,' I said. 'See you later.'

It was much easier to think about Natasha than Shazia and Jack. Drugs. Drink.

That phone call. Raf's dad. Surely . . . surely not. But Raf was definitely warning me about *something*.

Maybe I could retrace Natasha's steps, find out where she'd been, what she'd been doing. Her so-called friends must have some idea.

I went upstairs and found her address book. Nana Betty had given it to her at Christmas. Natasha had filled in as many friends as she could. It was as though Facebook wasn't enough for her, she needed to write them down herself, make them real. I looked at the smiley faces, the careful writing. I wished that people loved Natasha as much as she loved them.

Here they were. The girls we'd been shopping with. Molly, Keira and Sophie. They didn't live far away. I thought I'd pay them a visit.

There was no one at Sophie's flat. A curtain rustled when I rang Keira's bell, but the door remained closed. But at Molly's house I knew I'd come to the right place. Beer bottles in the garden. Vomit on the pavement. The whine of a Hoover as I knocked on the door.

The door opened slowly. A tall guy, year thirteen, I thought. Ed someone.

'Hey,' he said, 'it's the Lottery Girl. What do you want, Lottery Girl?'

'I have a name, you know,' I said. 'Is Molly in?'

'Moll!' he yelled, 'Lottery Girl here to see you.'

The Hoover was silenced. Molly yelled, 'Up here!' and I went up to find her, promising myself that when I moved to San Francisco – or possibly Sydney – I would never mention the word 'lottery' ever again.

I'd tell people I was independently rich or that I'd made a fortune by setting up a website. No, even better, I wouldn't tell people anything at all.

Molly was tidying her parents' bedroom. It wasn't too bad – just a massive stain on the pink carpet, a load of bottles on the floor and someone had scrawled a lipstick heart on her mum's dressing table mirror. I've seen worse. A lot worse.

Molly had a sly, fox-thin face and long blonde hair. She gave me a pained smile.

'My brother's birthday and I have to clean up. Lucky my mum and dad are in Croydon, staying with Nan.'

I didn't mess around.

'Was Natasha here last night? My sister?'

'Yes, she came with Sophie and Keira. What's the problem?'

'She got drunk. Very drunk.'

Molly shrugged her shoulders. 'So did lots of people.'

'She doesn't remember anything.'

'That's what she *says*.'

'No, she really doesn't. Come on, Molly, you know Natasha. She doesn't lie. I need to know what happened to her last night. I'm really worried.'

'There were loads of people here. Why should I keep an eye on your little sister?'

'I just want to know what you remember. Come on, Molly. Before the police get here.'

That got her attention. 'Police? What do you mean?'

'They think she might have been drugged. And we got a call last night . . . someone called me . . . made out they'd kidnapped her. What time did she leave? Could she have been picked up by anyone?'

'Well, I don't know anything about that. You'd better go.'

Her sharp eyes shifted away from me. She picked up an ashtray from her mum's dressing table.

'Come off it, Molly.'

She blushed, dropped the ashtray. Thirty cigarette stubs fell onto her mum's carpet.

'Look what you made me do.'

'Tell me about Natasha. Who made that phone call?'

'What phone call?'

I pulled my mobile out of my pocket. 'I'm calling the police right now.'

'Lia! I don't know about a phone call. I was totally wasted. Some people might have been, you know, messing around but I didn't have anything to do with it.'

'Who?'

'I don't know!'

'Who was even here?'

'I don't know – everyone. Loads of people from school. Look, I'll tell you who it might have been. You know Lindsay and Georgia? That lot. They were laughing, something about Natasha. Something about your mum wanting to know where she was. They thought it was a laugh.'

'And where was she? Where was Natasha?'

'I don't know. *Jesus*, Lia. There were loads of people here. She was probably sleeping it off in my room. Nothing funny, Lia, honest. There were a few girls in there. Had too much.'

'Did you know about the phone call? Someone phoned and said they'd got Natasha.'

'I don't know anything. They were laughing . . . talking about you and Natasha . . . that's all I know. Honest, Lia.' Molly hung her head. 'I'm sorry. You know what it's like. I was wasted. And Natasha, she was upset. She came down some time, crying. She said she'd get in trouble for staying out so long. Then she left.'

'What time was that?' I demanded, but she didn't know. She'd got so pissed at her own party that she didn't know night from day. It sounded like Nat had been here all night – but what if she hadn't?

'Great, thanks a lot, Molly,' I said. My shoulders were rigid with fury. 'My little sister came to your house and she got so drunk she could hardly walk straight. Anything could have happened to her.'

'She knew what she was doing,' said Molly. 'She wanted to get drunk. The thing about Natasha is – no offence, Lia – but she's so young. She's always trying to keep up with the rest of us. She's not quite there yet. She's sweet, I like her, I really do, but she's not as mature as we are.'

'Piss off,' I said. 'Get lost. You stupid cow.'

Molly eyed me. 'She wants to be like you. It was true even before you won the lottery and it's even more true now. She's not happy just being herself. She wants to be you.'

'I don't come to rubbish parties like this and get wasted.'

'Not since you've been a celebrity, anyway,' she said. 'But Natasha thinks she ought to be just like you.'

'Why couldn't you be a real friend to her, Molly? Why couldn't you just like her for herself? She's sweet, Natasha, and she wanted to be your friend so badly.'

Molly opened her eyes wide. 'Look, Lia, I don't

think you realise how much of a favour I was doing just letting her hang out with us.'

'Bitch!'

'You can get out right now,' said Molly's brother from the doorway. 'Don't speak to my sister like that.'

'Don't worry, I'm going,' I said.

Out on the doorstep I wondered where to go next. The internet café – Raf – but what about the police? And what about Raf's dad?

And then there was Jack – but I couldn't go to his house, could I? What if Donna was there? I needed help . . . needed someone to contact him, arrange for us to meet . . . smooth things over.

I needed Shaz. But Shaz couldn't be there for me. In fact, I ought to be there for her. There I was lecturing Molly about friendship, while my own best friend was crying . . . unhappy. . .

And then I realised that Molly's house was on the same street as the mosque that Shaz's family belonged to. Just a little mosque, really, set back from the road, brand new redbrick with a golden dome. On Fridays it was buzzing with people, men rushing in to pray. But on a Sunday it was quiet and there was no one hanging around outside.

I wondered if the imam was there. If I could talk to him. . . Maybe sort out this gambling business – surely he couldn't really think that the lottery was wrong? Maybe I could talk to him about Shazia.

Maybe I could do something good in a place where my money wouldn't help me at all.

Chapter 29

Money is not the most important thing in the world, especially if you've got lots of it.

A young woman opened the door of the mosque. She had a much more seriously heavy-duty headscarf than Shazia – one of those long white ones. I could see her whole face, though, and she didn't look unfriendly – just a little wary and surprised. The mosque smelled of new paint and furniture polish, shoes, coffee and spices.

'Can I help you?' she asked.

'I just wanted to speak to the imam,' I said. I could feel myself blushing – my face was hot as a toasted Pop-Tart – and my heart was thumping. What was I doing there? I already knew it was a stupid idea. I just desperately wanted to make things right for Shazia.

'He's away, I'm afraid,'

'Oh. Well, never mind. Sorry to bother you.'

'Is there anything I can do to help?' she asked.

'I don't think so,' I said miserably.

She laughed. 'Try me. You look like you've got some troubles.'

'Well . . . it's not me, really, that I came about. It's my friend.'

'Oh, your *friend*,' she said, as though strange girls turned up at the mosque every day, burbling about their friends. 'I'll tell you what, why don't you come and have a cup of tea with me? I'm teaching a girls' class in half an hour. Maybe I can give you some advice for your friend.'

So we went and sat at a Formica table in the mosque's sparkling clean kitchen and she made me tea and offered some biscuits.

'I'm the imam's niece,' she said, 'and I also work with ladies who wish to convert to Islam. So I may be just the person to help your friend.'

'Oh, right,' I said, nibbling my biscuit and wondering how to ask her about Shazia without telling her Shaz's name. Maybe she even knew Shazia. I'd have to be super-discreet.

'So, does your friend want to learn more about Islam?'

'No, no, that's not it. Actually, I think she might

286

want to know less about it.'

'Really?' The imam's niece looked a little confused.
I hoped I hadn't offended her.

'I think she's feeling, you know, repressed. Too
much religion,' I said.

'Really? But you . . . you don't look . . . you're not a
sister, are you?'

'I am a sister, actually,' I said, 'and I'm worried
about her as well. She went to a party and she got
horribly drunk and she's lost her memory.'

'I see.' She patted my hand. 'You've come to the
right place. You'd be surprised how many young
people come to us looking for a new direction, looking
to escape the excesses of secular life. They find
new meaning by embracing Islam . . . it's a very
beautiful process.'

Eh?

'No . . . it wasn't me . . . it was my *sister*. And anyway,
it's not her I'm here about. It's my friend. I think her
dad's making her be too religious. It's ruining her life.
She has to wear a headscarf and she can't go out with
this boy she likes. I was wondering if the imam could
. . . you know . . . soften the rules a bit.'

The imam's niece looked baffled, and a little bit less
friendly. She was looking at me closely, staring even.

'I know who you are!' she said. 'You're the Lottery Girl.'

'Umm . . . yes. . .'

'My uncle preached about you, only last week. Did you hear about it? It made quite a stir.'

'He preached about *me*?'

'He reminded the brothers and sisters who worship here of the dangers of gambling,' she said. 'The stories in the newspapers last week . . . they offered an excellent example.'

I was mortified. I imagined imams all over the country preaching sermons about my awful behaviour. Not just imams, either – vicars, rabbis, Buddhist monks, those Hare Krishna people . . . the Archbishop of Canterbury. The Pope. Jesus Christ himself, come down from heaven for a special guest appearance. . .

'I have done good things with my money,' I pointed out. 'And it's the lottery. Not really gambling, like a casino.'

She didn't answer. Hah! One-nil to me. Bring on the Pope.

'And I'm not a Muslim, anyway, so there are no rules against me gambling.'

'So you're Shazia's friend,' she said suddenly.

What the hell?

'Err, yes, but the thing I said before about my friend's life being ruined by religion, that wasn't about Shazia. That was about another friend. Another friend who sometimes comes here and sometimes goes to another, much stricter mosque. Much, much stricter. She's worried that her dad wants her to wear a burka.'

'Oh, I knew you couldn't be talking about Shazia,' she said. 'Shazia's the one who's got her whole family coming to the mosque. She's so enthusiastic about helping with the younger ones, doing good works. She's a real role model for the girls in our mosque.'

Shaz?

'She's very serious-minded, isn't she?' the imam's niece continued. 'She's full of passion for Islam. But she's loyal to her friends as well. She was quite troubled when you won your money, worried that it would come between you. But she was determined to remain your friend, despite the conflict involved.'

I had a gigantic lump in my throat. Maybe I was allergic to halal biscuits.

'She's a truly great friend,' I said.

'You couldn't do better than ask her advice about your other friend.'

'Who? Oh . . . err . . . that's a good idea.'

'And perhaps about your sister as well?'

'Umm . . . yes, right, maybe.'

'And Lia, if you feel you need guidance . . . advice
. . . then you are always most welcome.'

'I've got loads of advice,' I said. 'I've got a Winner's
Adviser and a personal bank manager and two
parents, thank you very much.'

'I mean spiritual advice.'

'I know. Thanks anyway.'

I couldn't get out of there fast enough. I didn't stop
until I was halfway down Jack's street passing *that*
newsagent, going up his front path.

The imam couldn't sort this out for me. I was going
to have to do it myself.

If Shazia wanted to be with Jack, and Jack wanted
to be with Shazia, surely religion wouldn't stand
in their way.

But that made it even more important that she
never found out I'd slept with him.

Chapter 30

'Life is a lottery.' People say that a lot. I don't really think it's true. Who expects to win when they buy a lottery ticket? Only the most stupid person imaginable. Mostly you think, it's only a pound or two, it's only a chance, I might win a tenner, it doesn't really matter. Imagine if life really was like a lottery. Imagine if every choice you made you thought, oh well, it doesn't really matter. It's all just chance and luck. I'm probably going to lose. You wouldn't care, would you? You wouldn't take care over your decisions. You wouldn't bother to think about what you were doing, work towards anything, make healthy or intelligent choices. Life isn't really a lottery at all. It's just that a lot of people act as though it were.

We'd planned it for months. Neither of us wanted to be virgins a moment longer than we needed to, neither of us fancied waiting to find the right person.

We wanted to know what we were doing when we met the right person.

We wanted to be in control. We wanted to be equally useless. We wanted to be experienced.

We didn't want it to be a big, big deal. We wanted it over and done with. We wanted to do it for the first time with our best, best mate.

So I went on the pill. I didn't go to our local GP's surgery – that would have been too embarrassing. I went to the family planning clinic at the health centre, where they took my blood pressure and explained how and when to take it. I'd been taking it for three months before my sixteenth birthday. I carried on taking it afterwards. It seemed like a grown-up thing to do.

Jack saved up so we could hire a room, and we found a bed and breakfast place in Finchley. I was going to say that I was staying at Roo's and he was going to make up some excuse, but in the end his gran was in hospital, and his parents went off to see her and left him all alone in the house.

So we did it on his Ikea bed, under his Tottenham

posters, after drinking a bottle of sweet white wine and watching a DVD. He wanted to watch some porn to get in the mood, but I didn't want him comparing me to those stupid girls with their satin undies and beach-ball boobs, so I said, 'Nah, let's get on with it.'

At first I didn't think it was going to work, because whenever he touched me I started shrieking with giggles, and he got all red in the face and said, 'Shut up, Lia, you're really putting me off. I'll never get it up if you're going to laugh like that.'

But then we started getting more into it, kissing and touching. I was pretending he was Robert Pattinson and God knows who he was thinking about, but we got enough into it to make it work. Just about.

He didn't last for long, and I was quite relieved, because it was a bit uncomfortable. My leg was squashed under his thigh. But it was dead exciting. Just thinking, I'm sixteen, I'm having sex, was enough.

At least, I thought it was enough.

It was absolutely OK, and good to have done it, and I felt like I was really, truly grown-up.

'Friends with benefits', they call it – at least that's what they call it on *Friends* – but we weren't going to be friends with benefits. We were going to be friends who'd done the benefits thing once. Just once. Only once.

And then I could continue dreaming about Raf – except I didn't tell Jack that. And he could go on yearning for Shaz – he didn't tell me that either.

Afterwards, I had a shower and used his mum's Radox gel, and then we walked down the road and I wondered if people were looking at my wet hair and what they were thinking about me.

When we got to the newsagent's, Jack said, 'Bollocks, Lia, I never got you a present,' and he went in and asked the guy how old you have to be to buy a ticket.

And the man said, 'You have to be sixteen to play the lottery,' and we both started giggling again and Jack bought me a ticket. I stood in that shop, smelling of Donna, laughing my head off, picking my numbers.

And I never thought, not for one tiny micro-second, that I might actually win.

Chapter 31

Get close associates and regular employees — cleaners, drivers, etc. — to sign a confidentiality agreement.

Jack opened the door. Jack in his trackies and a T-shirt. No Donna. No Shazia.

It all felt pretty normal. Just me and Jack. All the money and the mothers and imams and journalists in the world couldn't come between us.

'Hey, Lia,' he said. 'We need to talk, huh?'

I nodded. And we went on up to his room.

We sat on his bed, and I looked around at the comfortable sameness of it. His bookshelf – all horror, war, action, *Lord of the Rings* and Harry Potter – his model racing cars, his football trophies. Three cans of deodorant. One bottle of aftershave. High up on the bookshelf, tucked nearly out of sight, Mr Snowy, Jack's grubby polar bear. I remember when he wouldn't go anywhere without Mr Snowy. I remember when he had a tantrum because Mr Snowy got left in his uncle's car.

How could I be arguing with Jack? We shared so many memories, we were virtually the same person.

'Jack, what's going on? Are you going to tell the papers about us . . . you know. . .?'

'No!' I'd never heard Jack sound so definite about anything. 'No way. Don't worry about that, Lia. We said it'd be a secret and it is.'

'What about your mum?'

'She's just upset about the money. Don't pay any attention to her.'

'Bit late for that advice, isn't it?'

'You shouldn't have thrown a pie at her.'

'She shouldn't have called me a slut. I thought you'd told her.'

'Told my mum? Are you *mad*?'

'What about Shaz? What did you tell her?'

'Shazia? She's the last person on earth I'd tell. Wh . . . what did she say?'

'She said . . . she said . . . she said we were useless at secrets. That's what she said.'

He clutched his head in his hands. 'That's just Shaz trying to double-bluff you, Lia. She's clever like that.

She could work for MI6. She knows there's some mystery over when I bought you the ticket, but I'm certain she doesn't really suspect. And she must never know, we *agreed* that, Lia. No one must ever know.'

'I know that. God, Jack, I'm not going to tell anyone. It was just between us.'

'Yes,' he said. His voice was passionate. 'She mustn't know.'

'Yup.' My voice was a whisper. 'Why didn't you tell me, Jack? Why didn't you tell me what was going on with Shaz?'

'Come off it, Lia, nothing's going on. How can anything be going on with Shazia? With *Shazia*, Lia? Do you think she'd ever be able to go out with me? Do you think her family would ever accept me?'

I was trembling. 'They know you're her friend.'

'They don't, actually. I suppose you've never noticed that I don't go round there.'

I thought back. I supposed I did usually go round to Shaz's house on my own. Jack'd been playing a lot of football, though. How was I meant to notice stuff like that?

'No, I thought not. You don't really notice anything that's not directly related to you, do you, Lia?'

'I *do*. What do you *mean*?'

'Just that . . . it's Lia first, rest of the world second.' He grinned. 'It's part of your unique charm. Don't worry about it.'

I couldn't believe my ears. '*What*? Screw you, Jack! Just because you and Shaz have been sneaking around behind my back, suddenly it's *my* fault? *I'm* the selfish one? You're the one who slept with me when you really wanted to be with my friend.'

'I . . . err. . . It was completely separate from that, Lia. Anyway, you did it with me although you had the hots for posh-boy. It wasn't serious, you knew that.'

It wasn't. I did know that. But I hadn't quite realised how un-serious it was.

Time to change the subject. 'Are you going to sue me for half my money, Jack?'

He lay down on his bed. 'No, Lia, I am not. In fact, I should never have taken that bike from you. Mum won't let me use it, says she's going to send it back and you should give me the money instead.'

I said something very rude about Jack's mum.

'She is mad as a brush, true, but she thinks she's doing the right thing. She hates running that nail salon, and she really resents it that you've got so much dosh. But I'm not going to accept any money from you.'

'Why not? Look, Jack, maybe it's not fair. You did buy that ticket.' I gulped. 'Maybe I *should* give you half the money.'

He blinked. Then he shook his head, and said, 'No, I couldn't take it off you. I've been talking to Shaz's imam. People should make their own prosperity, not win it by gambling.'

'*You've* been talking to the imam?'

'Confidentially, Lia. The imam obviously doesn't know why I'm really there. I'm just trying to see. . .' he swallowed, 'if I could maybe, you know, go her way.'

'Oh my God! Jack! You're not even . . . I mean, you don't really believe anything, do you?'

'The imam thought that might help,' he said. 'Like I'm a blank slate, sort of. I don't know. It's asking a lot.'

'But she's really worth it, eh?'

'Yes.'

I was dazed. I hadn't slept for hours, and nothing in the world was the way I thought.

'Why didn't you tell me? What about all your strong Islamic principles when we . . . you know. . .?'

'I don't really have any strong principles, not yet,' he said. 'I'm trying to work out if I can develop some.'

'Oh, so you can resist four million pounds, but you couldn't resist a chance to get your leg over?'

He thought about that. Scratched his dumb head. And then he grinned and said, 'No, I couldn't. I'd been looking forward to that for *years*, Lia. Since we agreed.'

We were fourteen when we thought it up. We thought we were so mature. We'd wait until we were legal, and we'd do it, and we'd never have to do it for the first time with someone who'd laugh at us. And we wouldn't have to use a condom. We'd do it with our best friend.

Love had nothing to do with it. It was all about experience.

'When we decided . . . it was well before I had any feelings for Shazia at all. And if I really do become a Muslim I'll probably have to wait for *decades* . . . and I haven't even dared ask where they stand on, you know. . .'

I did know. 'You are *revolting*,' I said, throwing a cushion at him. 'I hope you do become a Muslim. I hope you grow a beard and wear one of those white tunics and pray all day long. It'll do you a lot of good. And it'll serve you right.'

'Huh,' he said. 'I'm starved. Want some toast?'

I was starving too. We went down to his kitchen and made tea and toast, which we plastered with crunchy peanut butter. I told him all about Darryl and Marcus, and he was highly impressed and wanted to know if I'd be seeing them again and whether he could come and hang out too.

'You're going to be living the high life, Lia,' he said. 'Tell you what, if you don't want to take over your dad's shop and Natasha doesn't either, then maybe I could.'

'You must be joking,' I said, spreading a layer of strawberry jam on top of my peanut butter.

'Not at all,' he said. 'It's always been my dream job. Imagine. All the cakes you can eat. Doughnuts for breakfast. All the kids in the area thinking you're the nicest person on earth. You know Food Tech's my favourite subject after PE, Lia. Miss Simpson said my Christmas cake was a work of art.'

'Yeah right, I'll mention it to my dad,' I said, licking jam off my fingers. I felt a bit irritated, though. Just because I'd won the lottery didn't mean I'd definitely decided to chuck Latimer's Loaves. Jack could keep his mitts off my birthright until I'd decided one hundred per cent that I didn't want it.

His mum had left the *Daily Express* on the table.

I started flicking through it, reading out stupid headlines, looking at pictures of celebrities in unwise bikinis.

Until I reached page seven. And I saw my name. And a picture of me and Raf taken in Hampstead. Smiling, laughing, arms around each other.

'Lottery Lia's new flame' said the headline. '"They were talking about moving in together," said taxi driver, Osman Botnick, 55. "They seemed very happy together."'

I stared at the newspaper in silence. Great. I couldn't even have a day out with Raf without everyone knowing about it. Soon they'd all be reading every detail of our night together. I'd won the jackpot, but I'd lost my right to privacy.

A big tear slid down my nose and landed on a story about immigration.

'What's the matter?'

I pointed at the paper. 'Look . . . Raf . . .'

Jack read it, face screwed up. 'What's the problem? Apart from you spending time with that weirdo.'

'He's not a weirdo. It's just . . . Jack, we spent the night together. A bit of the night, anyway.'

'You screwed him? Bloody hell, Lia. I thought he was gay. His clothes are gay.'

'He is absolutely, completely, definitely not gay.'

'Well, that's a relief. No offence, Lia, but I don't want you sleeping with some guy who'd rather be in bed with me.'

'Jesus, Jack, shut up. He's not gay. Definitely. But there's something weird going on.'

'Well, look, Lia, obviously I realise that no other guy's going to measure up after you've tasted the pleasures of my body—'

I clouted him with the *Express*.

'Not that, you moron. He was warning me about something. Something about his dad. Do you think he's after my money?'

'Well, how's he going to get your money? You're not offering four million quid to every guy you sleep with, are you, Lia?'

'Shut *up*! It's just . . . I don't really know anything about him. Not really.'

'Lia, if you want to find out about a guy, you'll have to interrogate him before you jump into bed with him. Because once you've done that, believe me, no one's going to stop to tell you his life story. Even gay boy here. Unless he is actually gay, in which case he'll be trying to put you off by telling you his entire family history in the hope that you'll fall asleep and he can escape to some club in Soho.'

'You are just vile and homophobic – not that Raf is actually gay – and I hate you,' I said. 'I'm going to tell Shazia that you are totally not worthy of her and never will be.'

'I've never felt that you appreciate my wisdom,' he said. 'More toast?'

'No thanks. I've got to find him.'

'Just remember what Uncle Jack told you,' he smirked. 'Keep your knickers on until you've asked your questions.'

Chapter 32

Do your research before important meetings.

Melbourne Avenue was on the outskirts of Tithe Green, the smarter, more expensive outskirts, where the roads were wider and the houses hadn't been carved up into flats and people had space to park multiple cars in their massive driveways.

Most of the houses seemed nice enough – based on their well-clipped hedges and doors glowing with stained glass. But number five was different. Almost hidden behind dark trees and overgrown bushes, I had to pick my way down the path. The iron gate clanged shut behind me, and a spider's web brushed my face. The sun hid behind a cloud, and a breeze rustled the weeds that choked the large front garden. A black cat burst out from the undergrowth, yowled at me, showing sharp white teeth, and then hid itself again. By the time I reached the front door – peeling mossy green paint, a blackened lion door knocker – I was slightly spooked.

Oh well. I'd just knock on the door and see if Raf was there.

The door creaked open. 'Why, Miss Latimer. How good to see you. Do come in.'

Oh God. Oh no. Raf's dad was standing in the gloomy hallway, dressed all in black, dark stubble shadowing his face, sharp gas-flame-blue eyes staring at me.

I considered turning and running. But nothing had actually happened. I swallowed.

'Hi . . . umm . . . I was just looking for Raf.'

'He's not here, I am sorry to say.'

'Oh, right, never mind,'

'But he will be here very soon. He's just called me. Please do come in, and you can wait for him.'

'Oh . . . well . . . I don't know.'

His gaze was hypnotic. 'Really – I insist.'

So I followed him through the gloomy hallway – dark wood panelling, a tinkling chandelier overhead – and through to a barely furnished living room, which had one dusty, plum-coloured sofa that looked like it had been there since Victorian times, a huge mahogany chest by the window, the kind of thing that pirates fill with treasure, and heavy, dark blue velvet curtains which were drawn closed.

'Oh!' I said.

'Let's let in some light,' he said, pulling one curtain a little way open, so I could see a glimmer of grey sky. 'I apologise for . . . for this. In the days when I lived here, things were very different. Please, make yourself comfortable.'

I sat down on the velvety sofa.

'Oh . . . *when* you lived here?'

'Long, long ago,' he said, smiling at me now, in a way that reminded me of Raf's heart-breakingly sad smile, but was somehow also deeply sinister at the same time.

'Umm, so, if you don't live here *now*, why are you here?'

'I have duties, apparently. And I am bound by terrible circumstances.'

God, he was even more cryptic than Raf. I was all over goose pimples. Long ago? Could he be . . . he surely couldn't be . . . a ghost, could he? Could he?

'Lia, I need to ask you something,' he said, leaning towards me. His teeth glinted as he spoke. I took a deep breath. He smelled of something spicy, something ancient and strangely attractive. I felt a little dizzy.

'I'm not . . . not sure. . .' I said in a small voice. And then it occurred to me. He'd said Raf had phoned him. But Raf never ever seemed to use his phone. Oh my God.

'I have a proposition for you,' he said, 'something I think you will like very much. Something attractive to both of us.'

Oh my God!

'I. . .'

'Hear me out, please,' he said. I held my breath. I could hear the wind crashing through the trees outside, the house creaking, and a strange rustling, crackling buzz in my ears, muffling his voice, working its way into my brain. I struggled to think clearly.

'Well, yes, but when you said Raf called, the thing is that he never actually uses his phone.'

Nick paused. His face flickered irritation and – I thought – a slightly guilty tinge.

'That boy is stuck in another age,' he said. 'He doesn't seem to engage with the world around him at all. He might as well live a hundred years ago.'

'But—'

'That's why I am so delighted that you are his friend. He needs friends. They will keep him here, with us, in the land of the living. Rafael has not had an easy life, and I feel responsible for that. But you, my dear Lia, you can help me make life very much easier for him. You can transform his existence.'

I was being drawn in – I couldn't help it – by his intense stare – did he ever blink? – and his heady scent.

'Oh . . . right . . . well, I'd like to help.'

'Here, in this house, we are in the power of an evil woman. A vengeful, bitter woman who has all the power, while I have nothing.' His face twisted. 'I need to get back what is rightfully mine. You can help me, Lia, help me and my unfortunate son.'

'Oh . . . right, but how?'

'It's very simple,' he said, leaning towards me. I inched backwards.

And then the buzzing noise got louder and louder, and turned into a wailing cry, a piercing, miserable sob. And I opened my mouth and screamed.

Chapter 33

Always pay your taxes.

Nick jumped away from me, burbling, 'I. . . Are you OK? There must be some mistake. . . Oh, God. . .'

'What the hell?' Jasper's cold voice came from the doorway. I stopped screaming. But the buzzing wail went on. Neither of them seemed to be able to hear it. Was I going mad?

'There's nothing . . . we were just talking . . . I was making a proposition to Miss Latimer . . . a purely *business* proposition. . .'

Jasper said, 'Oh yes, right, Dad, with your track record, I completely believe you. Lia, I must apologise for my father's behaviour. Dad, for God's sake, she's at school with Raf. A bit young, even for you. At least Carmen was nineteen.'

Nick looked as horrified as I felt. 'No, no, Jasper, I assure you, really nothing happened. . .'

'No, nothing at *all*,' I said. 'It was just, Raf said . . . he said you were dangerous.'

'Huh,' said Nick. 'I do everything for him, only for him, and he runs around telling you . . . what did he tell you? That I'm some sort of bloodsucker?'

Oh my God. Oh my God.

I decided to ignore that question. 'And then there's that noise. . . I don't know if you can hear it?' I mumbled.

'I don't know why you bother to have it on,' said Jasper mysteriously. 'You never seem to react.'

'I just wanted to talk to Lia while I had the chance,' said Nick. 'I really didn't mean to scare you . . . I . . . what did I do to scare you?'

What did he mean about sucking my blood?

'I'll go,' said Jasper, picking up a little white box from the window sill and switching it off. The awful buzzing noise stopped, just like that. But there was still a dim wailing cry.

'No . . . don't. . .' I said, but he'd gone already. I could hear the creak of his tread on the stairs. The crying stopped.

'I'm looking for investment,' said Nick, 'and I thought of you. I used to be in the fashion business and I can see you're a stylish girl . . . you understand

vintage too, which neither of my sons do. I was once
. . . well, people called me "tailor to the stars".
I designed for many big names, you know . . . Mick
Jagger, Joan Collins . . . I was the first to put Princess
Diana in a catsuit. . .'

Despite everything, I was fascinated. 'Really. . .?
Wow. . .'

'But times are hard, my dear, times are hard. My
business ran into difficulties. It started with the divorce,
I suppose, but you know, I was so busy, so busy opening
shops, designing, travelling here and there. . .'

'Partying with your celebrity friends, spending
money left, right and centre. . .' Jasper was back again,
holding a little boy in his arms. A tiny boy with Raf's
dark hair and Nick's arched eyebrows and the same
crooked smile that they all had. A little boy clutching
a wooden red building block in his hand, which he
lifted and—

'Duck!' yelled Jasper as the block flew through the
air, missing my head by a millimetre.

'George! I've told you not to do that! No!'

The little boy was laughing his head off.

Nick viewed him with suspicion. 'Jasper, I know
you don't like me saying this, but I think you should
get George checked out. . . I mean, I don't want to

believe there's something badly wrong with my own grandchild, but I don't think he's normal. Ever since he hit Rafael in the eye with his damned bricks, he's been trying to blind everyone else.'

'Nonsense,' said Jasper. 'He's just upset because you were ignoring the baby monitor. Where the hell is Rafael, anyway? Lia, I can't believe my father was trying to tap you for money. He can't set up any kind of business for at least another year, you know. He's been declared bankrupt, and there are rules against him asking for investment when he owes thousands to all sorts of creditors, particularly the Inland Revenue.'

Nick looked a little shifty. But he rallied quickly. 'The infernal tax collectors!' he said. 'Now, they are the real bloodsuckers! Taking money to pay for fripperies like universal education for the unwashed masses . . . benefits for the undeserving poor. . .'

'That'd be you, then,' said Jasper, putting the little boy down so he could cannon into Nick's knees. 'You're living off benefits at the moment. And education for your son, whose expensive private school is yet another one of the organisations to which you owe money. Where *is* Raf? There's no one at the café. That's two shifts he's missed.

The police were asking about him. I'm worried.'

I was worried too. 'He was at my house this morning – my sister, she'd gone missing and Raf found her in the street. The police said they wanted to talk to him – they wanted to know about the office above the shop.'

Jasper shook his head. 'That's not good . . . not good at all. Was he all right?'

'I don't know . . . he went off.'

'Dad – would he go to your bedsit, do you think? Should we go there?'

'He never ever comes to see me,' said Nick gloomily. 'It's your fault. You've stolen my son.'

'Oh, come off it, Dad. The poor kid's my brother, even if you kept us apart all these years.' Jasper turned to me. 'Raf's told you his story, no doubt. How Dad got the au pair pregnant, packed her off back to Spain, and failed to tell anyone – including my mum – that he was supporting her and her child, until Raf was seven and his mother was killed in a car accident, and suddenly he had to be brought back to England.'

'Oh! No—' I said, but Jasper was in full flow.

'And Dad still blames Mum for reacting to this by divorcing him, which anyone in their right minds would do. And she was perfectly entitled to this house.'

Ah, I thought, the evil woman! A long time ago!

'And how lucky for me and Sylvie and little George that Mum was prepared to move upstairs and make room for us when Dad's business went bankrupt and I was out of a job. And lucky for Rafael too that she didn't mind him coming to stay with us. I know it's not easy for him – and God knows, it's not easy for any of us, with George's sleeping problems—'

Little George gave a joyful cackle, and ran his scooter over Jasper's foot.

'Argh. . . But at least it's better for Raf than staying with Dad in his bedsit and having to listen to him going on and on about himself and his own problems the whole time. No wonder Raf's eaten up with anxiety. No wonder he tried to kill himself.'

He tried to kill himself? Oh God . . . is that what Olivia meant. . .?

'So,' I said, 'where is he now?'

Chapter 34

You need to work out which instincts to trust.

Nick and Jasper were useless, really. They called the local police, who said they'd taken his details and were planning to contact Raf's family, but they hadn't questioned him because of his age.

'We will be doing so in due course.'

'So where is he?' demanded Jasper.

'We have no idea. He said he was going home.'

Jasper put the phone down. 'Sounds like the policeman just wanted to give him a scare.'

'Jesus,' said Nick. He'd sat down on the sofa and was turning George's wooden block over and over in his hands. 'He'll be with his friends,' he said. 'He tells me he's made lots of new friends at his school. He seems quite happy there, working hard, much less worried. Who would he be with, Lia?'

I shook my head. 'I don't know. Look,

I'd better be going. He'll turn up, I'm sure of it.'

'Lia—' said Nick, but Jasper said firmly, 'Thanks, Lia, for coming over. I'm sure Rafael will be in touch soon.'

I fled down the path, headed back to the Broadway. My mind was thinking furiously, about Raf, about who he was, where he could be.

The last person I needed to bump into was Georgia.

'Hey, Lottery Girl,' she sneered. 'Looking for your little sister? I hear she's gone missing.'

I was not in the mood. 'Leave me alone, Georgia.'

'Bet she gave you a scare.'

Hang on a minute.

'No, Georgia, *you* gave us all a scare. You made that phone call, didn't you?'

'What phone call?'

'Spare me, Georgia. Save it for the police.'

'What do you mean, the police?'

'Well, you can't really go around threatening to kill people and trying to get ransom money without getting the police involved.' I looked at her face – half defiant, half scared – and took a risk. 'They know it was you, you know. They can trace calls.'

'What! What! It wasn't me. It was Alicia's phone!'

I shrugged. 'Whatever. Don't tell me. Tell the police. Natasha's fine, by the way.'

She realised just too late. 'You bitch! You didn't know a thing, did you? Jammy cow!'

'Not difficult to guess, Georgia. I look at Facebook, you know, I know how your small mind works. Now, excuse me, I'm looking for someone.'

'Who?'

'None of your business.'

'It's Raf, isn't it?' Her voice was mocking. 'Raf the vampire. How much did you pay him to go out with you?'

I swung my bag (Fifty pounds. Top Shop. Leather slouch.) at her. 'Take it back!'

'No! It's true! He never looked at you before!'

'He did!'

'He never! Anyway, who wants him? He's weird. He never talks to anyone, and he spends all his time hanging out with dead people.'

'He doesn't . . . he's completely normal . . . he's . . . what do you mean?'

She cackled. 'You don't even know that he hangs out at the cemetery. Alicia and I have followed him there loads of times. He's strange, I'm telling you. He just sits there, staring into space. Or sometimes he *reads*.'

Georgia made it sound as though reading was one of the most disgusting things anyone could do in a public place.

'Bye, Georgia!'

I sprinted in the direction of the cemetery. It was only when I got to the cemetery gates that I slowed down and wondered if I should call Jasper . . . but I didn't have his number . . . or Shazia . . . or Jack. What if Raf was . . . but I couldn't even think about that. What if . . . what if I couldn't find him? I had to find him. Oh God. I vowed that if he was all right, I was going to buy him a phone with a secret tracker device, so I could always locate him.

The old cemetery hadn't been used for years. It was overgrown and neglected, big cracks in some of the granite tombs. Crumbling angels with blank faces adorned some graves, but most were just engraved with names and dates disappearing under years of rain and grime. This wasn't a grand impressive graveyard, full of important people. This was where ordinary Londoners came to fade away. It wasn't a place for guided tours or romantic walks. It was dank and depressing and miserable.

It was a place of whispered rumours, of paedos and perverts and black masses. Ghosts and ghouls and phantoms lived there alongside the glue-sniffers and junkies. It made me shiver. It made me scared.

But Rafael was most probably hidden away somewhere here, and he might need my help.

I scrambled through brambles, pushed aside ivy, winced as a nettle brushed my ankle. My eyes darted everywhere, looking for signs of him. What if he wasn't here? What if Georgia had tricked me . . . tracked me here?

And then I realised that someone *was* following me.

It was just a small rustling noise. But it stopped when I stopped. And then it started again. A crackle, a shadow, a glimpse of someone lurking in the bushes.

I shrieked and ran, stumbling over stones, leaping puddles, dodging trees and statues. And someone was running after me . . . the rasp of heavy breathing, a face glanced out of the corner of my eye. I'd lost all sense of direction . . . I fumbled for my phone – tripped, fell – the phone flew out of my hand. . .

'Lia!' Raf appeared from nowhere, catching me as I crumpled. 'What's going on? Lia?'

'Someone's . . . someone's chasing me. . .'

Raf held me tight. 'It'll be some girl. They seem to come here all the time. I try and ignore them.'

Out of the corner of my eye, I caught a glimpse of Alicia's skinny bum disappearing into the undergrowth. I hugged Raf even closer.

'Are you all right?'

'I'm fine,' I said. How stupid did I feel? I'd come to rescue him, and I'd ended up having to be rescued myself. From Alicia, for God's sake.

'I didn't know you came here,' said Raf. 'It's great, isn't it? So quiet, and history everywhere. All these names, all these people, all these stories. I come here a lot.'

'You do?'

'It's my sort of place.' He shot me a glance. 'You think I'm mad, don't you?'

'No. . .' I said, because I couldn't really say yes. 'Raf, I talked to your dad and Jasper. They said you tried to kill yourself. I was scared . . . I was worried.'

He seized my shoulders.

'I didn't really. . . Look, it was a difficult time. I couldn't remember ever not being at a boarding school. I was institutionalised. And my dad used to come and talk to me about all his money problems . . . everything he was worried about. He was really down. His girlfriend had left him and he wasn't coping. You've met him. He's kind of . . . he takes over your mind. I got to a point where I couldn't sleep. Still can't, most of the time. I get anxiety attacks. It's . . . it's humiliating, Lia. I feel like I'm having a heart attack. I have to breathe into a paper bag. Then I worry about it happening where people can see – I avoid people, most of the time.'

'That time in school . . . when you wouldn't talk to me. . .'

'I *couldn't*. I probably would've passed out. When you fainted at the café – I felt like we had something in common. That you'd understand. . .'

'Yes, but *Jesus*, Raf, you took an overdose? You wanted to die?'

'No . . . not really. I didn't think I would die exactly. I just didn't care if I did or not.'

I tried to ooze silent sympathy from every cell of my body.

'I took some pills – they'd given me stuff to help me sleep – and I washed them down with some vodka. I just thought I'd take a chance, that's all. I didn't really care about the result.'

'You could have *died*.'

'I was lucky, I suppose.'

I was trembling. Raf had gambled with his life. Just a few more pills, another sip of vodka. . . What if he got sad again? What if he felt so lonely, or desperate or so reckless that he didn't care about the future?

'Do you think . . . would you ever. . .'

'The strange thing is,' he said, 'that when Dad did lose everything, and I had to leave school and we ended up staying in some revolting hotel place – truly disgusting, Lia, there were bed bugs in the mattress and it stank of dead mouse – it was actually easier than worrying about it.'

'It must've been horrible, though.'

'Jasper saved me. He said I had to come and live with him and Sylvie – that's his wife – even though it would be awkward because their little boy George doesn't sleep and they were living at his mum's, which isn't easy. . . I mean, it was my fault she got divorced in the first place.'

'That must be so difficult.' Oh my God. And I thought things were tough living with my parents.

'She's always very nice and polite to me, but I know she must hate me – I try and keep out of her way. And Jasper and Sylvie, they're great, actually, but so tired all the time, because George never sleeps. Jasper gets really bad-tempered sometimes because he hasn't slept enough. And Sylvie keeps on bursting into tears which is kind of embarrassing. My dad, he's got a lock-up full of clothes and he sells them. It's totally against the rules. If the authorities found out, they could prosecute him. Lia, I know he wants you to invest – you mustn't. . . He'll take all your money!'

'Don't worry,' I said. 'Blimey, Raf, I can see why you wanted to move into that office.'

'Yeah. I don't know what I'll do now.'

I knew I had to ask. 'You won't ever do it again, will you?'

'What?'

'You know . . . the pills and vodka. . .'

He stared at me. 'Why would I do that, when the best thing that's ever happened to me just happened?' And then he looked away. 'I'm sorry, Lia. Maybe you just want to forget it . . . forget we ever. . .'

'No, I don't, it was great, but Raf, I don't know . . . how I feel. I don't know what's going to happen.'

'No one knows what's going to happen.'

'I never want to hurt you. But I don't want to make you promises I can't keep.'

'It's OK,' he said. 'I'm OK. There are lots of good things happening in my life, Lia.'

'But, Jasper – he works you like a slave.'

'He thought it would help the anxiety if I was busy all the time. And I am, and it does. He made me join the football team as well. It all helps. I'm actually excited to have that job in the bakery – I've got loads of ideas about your dad's development plans. And one day I want to set up my own thing – maybe antiques, something like that – but till then I need to learn how to run a business and not end up like my dad.'

'But you like history . . . and literature. . .'

He shrugged. 'I can always read. The way things are at the moment, you have to be a millionaire to devote your life to stuff like that. You could, I can't.'

'I could . . . I could help you.'

'You do help me. But not with money. Much more than that.'

And then his arms slipped around my waist and, he bent his head and I tasted the warm, salty softness of his mouth.

It was strange, I thought. All those months thinking Raf was like a hero in a paranormal romance, that he might be one of the living dead. And none of us realised how close he'd been to being just plain dead and gone, ashes in the air or rotten flesh in the ground.

'Just think about it,' I said. 'I can't keep all the luck to myself. I have to share it around.'

Then we walked around the park a bit, and then he said, 'I'm due at the internet café, I think. . . I'm hours late, actually. Jasper will kill me.'

And I looked at my watch and said, 'Oh God, I've been out for hours, I'd better go home.'

The minute I walked through the door, my mum pounced.

'Where have you *been*? I've been worried *sick*. We came back from the hospital and there was no sign of you. I've been phoning and phoning, texting and texting. Good Lord, Lia, I'd have thought you had more consideration.'

I had no energy to fight at all. I fell into her arms. 'I'm sorry . . . it's been a really difficult day . . . I didn't mean to scare you.'

She looked as amazed as if I'd grown another head.

'Well! As long as you're all right. Come inside, darling and I'll make you some tea. You look done in.'

'Where's Natasha? What did the hospital say?'

'She had an acute reaction to alcohol. Some people do. It's like an allergy. She's sleeping it off.'

'What did about the phone call?'

'She knew nothing about it. She just passed out at her friend's house, then tried to walk home. No, the police think that phone call came from some girls at

326

your school. Shazia – she called them. Told them to look at that disgusting Facebook page. There were all these comments there about playing a trick on you . . . making you suffer. Ugly stuff. They're going to have a word with those girls. It's disgraceful. Cyber-bullying, it's called. I think the school should take some action. Get those girls suspended, at least.'

She made tea and came and sat on the sofa next to me. I leaned against her, just like I used to when I was little and she'd read to me, for hours and hours – *Little House on the Prairie*, *The Secret Garden*, *The Little Princess*.

'Mum,' I said, 'what if someone loves you more than you love them? What if you think you'll end up hurting them? Should you just finish it?'

She smiled. 'That's a difficult one. Is it . . . are you. . .? Never mind. I think you have to be honest, and try not to get in too deep. Take it easy. Love can grow, you know. Don't rush at things.'

'Oh, right.'

'Sometimes that's how I feel with you girls,' she said. 'I love you so much, and all you want to do is break free of me. Sometimes it feels like you hate me. I have to remember that it's quite normal – and it's what I did to poor old Nana Betty in my time.'

My eyes filled with tears. 'I haven't even bought Nana a present. I've got all this money and I haven't sent her anything. I'm so selfish.'

'No you're not. You're just young and you've got a lot to deal with. There's plenty of time to sort yourself out. And I sent her some flowers from you, a week ago, to keep her happy.'

'Mum, you are brilliant,' I yawned.

I needed to sleep for a hundred years. But I logged onto Facebook, called up the hideous page. And it was hard to know what to write on the wall, without looking paranoid or needy or sad.

But in the end I put this: *You know, I couldn't help it that I won loads of money. I'm just the same as you, just doing the best I can. OK, if you want to hate me there's nothing I can do about that. But what happened to me could still happen to you.*

Chapter 35

Money can't buy you love. But it can buy
many other very nice things.
Winning the lottery exaggerates your
normal life. If you're basically happy,
you'll be even happier. If you're screwed up,
you'll be even more screwed up.
Independent financial advisers are the most
trustworthy. Other people might make
big promises, but they won't tell you
that they're raking in a ton of commission
on the side.
It's worth spending money on
great underwear, because it makes cheaper
clothes look really good.

'What are you *doing*? I thought you'd finished with
your GCSEs . . . what are you scribbling in
that notebook?'

Even though I'd acquired a massive suite all of my own, even though I had my own bathroom and living room – a purple velvet sofa, a forty-two-inch plasma screen – and a deluxe super-stylish bedroom, Natasha *still* constantly invaded my privacy. Huh.

'Mind your own business,' I said, chucking a purple satin cushion at her head. I missed.

'Oooh . . . what are you hiding? A love letter?'

'Why would I be writing a love letter?'

'Well, I don't know . . . you're the one dating a vampire. . .'

'For God's sake, Natters. . .'

Honestly. The stupid year tens *still* thought Raf was paranormal. Talk about immature. Thank God we'd be escaping to sixth form college in a few months. Although, mind you, Raf was still insisting that he wanted to leave school and concentrate on making his fortune. I was trying to work out how I could persuade him. Emotional blackmail? A mysterious scholarship fund?

I sucked my pen and wrote: *Having lots of money doesn't mean you can control everyone's life.*

'Anyway. . .' she said. 'I just came to ask you for a loan, Lia. Twenty pounds, only . . . although if you've got it, I could do with forty.'

'*What?* Why don't you ask Mum?'

'Lia, you *know* she's cut off my allowance since I broke curfew last week. Honestly! She's such a cow. So full of herself too, since she got her new boobs. Dad's just as bad since you gave him Jack's motorbike. Such a big fuss because I came home fifteen minutes late. I don't understand you. You had the chance to escape, and you bottled it. I mean, this house is great, but we still have to live with *them*.'

'Oh, they're OK, really.'

I'd looked at a few flats. Gorgeous modern penthouses, with walls made of glass and views all the way to the London Eye. Flats carved out of old houses, with stained glass and high ceilings, rooms large enough for grand pianos. I imagined myself living in this flat . . . in that one. All that freedom. No parents telling me what to do. Raf could come and live with me . . . we could do whatever we wanted. . .

Financial independence is the best. But actual independence . . . you'll know when you're ready. If you feel scared and anxious at the thought of living on your own — you're not ready.

So I instructed Kevin the Bank Manager to help my mum and dad find a nice big house in Tithe Green where everyone would have loads of space; and he worked out some sort of deal where we all paid part of the mortgage, and I put down a lump sum and they hung on to their house and rented it out.

A personal bank manager is a great help in knowing how to organise complicated deals and investments, and a trust fund that gives you a regular income but protects most of your money.

Just about that time, Jasper's mum sold the house in Melbourne Avenue and moved to Bournemouth, and Jasper and Sylvie and George rented Mum and Dad's house. So mostly Raf sleeps in my old bedroom, and occasionally, when Mum and Dad and Natasha are elsewhere, he sleeps in my new one.

Natasha clicked her fingers under my nose. 'Wake up, dreamer! Am I getting the money or not?'

I stretched out on my completely amazing, bouncy, wrought-iron, satin-spread-covered double bed. 'Natasha, you know very well that Mum would kill me if I undermined her authority. Plus, you've got to learn the hard way that money doesn't grow on trees.'

Her eyes grew wide. Her mouth formed an outraged O shape and she took a deep breath.

'Only joking!' I trilled, and pulled twenty pounds out of my purse. 'But don't tell Mum and Dad.'

'Of course not! You had me worried there – thought you'd flipped over to the Dark Side.'

'Maybe I will, if I don't even get a thank you—'

But she was already talking on the iPhone that I'd bought her for her birthday.

Christmas and birthdays after you win the lottery are a nightmare. Everyone's not-so-secretly expecting the best present ever. Months and months of dropping unsubtle hints. Huge pressure. I wished they'd all convert to Islam. Next year they're all getting personalised donations to charity. Almost definitely.

'Hey, Molls, I stung Lia for twenty quid, meet me at Starbucks down the mall, OK?'

Huh. I wasn't all that sure about the new Natasha. OK, I enjoyed all the rows she had with Mum and Dad – it was so nice to be out of the firing line. But she'd got a little too assertive for my liking. Even though I'd kindly offered to arrange for her to meet Marcus and be told the truth about the music business, she was still completely certain that she was going to win *Britain's Got Talent* and become a big star.

Oh well. We all have to make our own mistakes.

I put the notebook in my bag and walked down to the Broadway to meet Shazia at the café. She was there already, sipping her hot chocolate. I don't know what I'd do without Shazia. Now I'd got used to it, I really appreciated that she was so hands-off about my money. Although I wished she'd agree to come with the rest of us to Ibiza for the summer.

Specialist travel agents are the best. They've usually visited the places they're selling you.

'Hey, Shaz, had second thoughts?' I knew she'd say no. Where Shaz and I differ, fundamentally, is that she loves not having to worry about what her decisions should be, whereas I quite like working things out.

But even Shaz could surprise me. She gave me a huge grin and said, 'Well, not exactly, but guess where my parents are taking us on holiday?'

'No! Shaz! No! *Squeee!*'

'Just a few miles away! We'll be able to meet up!'

'Oh, Shaz, that's the best news ever!'

'What's the best news ever?'

'Jack! Shaz is coming to Ibiza.'

Jack's smile was straight from a mouthwash ad.

'I'm not staying with you lot . . . we'll be a few miles away,' said Shaz, hastily, dipping her head to hide her blush.

Jack sat down heavily on the chair next to her and said, 'That's the coolest thing I've heard since Lia said she was going to buy Hard as Nails from my mum.'

'It was the best way of expanding the bakery,' I pointed out. 'It wasn't because it was your mum, or because I felt bad or guilty or anything. A purely business transaction. We're never going to develop the brand unless we have a bigger kitchen.'

'You've got the builders in now, haven't you?'

'Yeah, and I've been talking to the architect about making the upstairs a kind of workshop. So I can do more with the vintage clothes side of things, the customising, you know. I've got some great ideas. I know I won't be able to do much until I've got my A levels and been to uni, but I can start things up, can't I?'

Without qualifications you could end up with a pretty boring life, even if you're not worried about money. In fact, not worrying about money might make it even duller. . .

'Why are you writing in your notebook all the time?' demanded Jack.

'Oh . . . I'm just noting things down when they occur to me. I'm thinking of writing, you know, a book. A guide for people who win the lottery. Young people like me. It's much more difficult than you'd think.'

Jack spluttered a cloud of croissant crumbs. 'Who's

going to read that? A self-help book for teenage millionaires? *Lia's Guide to Winning the Lottery*? You must be joking.'

'It's a great idea,' said loyal Shaz.

'Well, I hope you're going to spice it up with highlights of your love life, Lia, or it'll be pretty dull.'

I thumped him gently. 'Oh, do you? Well, I don't go in for kiss and tell. And it's not going to be for sale. I'm going to give it to Gilda, so they can hand it on when teenagers win the lottery.'

'Blimey, Lia, you've got enough money to help thousands of people all over the world, and the ones you're worrying about are the lottery winners?'

'Not just them,' I said, 'but we matter too. And I am trying to help lots of other people in other ways.'

'Yes she is,' said Shaz. 'Why do you think she wants to study International Development at uni?'

'I know, quite saintly, young Lia, isn't she? Must be our good influence, Shaz. I knew we'd get through to her in the end. Oh, by the way, Lia, Rafe says he's got to cover for his brother across the road. I think he'd be glad to see you.'

'Don't call him that!'

'My good friend Rafe? He won't mind. . .'

And he wouldn't, I knew it, because since Raf got a

place in the school's A team, and Jack started doing shifts in my dad's bakery, they had become quite matey.

Luckily, I could trust Jack to keep a secret.

So I walked over the road, and found Raf in the internet café, and listened to him enthuse about the new recipes he was printing off for my dad to try, and how he'd been researching local farmers' markets, and how, if my dad would start making stoneground, organic loaves with seeds and apricots, he reckoned we could do really well. . . Sometimes it felt like I was dating a candidate from *The Apprentice*.

'Enough!' I said. 'Way too much detail. Talk to my dad about it. I want to know if you've heard from *your* dad. How did he get on?'

'How would I have heard from him?'

'On your *phone*, Raf, for God's sake. I told him to send you a text.'

Raf shuddered. 'I don't want to hear about it. It was your mum's worst ever idea, putting him in touch with those television people.'

'It's fine. He'll be brilliant. Telling his celebrity anecdotes and advising people on their clothes.'

'It'll just feed his gigantic ego. I'm not having anything to do with it.'

Raf hadn't actually spoken to his dad since he

discovered he'd sold loads of his amazing vintage clothes on eBay. I'd had to dissuade him from reporting his dad. I'd certainly never admitted that I'd taken more than a few choice items off Nick's hands. Some people, like Shazia and Raf, like rules. Others – like Nick and me – prefer to be more flexible.

No one could say that Raf's life was easy or simple. And there were times – when he got tense and pale and sleepless – that I worried about him. He wasn't mysterious any more, but he wasn't exactly your normal boy. But then I wasn't really a normal girl any more.

Raf shut the computer down, collected his printouts and put them carefully into a folder.

'Shaz is coming to Ibiza!' I said, hoping Raf would be pleased. Ibiza had been a difficult subject ever since I booked his ticket without telling him. In the end, my dad had persuaded him that he deserved a bonus for being Top Bakery Employee. Rita and Norma were fine about it, because I bought them cruise tickets for Christmas.

'I'm writing a book,' I told him. 'A guide, to help people who win the lottery. So they're prepared for some of the stuff that happened to me . . . so they don't make stupid mistakes.'

And he laughed at me, and said, 'Oh, so you'd have read a guide, would you? Something telling you what to do?'

'Well . . . I'd have been interested. . .'

'Yeah, but you wouldn't have actually followed anyone else's advice, would you? You'd have just rushed ahead, done your own thing.'

'Well . . . I would. But not everyone's like me.'

'No, that's true. You're unique.' He smiled at me, and he put his arms around me, and it was just like the night I won, all over again.

All the very best things in my life didn't come because I won the lottery. They came from the people that love me. That's why I'm lucky.

But I'm still glad that I won.

Acknowledgments

Many thanks to Liz Parker, Andy Carter and Irma Dawkins of Camelot who contributed so much information and ideas. Getting their help was invaluable. I take full responsibility, however, for the inaccuracy of some details of the 'whole winner experience', introduced for story-telling reasons. Rest assured that if you win the lottery, the help you get will be even more professional and caring than that given by Gilda and Kevin the bank manager.

And thanks to Marsha Healey, Andrew Wigman and Jessica Pitcairn for telling me about debt, money management and Islam.

Thanks to Deborah Nathan for the palatial office space, and to Katie Frankel, Mark, Hannah and Zoe Berman for allowing me to hijack their home.

Thanks to all at Frances Lincoln, especially Maurice Lyon and Emily Sharratt, and to all at Andrew Nurnberg Associates, especially Jenny Savill and Ella Kahn.

Thanks to the Finsbury Library ladies – Anna, Amanda, Jennifer, Lydia, Becky and Fenella – and to Mum, Hannah and Jimmy for reading.

Most of all, thanks to Laurence, Phoebe and Judah for putting up with a lot of grouchiness and for going on holiday so I could finish this book.

If you enjoyed *Lia's Guide to Winning the Lottery*,
you can go to
www.liasguidetowinningthelottery.co.uk
for more news and information.

Keren blogs about her life and books at
www.wheniwasjoe.blogspot.com

You can also follow her on Twitter
@kerensd

or find out more about on the **When I Was Joe**
and **Lia's Guide to Winning the Lottery**
pages on Facebook.

Growing up in a small town in Hertfordshire, **Keren David** had two ambitions: to write a book and to live in London. Several decades on, she has finally achieved both. She was distracted by journalism, starting out at eighteen as a messenger girl, then working as a reporter, news editor, features editor and feature writer for many and various newspapers and magazines. She has lived in Glasgow and Amsterdam, where, in eight years, she learnt enough Dutch to order coffee and buy vegetables. She is now back in London, and lives with her husband, two children and their insatiably hungry guinea pigs.

Keren's debut novel was the award-winning *When I Was Joe*, which was nominated for the Carnegie medal; followed by the thrilling sequel, *Almost True*.

Lia's Guide in Numbers. . .

- In most American and Australian states you have to be **eighteen** to play the lottery. In the UK the age limit is **sixteen**. In France there is no minimum age at which you can start playing the lottery.

- Your chance of being a jackpot winner in a standard lottery is **one** in 13,983,816.

- Callie Rogers was one of Britain's youngest ever winners in 2003, when, aged **sixteen**, she won **£1.9 million**. Seven years later, she told a magazine that she was down to her last £100,000 and wanted to train as a counsellor.

- In some American states you can get a learner's driving licence at **fourteen** (**eighteen** in New York City). In New Zealand the age limit is **fifteen**, in the UK, **seventeen**.

- The Great Wall of China is believed to have been funded by one of the world's earliest lotteries.

• The age of consent for sex varies around the world: **fourteen** in Hungary, **twenty** in Tunisia, **sixteen** in the US and the UK. In Columbia and Peru the age of consent is **fourteen** for boys, **twelve** for girls.

• England's first recorded lottery was in 1566 – the draw took place three years later by Queen Elizabeth I. Every ticket won a prize.

• Dr Chris Boyce, Economic Psychologist at Warwick University, compared the happiness levels of lottery winners with those of people who had psychological therapy to improve their mental health. He found that a course of therapy costing **eight hundred** pounds provides the same amount of happiness as a **twenty-five thousand** pound windfall, and concluded that therapy was therefore **thirty-one** times more cost-effective in making people happier than a lottery win.

• **Ninety-eight** percent of UK lottery winners say they are as happy or happier since their win. **Ninety-seven** percent give money to family and **sixty-nine** percent give presents to friends.

19 • Tabloids called Michael Carroll, **nineteen**, the 'Lotto Lout' after he won **£9.7 million** in 2002. The former binman collected his cheque wearing a prison monitoring tag, and has many convictions. He immediately bought **four** homes, a holiday villa in Spain, **two** convertible BMWs, **two** Mercedes Benz cars and several quad bikes. He was declared bankrupt in 2010, and said he had reapplied for his old job as a binman.

• In most countries, including the UK, the legal age for drinking is **eighteen**, but in most American states it is **twenty-one**. In many Muslim countries the consumption of alcohol is illegal at any age.

• The UK lottery has raised more than **twenty-five billion** pounds for good causes.

• **Thirty-seven billion** pounds has been paid out by the UK lottery in prizes, creating more than **two thousand, four hundred** millionaires or multi-millionaires.

- Tracey Makin from Belfast was just **sixteen** when she won just over **one million** pounds in 1998. Tracey invested her money and stayed in her office job.

- The minimum wage in the UK in 2011 is **£5.93** an hour. A specialist nurse gets **£10.22.** Wayne Rooney's contract with Manchester United is estimated to pay him **£936** an hour.

- Roughly **one** in **eight** of the world's population do not have access to safe water. **2.6 billion** people in the world do not have access to adequate sanitation, this is almost **two fifths** of the world's population. **1.4 million** children die every year from diarrhoea caused by unclean water and poor sanitation. It costs just **one hundred** pounds to build a well in Nigeria (source wateraid.org).

- In most countries, including the UK, the legal voting age is **eighteen**. However some countries give you the vote at **sixteen** – including Austria, Brazil, Jersey and Guernsey – or at **seventeen**, for example, East Timor and the Seychelles. In Uzbekistan the minimum age for voting is **twenty-five.**

- Breast enlargement prices at one of Britain's leading cosmetic surgery groups start from **£3,695.** This includes a **ten** year breast implant warranty.

- In 2008, **eighteen**-year-old student Ianthe Fullagar from Cumbria won **seven million** pounds with her second ever lottery ticket. She said she would still go to university to study law, and would invest most of the money for her future. She said: "I have worked very hard to get where I am and I still plan to go to university. I just plan to live like a normal student and not like a millionaire."